Austin McDonnell was born in Coventry and after the Coventry blitz went to live with his grandparents in the Connemara. He was educated at Bablake School Coventry. He is married and has two children. After a varied career in banking he retired in 1989 as Senior Manager of NatWest Bank Stevenage. He now lives in Cambridgeshire and since retirement has been a financial consultant and a property company director.

Writing has always been a passion, but other careers got in the way.

A PARALLEL LIFE

Austin McDonnell

A PARALLEL LIFE

Olympia Publishers
London

www.olympiapublishers.com
OLYMPIA PAPERBACK EDITION

Copyright © Austin McDonnell 2012

The right of **Austin McDonnell** to be identified as author of
this work has been asserted in accordance with sections 77 and 78 of the
Copyright, Designs and Patents Act 1988.

All Rights Reserved

No reproduction, copy or transmission of this publication
may be made without written permission.
No paragraph of this publication may be reproduced,
copied or transmitted save with the written permission of the publisher, or in
accordance with the provisions
of the Copyright Act 1956 (as amended).

Any person who commits any unauthorised act in relation to
this publication may be liable to criminal
prosecution and civil claims for damage.

A CIP catalogue record for this title is
available from the British Library.

ISBN: 978-1-84897-222-3

This is a work of fiction.
Names, characters, places and incidents originate from the writer's
imagination. Any resemblance to actual persons, living or dead, is purely
coincidental.

First Published in 2012

Olympia Publishers
60 Cannon Street
London
EC4N 6NP

Printed in Great Britain

Dedication

To my wife Celia for her constant help and support during the writing of the book.

Acknowledgements

My friend Roger Lane for technical support.

PART 1

1

The fog wrapped itself around the house like a grey blanket. It had persisted since early morning, when the lawns had been covered by a white frost. It had not lifted and had grown denser with the approach of darkness.

The old man shivered and pulled the blanket firmer around his shoulders. He could see only the blurred outlines of the trees as he gazed through the French windows. The rose beds beyond the end of the lawn had disappeared completely. He sighed deeply, lost in his own misery.

He gazed into the fire and watched the logs as they burned with a cheerful glow. He had always loved a real fire; none of these gas or electric fires for him. He remembered his mother's joy when she had bought her first gas fire. His thoughts floated back into the past, as they often did now.

Then he was there again: in that room, at what was possibly the defining moment of his life. She stood in front of him; a vision of loveliness and he ached for her, but his shyness numbed his body. Then he moved forward, encouraged by her smile and put his arms around her. He kissed her lightly on the cheek and caressed the hair at the nape of her neck. Then, for some inexplicable reason he had let her go, feeling the softness of her waist through her thin dress. Their lips had not met and he had lived a lifetime of regret since that moment.

The door to the living room opened, disturbing his reverie and Mrs Blakewell came in. She had been his housekeeper for over ten years and had looked after him as well as, if not better, than any wife. She had answered his advertisement in the local paper, having recently lost her husband through cancer. Mr

Blakewell had not been a wealthy or even careful man where finances were concerned and as a consequence his wife was left virtually penniless, necessitating some form of employment. Her new situation was heaven sent in her opinion. She had her own suite of rooms in the grandest house in the district, lovely grounds to walk in, all shopping paid for and a generous salary. In addition she had no sexual demands to meet; that had always been the part of her marriage she hated the most.

Now though, the world had suddenly turned against her. Sheila, her sister, who lived alone in Wales, had been struck down with Parkinson's disease. They had always been close and she could not desert her in her hour of need. Sheila had written to her, begging her to come and live with her. If she did, she would name Margaret as her sole heir. She had no children to leave her house and her wealth to, and they had been wealthy, she and Ernie.

"It's nearly time sir," she said quietly. She had always insisted on calling him 'sir', even though he had asked her to call him by his Christian name. "The taxi will be here any minute."

His heart sank. "Do you have to go?" he pleaded.

"The decision has been made," she replied. "There is no going back now."

Just then they heard the approaching car crunching up the gravel drive, followed by the sound of a horn.

"Have you had any replies yet from the advert?" she asked.

He shook his head. "None. I was hoping one of my nieces would be able to help out temporarily, until I found someone, but I had a letter today saying they are both too busy. If I died they would be here quickly enough."

"That's the way of the world now," she said, turning to go.

"Wait! There's an envelope for you on the mantelpiece. I almost forgot."

She walked across and picked up a plain white envelope addressed to her.

"It's a going-away gift. Call it a bonus. You may need it in Wales. It's a wild and lovely country, as I know from my youth, when I used to climb the mountains there. It's a thank you for all your help."

"Bless you," she said and walked over and kissed him lightly on the forehead. It was the first time they had ever had such close contact and she could see the tears welling in his eyes.

The taxi's horn blared twice impatiently.

"I must go," she said and fled from the room.

He heard the taxi's engine fading into the mist and gloom. Night had almost descended and only the flickering logs in the hearth shed any light in the room.

2

He must have slept for several hours. Outside, the fog and total darkness obliterated everything. Inside, the living room was cold, lit only by the dying embers from the log fire. At first he wondered why Mrs Blakewell had not made up the fire, drawn the curtains and brought his tea. Then he remembered, she had gone and he was on his own.

In sleep his body had stiffened, as it always did. He rose awkwardly from his armchair, his legs and feet numb with cold. He moved automatically to the French windows and after a quick glance into the darkness, drew the heavy curtains and put on the lights. After piling some fresh logs on the embers he collapsed again into his armchair.

The dream he had been having came to him clearly. He was a child again, running up from the lake, following his older sister across the lawn to where his parents sat under a canopy, to shade his mother from the sun. She maintained she had a delicate complexion, which would not allow her to have too much sunlight. She was dressed in a vividly-patterned cotton dress, and rocked herself gently on the swinging seat. She looked very beautiful. His father sat in a deck chair alongside her, puffing gently on his pipe. Between them there was a small round garden table, on which rested a glass of apple juice for his mother and a glass of white wine for his father.

He could not keep up with his sister who arrived ahead of him and blurted out their news. They had been down at the lake, looking for fish, but suddenly they had seen the most startlingly beautiful bird. He could not believe such birds existed. It skimmed across the water, its pale blue reflecting the sunlight. It seemed to hover for an instant and then it darted away into the wood. Elizabeth bent her head and whispered in his ear that it was a kingfisher. At once he set off to tell his parents, but she was older and faster and arrived well ahead of him. It was only a small regret that he had not won the race and had the pleasure of telling his parents. He felt such joy now recalling the dream, being there with his loving family.

His father had been a solicitor who started as a junior in a local firm and rose to be the senior partner. He was meticulous in his professional life and often worked long into the evenings. His hobby was investing his surplus money in property, domestic and commercial, but his main investment was in his own house, which he adored. He lavished time and money on it to make it a showpiece for the area and was proud to show it off. There was always another scheme in his mind to further his ambition. It gave him such pleasure to invite his friends and business colleagues to share the delights of 'Highfields', particularly in the summer, when they could explore the acres of grounds, woods, lake and gardens.

His mother loved his father and adored her two children. She looked after them to the exclusion of all else. They were her sole raison d'être and no sacrifice would have been too great to satisfy their desires.

Elizabeth was two years older than Edward and he loved and admired her greatly. She seemed to know the answer to all his questions and he would visualise the cheeky smiling way she would look at him if he asked what she thought was a particularly stupid question. Her clear blue eyes would smile at him mockingly and she would purse her lips and then very seriously and slowly give him the answer, emphasising every syllable as though it was a state secret. Then she would giggle at the expression on his face.

Suddenly he was gripped with that old familiar pain in his shoulder. At times he felt like screaming, it was so sharp, like a knife in the shoulder blades. At other times it caught him in the small of his back, stiffening him to the point where he would think he would never straighten again. If he kept quite still for a minute it sometimes eased off. Perhaps Elizabeth was the lucky one. She had avoided these aches and pains. He tried to get back to his dream, but it had gone. Rising painfully he threw a few more logs onto the fire, which had begun to burst into life.

The clock in the hall struck ten o'clock. "Have I been asleep as long as that," he thought. He had had nothing to eat since Mrs Blakewell had given him his lunch, but he did not feel hungry. She had told him she had left some sandwiches in the pantry but he had no inclination to go and fetch them. The pains had started again in his shoulder, his knees and his feet, which felt cold and numb. When he had been up high in the mountains the one thing he used to worry about was getting frostbite. No matter how bad the weather he knew he could find his way down as long as his feet did not become frostbitten.

He moaned aloud as he sank back into his chair. "How long have I got to put up with this?"

Suddenly he shivered. It was as though someone had just come in through the French windows. Or maybe walked over my grave, he thought, remembering one of his mother's favourite sayings, but then he felt rather than saw another presence in the room. He glanced round and saw a figure dressed all in black standing just inside the French windows, as though indeed he had just stepped in from the garden. Edward was fearful. There were so many stories now of forced entry, robbery and assault, even in one's own home.

"You have no need to be afraid," the stranger said in a strong commanding voice. He was about forty years old, Edward estimated. His face was lean and weathered by wind and sun.

"I'll take my coat off, if you don't mind," he said and unbuttoned it without waiting for an answer. Underneath the black coat he wore a black suit, with matching black shoes and black tie.

"Won't you take a seat," Edward said, beckoning to an armchair close to the fire. The man ambled across, his eyes taking in every detail of the room. He lowered himself noiselessly into the chair. He seemed to move like a cat prowling the street, lithe and controlled. He turned his head and gazed into Edward's eyes.

How did you get in?" Edward asked.

"You invited me in," was the strange reply.

"I!" He struggled for the right words, "invited you in."

"Yes. Your thoughts reached me and in obedience I came." Seeing the puzzled expression on Edward's face, he added, "you don't have to specifically invite me. I can see into the deepest recesses of your mind, your subconscious thoughts and innermost secrets. I can even clarify your words and actions, explain them in a way you couldn't understand." He smiled. "Not many people can fathom their own sub consciousness and therefore cannot fully understand themselves. That's probably a good thing; it hides the truth. Most people could not bear to understand the reality of themselves."

"So what prompted you to come?" Edward asked. His mind was in a turmoil and he was not sure whether he was really talking to this stranger or having another vivid dream.

"You thought about ending your own life, the man replied calmly. "You did not think that in so many words but it was there, in your mind, the hidden recesses, but it was struggling up to the surface and would reach the conscious expression within hours.

Edward sighed. He recognised the truth of what the stranger was saying. "I have to admit that life has become very difficult and I am at a low ebb at the moment, but I am sure I was not about to end it all."

"You feel your life has been a waste, a lack of achievement, a lack of love and a lack of friendship."

Tears welled in Edward's eyes. After University he had taken a job with a merchant bank in the City and was making steady progress until his father died suddenly. He could see the crowded pews in the church as the coffin was carried in, his mother and sister following, weeping profusely. Then the reception back home. There was a crowd of people, friends and neighbours of his parents. He did not really know any of them, but they were all very sympathetic. It was tragic to die so young from a heart attack. His father would have enjoyed the reception, he could be the life and soul of a party, liked a drink and a joke and to tease and flirt with the women. Edward was not like that, and was grateful when the last one had departed.

In the evening there was a serious conversation with his mother and one of his father's law firm's partners. By then there was a large portfolio of properties in his father's property company and it seemed the obvious solution for Edward to acquire his father's shares and become Managing Director. It would mean giving up his job in London, but he felt no regrets about that. He would move back home to live with his mother, his sister having already married.

He enjoyed his new responsibilities and living back in the house he loved so dearly. In truth his responsibilities were not that great. His father had been such a good businessman that the Leases ticked over and the rents flowed in. Soon he was buying more properties. He sold all the domestic houses and ploughed all the money back into commercial buildings; shops, offices and warehouses, where there was less hassle with occupiers and the rents were paid direct to the bank account.

"And all that gave you great satisfaction," the stranger said.

Edward was startled. It was as though he had spoken all his thoughts aloud.

"Yes. It did," he said.

"And now you have your doubts?"

"I don't know. When I look back my life seems to have been successful and comfortable, but it lacked excitement. I think it was too cosy." He paused. "And there was something else."

"Your lack of success with the opposite sex," the stranger suggested.

"Yes. I found them unapproachable. I was totally fearful of rejection. That's where women have the advantage."

"You think so."

"Yes. They get to choose. They can sit back and wait for the advances and reject or accept them, as they wish. If I could come back I would choose to be a female. I did once toy with the idea of becoming a Buddhist, but I would probably be reborn as a toad or a worm, knowing my luck."

"You don't believe in religion, do you?"

"No. My parents both attended church frequently and I was dragged along, but as soon as I went to University I had nothing more to do with religion, much to my mother's disapproval. Now I have come to the conclusion that religion causes all the havoc in the world. Each religion professes to believe in god, but it has to be their own particular version of god. They fight and kill each other to make their point."

The stranger chuckled. "Yes," he said. "People all believe that god is good and the devil is bad. If something turns out right: someone is rescued from a fire or a sinking ship, god is praised and thanked for the deliverance. What about those who perished in the flames or drowned when the ship sank? Everyone says that was the work of the devil." The stranger laughed heartily. "It is so convenient to have someone to praise for the good things in life and someone to blame for the bad. Have you ever thought that god and the devil are the same?"

"I think we were better off thousands of years ago when men worshipped the sun," Edward said. "At least there was a fundamental truth in that religion. We do all depend on the sun to keep us alive. But you must excuse me. I haven't offered you a drink. Would you like something?"

"No, thank you." He waved his hand dismissively.

"I never even asked you your name."

"Names don't matter much to me, but you can call me Michael. The clock in the hall began to chime again.

There was silence between them as the clock struck eleven times. Had it only been one hour since his visitor arrived? It seemed much longer than that.

"I have decided to extend your existence," Michael said, "but you must do exactly as I ask. Are you prepared to do that?"

Edward was sure he had not been contemplating suicide, as Michael implied, but what if he had. Michael seemed to know what was in his mind better than he did. Certainly he had reached a low ebb with the departure of Mrs Blakewell and the contemplation of the rest of his life alone, while his arthritis progressed.

"I will do as you say," he said at last, resigned to his fate.

"Tonight you must write a letter authorising an unnamed person to have power of attorney over all your affairs. The name will be left blank. Leave space for it to be inserted. Date it today and sign it. Is that clear?"

"Yes. I understand."

"Finally, you must pour this liquid into a glass, get into bed and then drink it." Michael took a small brown bottle from his pocket and, rising from his chair, handed it to Edward. It seemed to burn Edward's fingers and he stared fixedly at the bottle to see if it bore any label or words of any kind, but there was nothing. Then he raised his head to speak, but there was nobody there. Michael had disappeared as suddenly as he had arrived. Edward could have believed it was all a daydream, but for the small brown bottle in his hand and the tingling sensation in his fingers.

He rose and poured himself a whisky. A few sips brought some of the colour back into his pale cheeks. Then, carrying the glass and the bottle, he left the living room, crossed the hall and entered his study. Pushing aside the papers on his desk he found some clean sheets in one of the drawers and began to write. Thanks to his father he had a fair idea of how to compose a legal document. As he wrote, his mind was in turmoil. What if the bottle contained poison and the blank space would bear the name of his visitor by the time his body had been found. Michael had shown that he could enter and leave the house at will.

The pen hung in the air as doubts crawled through his mind. He had never taken any bold chances or been a gambling man throughout his life. With each major decision there had always been at least one alternative if things went wrong. The bottle did not offer any alternative. There was no get-out clause in this contract. The pen hovered above the page while he tried to decide and then descended to the paper and completed the document. He signed it with a flourish and then placed the date beneath his signature.

With a sigh he threw the pen down onto his desk, picked up the whisky and drained the glass. Taking the empty glass with him he left his study. The huge hallway seemed somehow menacing. The only sound was the tick tock of the grandfather clock, which stood further along the hall outside the door to the dining room.

The great oak staircase climbed up to a half landing, from where it curved round and continued to the upstairs corridor. He slowly mounted the stairs, pushed open the door to his bedroom and saw that Mrs Blakewell had left his neatly folded pyjamas on the pillow. He knew it was the last time she would do that for him. Quickly undressing he pulled on the pyjamas and slid into bed. Only then did he take up the glass and the brown bottle from the bedside table. Even then he hesitated a little longer, but eventually putting aside his doubts and fears, he unscrewed the cap of the bottle and poured the contents into the empty whisky glass. The liquid gurgled into the bottom of the glass, no more than a double measure of scotch, but far less appetizing. It was a dull green colour and looked completely opaque.

After contemplating it for a few seconds, with a gesture of resignation, he raised the glass to his lips and swallowed the contents. There was no particular taste, but he felt a slight burning sensation in his throat. He put down the glass and laid his head back on the pillow. In that instant he was asleep.

3

Sunday 14th February

Edward could not remember having such a long and peaceful sleep. His eyes flicked open and he could tell from the sunlight trying to penetrate the heavy curtains over the windows that the fog from the previous day had been swept away, to be replaced by bright winter sunshine. He stretched his legs and amazingly felt no pain at all. On the contrary he felt as though he could leap out of bed and run around the room. There was one thing puzzling and disturbing him however. His head seemed to have slipped off the pillow, but at the same time his toes seemed further from the end of the bed than usual. Surely he had not shrunk in the night.

    Feeling some alarm now he threw back the bedclothes and swung his legs out effortlessly and stood up. Almost simultaneously his pyjama trousers fell down around his ankles. He looked down in amazement at two small perfect white feet. At the same time he was aware that the pyjama jacket was slipping over his shoulders and after a few tugs to attempt to keep it up, he let it go. The garment slid down his body to join the trousers in a heap at his feet. He looked down and then sprang back in alarm. This was not his body that he was looking at, but that of a young woman. He ran to the curtains and pulled the cord to open them fully. Then, stepping in front of the long mirror on his wardrobe door, he surveyed the reflection of a lovely girl; completely naked, with perfectly formed breasts and long smooth legs. She had brown eyes, like his own and in the face he could discern some familiar features. Her hair was dark brown, as his had been when young. It framed her face in soft natural curls. Her nose and mouth seemed familiar to him. She was very beautiful. He put his left hand out and touched her lips in the reflection. Then he touched his face and explored it, feeling the softness of the skin. There was not a mark or blemish on it, or anywhere else from what he could see. He ran his hands over the beautiful breasts, the flat stomach and explored the thighs and legs.

"There's no doubt about it. I'm a girl," she said aloud, and heard her soft female voice for the first time. The metamorphosis was complete.

And now I must get dressed, she thought. She opened the wardrobe to find, as expected, Edward's suits, jackets, sweaters and shirts hanging there. She took out a dressing gown, which was far too big for her, but at least it covered her nakedness, and then, in bare feet, proceeded to go from bedroom to bedroom in search of clothing. Each room was exactly as she expected to find it. Finally, in desperation she opened the door to the small room at the end of the corridor. It had been used as a storage and box room in the past, but now there had been a complete transformation. The junk had disappeared and in its place she found a clean well-decorated room, with a new soft pink carpet beneath her feet. There was a single bed, with an attractive rose pattern on the bedspread, matched by the curtains. A dressing table stood against the wall, covered by an intricate lace cloth, on which stood an assortment of perfume bottles and all the accoutrements she could possibly desire. She crossed to the window and looked out at a sweeping view of the grounds, down to the lake and beyond to the woods.

The whole room smelled clean and fresh and cared for. It made her feel very happy to think that someone had gone to such trouble to prepare it for her. She noticed a large wardrobe in the corner and gave cry of delight when she opened the door, to find rows of hangers full of every variety of female attire and she knew instinctively that they would all fit her.

Without hesitation she threw off the dressing gown and began to select a few items. She found all the underclothes she needed in the drawers of the dressing table, but had a struggle putting on a bra for the first time. Eventually she realised that the correct method was to turn the clasp to the front and after it was fastened, reverse it to the back. She chose a pair of trousers and a sweater as she felt she would feel more comfortable in them. They fitted her perfectly and after she had found a pair of fairly sturdy shoes with a low heel, she felt ready to face the world. Dressed and feeling happy she skipped down the great staircase and along the hall to the kitchen, where she stopped dead in her tracks. There was a woman standing at the sink, washing up some cups and saucers, gently humming to herself. She turned when she heard the door opening and smiled warmly.

"Good morning," she said. "You must be Edwina. I didn't think you would be up yet, after such a tiring journey." She dried her hands. "I'm Mrs Pearson. I'm sure your father must have mentioned me to you." They shook hands. "If you take a seat I'll make some tea for you, or would you prefer coffee?"

"No, tea will be fine," Edwina said.

Mrs Pearson was probably in her mid forties. She was fairly plump, with a round happy face, and a cheerful smile. She spoke with a distinct Midlands accent. The end of the large kitchen had always served as a breakfast room. The table could seat six comfortably, but only one place was laid now. She was obviously expected, so without demur she seated herself. Mrs Pearson had called her Edwina, so that must be her name. She was satisfied with that; it was not so different from Edward. There was a selection of breakfast cereals on the table, a large jug of milk and pots of jam and honey. She felt ravenously hungry. Before long she was served with orange juice, tea and toast. When she picked up the glass of orange juice in her right hand it didn't feel right, so she switched hands and realised she was left-handed, whereas before she had been right-handed. Just another reversal she supposed. The housekeeper jabbered away throughout the meal, talking of things Edwina knew nothing about. She tried to make conversation but it was difficult, so she covered up by keeping her mouth fairly full.

"That was so good," she said, rising, "shall I help you clear away?"

"No dear, I'm sure you have lots of things to do. Your father said he had left quite a few things for you in his study."

"My father?"

"Yes dear."

"When did you speak to him?"

"Why, yesterday of course. He was so sorry that he could not be here to greet you, but said he couldn't postpone his trip. He had been planning it for months and was so looking forward to it. We only knew you were coming yesterday, so it was far too late to change his plans."

"Where has he gone?" Edwina asked hesitantly.

"To Italy, of course. Surely he told you. Don't tell me you have forgotten."

"No, of course not. I'm sure he will have a wonderful time. I'll go along to the study and see what he has left me."

"Mr Pearson will be in for his mid-morning coffee at eleven. Shall I bring you a cup?"

"That will be nice," she said, trying to keep calm, and made a leisurely exit.

She crossed the hall to the study and closed the heavy door behind her. She stood still for a moment, listening. All was quiet, but she could feel her heart thumping in her chest. It was hard to believe that she had sat at the large desk only hours before, writing her power of attorney.

She walked over to the desk, catching her breath when she realised the letter Edward had written was no longer where she had left it. She pulled forward the pile of papers he had pushed to one side the previous night, turned over the first two and there she saw an official printed document headed 'Power of Attorney'.

She sat in the large armchair and slowly read the document. It had been prepared by Edward's solicitor, Bruce Collinridge, and was dated three months previously, on the 13th November. How could that be, she wondered? Edward did not have any idea that she would be here then. Just when she thought the situation was becoming clearer it became more confused. She read through the document, which named Miss Edwina Cabrossi as Edward Grangelove's attorney. It bestowed a lasting power of attorney on her, from which she gathered she could act on his behalf in all his affairs. It covered property, financial affairs and even personal welfare. The document had been registered with the Office of the Public Guardian and there was a letter attached from Edward's bank, acknowledging the existence of the arrangement.

So, her name was Cabrossi. That did not convey anything to her. She had a new body, a new name and a new personality, but she was a stranger to herself. "Who am I?" she whispered. "Really, who am I?"

She rose and went over to where the wall safe was hidden behind a picture. Moving the picture aside, she was relieved to see the old familiar safe. There were no keys, just a three-figure combination. Would the combination be the same, she wondered? If it had been changed in this unfamiliar world, how would she open the safe? With trembling fingers she placed the marker on zero and spinning the wheel to the right stopped on sixteen, then two spins in the opposite direction, stopping on thirty, followed by once to the right again to seven. Please be the same combination, she thought, and turned the marker left to the zero. There was a recognisable click and the door swung open. Edwina heaved a sigh of relief. She reached inside, gathered up the pile of papers and carried them over to the desk.

She was familiar with all the contents; deeds of the house, insurance policies, share certificates and the will. There was nothing else. Everything looked the same but, on closer examination, the envelope containing the will looked cleaner and newer than she remembered it. The envelope was unsealed, as his solicitor had asked Edward to keep it that way, so she slid the will out. It was clearly of recent origin and a fairly simple document. After the usual opening legal phrases, there were several bequests of five thousand pounds each to various charities Edward had supported throughout his life, the sum of fifty thousand pounds to Alfred Pearson and Mrs Lucy Pearson of Hollytree Cottage for the way they had looked after Highfields house and grounds. In addition they could live rent free in their cottage for as long as they wished. The next bequests left the sum of one hundred thousand pounds to Mrs Martha Bracken, followed by a similar bequest to her sister Mrs Kathleen Hastings, her two cousins. Finally the will named my beloved daughter, Edwina Cabrossi to inherit the residue of his estate. Instantly Edwina could see trouble on the horizon. In Edward's previous will the sisters were due to receive a half share in the residue, worth several million pounds, as his sole heirs. At a guess she thought they would have received approximately six million each. Most of the residue was invested in property, but there was also a substantial portfolio of stocks and shares.

"I am my own daughter," she said aloud, and laughed. She had not heard herself laugh before and was pleased with the merry sound. The will was signed Edward Grangelove and witnessed by Bruce Collinridge and his secretary, Annette Hyde-White.

There was a knock at the door and Mrs Pearson entered with a small tray. "I've brought you a coffee and some biscuits, in case you are hungry," she said. She placed the tray on the corner of the desk.

"How long have you been working here now?" Edwina asked, trying to keep the question casual and conversational.

"Oh, the best part of two years. Me and Alf love it here."

"Does your husband look after the gardens?"

"Yes, and everything else. He's a proper Mr Fix-it. So, if there's any odd job you need doing, just you let me know."

"And where do you live?" she asked.

"Why, bless you, in 'Hollytree Cottage', at the end of the drive. Mr Grangelove had it specially done up for us."

Edwina knew that the cottage had been unoccupied for several years and needed a lot of money spending on it, to bring it up to a state where it was fit for habitation. Edward had planned to do it, but had kept putting it off, as he was not sure that he wanted people living in close proximity to him.

"We're very cosy there, and Alf loves it. Didn't Mr Grangelove mention it to you?"

"No, we didn't correspond very often."

"I'm not really surprised. I didn't even know of your existence until yesterday. Then Mr. Grangelove calls me in and says you will be coming to stay, but that unfortunately he will not be here, as he can't change his plans. You could have knocked me over with a feather. I didn't know anything about his plans. Anyway he was most anxious that you were made to feel at home."

Edwina smiled. "I certainly feel at home," she said, smiling. "Did my father say how long I would be staying?"

"No, but he said he was hoping to persuade you to make this your permanent home. That would be so nice for him if you could. It must be very lonely in this huge house without any companionship."

"Yes, it was terrible," Edwina said and then corrected herself. "I mean it must have been terrible."

"Well, I must get on," Mrs Pearson said. She picked up the tray and went back to the kitchen.

Her husband, Alf, had come in from the garden and was seated at the table, sipping his coffee. He was a few years older than his wife, thin but muscular, from years of hard manual labour. His lean craggy face was weather-beaten by sun and wind.

"She didn't touch the biscuits," Mrs Pearson said, putting the plate down on the table. "Would you like one?"

He reached forward and took one. "How is she?" he asked.

"Very pretty and very pleasant. I think she's feeling a little lost at the moment, poor soul. It must be difficult, coming to a foreign country and having no friends."

Alf nodded and helped himself to another biscuit.

After Mrs Pearson's departure, Edwina searched through all the papers on the desk, but could not discover anything she was unfamiliar with. She had picked up a pen to doodle on the blotter, but found that it felt unfamiliar in her right hand. Even so, she tried the familiar signature and with a natural flourish signed Edward's signature. She then tried to sign as Edwina Cabrossi, but could hardly hold the pen. Switching it to her left hand she signed, 'E.Cabrossi' fluently and firmly. Looking at the two signatures, side by side, she laughed.

4

Edwina sauntered through the garden, admiring every flower and bush, and relishing every breath of fresh air. It seemed like years since she had been able to walk without stiffness and pain, but in reality it was only a matter of months. She felt strong and athletic and it was as though she was discovering the garden for the first time. The crocuses and snowdrops were past their best, but still gave a colourful show. The daffodils were about to burst into flower and the tulips, which she loved the most, were just pushing their heads above the soil. All the beds were well cared for and it was obvious that Alf knew his job and worked hard to keep everything tidy. There were no weeds in the beds, the hedges were well trimmed and the trees and bushes well pruned.

Her footsteps led her down to the lake. There were two swans sailing serenely on the far side. They had nested there, undisturbed, for years. She was sure they were the same pair. Moorhens and coots also nested on the margins of the lake and ducks found a sanctuary where they would not be hunted. She preferred to enjoy the company of the living birds than to see them on her dining room table.

She skirted the lake and entered the wood through a kissing gate. The view back to the house from that spot was magnificent. Soon she was following the old familiar path through the wood, which covered almost ten acres. The path ended close to the road and then veered to the left, skirting the wood, separated from the road by a thick thorn hedge. At the corner of the wood the path turned again to the left and followed the boundary between 'Highfields' and 'Greenblade

Farm', which was owned by the Skefford family. Robinson Skefford was married to Emily and they owned about one thousand acres. They had always been friendly on the few occasions they had met, but as Edward had not been married and, through his shyness, had shunned social gatherings, they could not be counted as friends. Even to call them acquaintances was stretching a point. She recalled that there were two sons and a daughter, but she could not remember seeing any of them for years and could not recall any of their names.

Engrossed in these thoughts she was startled to hear a man's voice calling.

"Hello there." She did not think the call could be addressed to her, so she continued her slow progress, deep in thought.

"Hello, there," the voice called again, louder and more insistent.

She stopped and looked towards the hedge.

A young man, probably about her own age, was gazing at her in astonishment. "How on earth did you get over there?" he asked. "Did you know they were private grounds?"

"Really," she said innocently, deciding to tease him a little. "To whom do they belong?"

"A man called Edward Grangelove."

"I'm sure he wouldn't mind me having a walk through his wood."

"I don't know about that," the young man said seriously. "He keeps himself to himself and doesn't encourage people trespassing on his property. He's a real recluse."

"So he might set the dogs on me," she said. "Well, I can't jump over that hedge, so I will have to go on trespassing for a little longer."

"If you follow the hedge along you will come to a cottage eventually and that's where the drive from the house comes down to the lane."

"That's very helpful," she said with a smile and turned to go.

"Don't go," he said. She stopped and turned towards him again. "I think you know the way out, don't you? You've been pulling my leg." He laughed and she joined in.

"Are you staying at 'Highfields?" he asked. "I don't think there have been any visitors there for years."

"I only arrived yesterday, but I will be staying for some time."

"Are you with your parents?"

"No. All by myself."

"Then you must be one of the mythical nieces we have heard about, but no one has ever seen."

She laughed. "In fact I'm the mythical daughter that nobody has ever heard about or seen."

His face was a picture of complete disbelief. He obviously thought she was teasing him again. " Do you," he stammered. "Do you mean to say Mr Grangelove had a family all along and kept it to himself?"

"I said nothing about a family," Edwina corrected him. "Just a daughter." Looking at her watch she said, "I must go. Mrs Pearson will have lunch ready and it would be very rude to be late on my first day."

"Please, don't go," he pleaded, as she turned away. "I don't even know your name."

"It's Edwina," she said.

"That's lovely. I'm Robert Skefford and I live at the farm up on the hill over there." He waved his hand towards the large white farmhouse perched at the top of the distant hill. "I have an older brother, Rupert and a younger sister called Margaret. You must come over and meet us all."

"I would like that very much," she said, "but now I really must go."

"I'll have a word with mother. Would you like to come over for lunch one day?"

"I'd love to," she said, half turning, to see his face light up, and then he was bounding across the field towards the farmhouse.

5

Mrs Emily Skefford, like most farmers' wives, was a very well organised woman. She worked hard and supported her husband, Robinson, in all his undertakings. In the early years of their marriage she had laboured on the farm, in addition to raising three children, born at approximately two yearly intervals. She could plough a furrow as straight as any man and could operate most of the other machinery, but drew the line at the huge harvester.

She was a farmer's daughter and had met Robinson through the local Young Farmers Club. It did not take long before they were holding hands and attending club functions as a pair.

Robinson was an only child and received a good education before the natural progression to an Agricultural College. He had to be equipped to take over from his father one day, just as his father had taken over from his grandfather. He was a very contented man, always busy and certain that he had the best wife, the best children and the best life anyone could wish for.

Mrs Skefford was just putting the finishing touches to the lunch when Robert came into the kitchen, red-faced and slightly out of breath from his jog up the hill.

"You will never guess who I have just met," he announced, and paused for effect.

"His mother glanced up at him, as she slid the joint out of the oven. He looked excited and bursting to tell his news.

"Edwina Grangelove," he blurted out, unable to contain his secret any longer.

"Who?" his mother asked, doubtfully.

"Edwina Grangelove. Edward's daughter."

"Don't be silly," his mother chided him, "Edward doesn't have a daughter or any children. He's a confirmed bachelor. He would run a mile if any woman came within a mile of him. Someone has been pulling your leg."

"She wouldn't do that," Robert protested, but then recalled that she had let him think she was trespassing on Edward's land. "I'm sure she was telling the truth. She's the loveliest girl I've ever seen," he added.

"It seems you have fallen hard." Mrs Skefford laughed.

"Maybe I have," Robert said thoughtfully. "That wouldn't be difficult."

"Perhaps you met one of his nieces."

"No," Robert insisted. "I thought that and asked her if she was. She insisted she is Edward's daughter."

"Well I'm blessed," she said. "So the old man has a skeleton in his cupboard. I wonder where he has been hiding her."

"I've invited her to lunch," Robert said.

Mrs Skefford stopped carving and looked hard at him. "She isn't coming today, I hope."

"No. I said I would talk to you and then let her know."

"And how do you propose to do that?" she asked.

"By telephone of course."

"Mrs Skefford shook her head. I doubt if we have a note of his number. We may have had it once, but it's probably changed since then. You could ask Mrs Pearson, who lives in 'Hollytree Cottage'; she'll let you know the current number. She will also probably tell you there is no such person as Edwina Grangelove. If you track her down, I think I would quite like to meet this young lady and solve the mystery of who she is and where she has come from."

"So it will be alright to invite her then?" he asked.

"Yes. Invite her over on Thursday. There's one snag though. We will have to invite Edward as well."

"If he's such a recluse he probably wouldn't come," Robert suggested.

"If he has a daughter he can't be such a recluse as we thought," she said. "Yes, invite them both. I can't wait to meet this Edwina."

6

When she returned to the house Edwina received a shock; one she had been expecting, but hoped to put off for as long as possible. Mrs Pearson told her there had been a telephone call from Martha Bracken, the oldest of her two cousins.

"She was enquiring about your father," Mrs Pearson said. "I told her your father had gone away and that you had arrived."

"I suppose she was surprised to hear that."

"Yes. Very surprised. In fact she said she had never heard of you."

"I can imagine her concern," Edwina said, trying to remain calm and keep the sarcasm out of her voice. "I don't think my father told anyone about me."

"She would like you to call her back," Mrs Pearson said. Obviously her curiosity had been aroused.

"Have you ever met either of my cousins?" Edwina asked.

Mrs Pearson answered immediately. "Neither of them has been here in my time."

Edwina decided the call to Martha could wait, indefinitely, if she could manage it. Neither Martha nor her younger sister, Kathleen, had ever put themselves out for their uncle and the last thing she wanted was a stream of questions she would have difficulty in answering.

"I'll give her a call after lunch," she said. "I'll relax for a few minutes in the living room."

"I will call you when lunch is ready," Mrs Pearson said.

Edwina walked down the corridor to the room she had not entered since her meeting with Michael. She flung herself into the familiar armchair. Now what shall I do, she mused. Thank goodness I was out when she called. She could imagine the consternation in the Bracken and Hastings families when the two sisters discussed the implications of the news imparted by Mrs Pearson. They would probably have their heads together at that moment and would be asking who was this mysterious interloper, who threatened to do them out of what they almost certainly considered to be their just deserts on the death of their uncle. They must have been rubbing their hands in glee for years at the prospect of inheriting dear old Edward's fortune, even though it had been far too much trouble to visit him. They would not give up those prospects without a fight.

I could always go abroad; that would postpone any meeting until I have had time to work out a strategy, Edwina thought. But where should I go? That was the next question. She had no idea of her own background, but presumably she must have been born somewhere, have lived somewhere, gone to school, made friends. It was all just a blank. Her memories were all Edward's memories apart from the time when she woke up. I need to find out about myself or the happiness I feel in this new existence could be snatched from me and my cousins are the ones who have the power to destroy me, unless I can come up with the answers. Do I have a passport? Do I have a birth certificate? When she examined all the documents from the safe, neither of those documents was present.

Just then she heard Mrs Pearson calling her in to lunch.

She crossed the hall to the dining room where she found that a place had been laid for her at the head of the long oak table. There was room to seat eighteen people and from where she sat she looked down the length of the highly polished surface to the huge bay window, and beyond that to a large gravelled parking area, surrounded by bushes and trees. From there the drive disappeared to the right, round the corner of the building and then straight on towards Hollytree Cottage, before joining the lane.

The walls of the dining room were hung with expensive oil paintings, mostly depicting landscapes. A large antique mahogany sideboard, adorned with equally ancient bowls and vases, stood to the left as she looked towards the window and there was a large open fireplace to the right. The fire had not been lit and Edwina shivered as she ate her solitary meal. This was a room for a crowd of happy laughing people, as it had been, for a time at least, in her father's day. Even the pictures, which usually gave her such pleasure, seemed to glare down at her in disapproval.

She ate her meal quickly and returned to her armchair in the living room, where there was a cheerful fire blazing in the hearth. As she sat contemplating the flames, she wondered why she had no memories of her earlier existence as Edwina. All her memories were those of Edward. She had thought that by now she would begin to recall something of her early life as Edwina, to picture her mother and the place where they lived and she had been brought up, but there was nothing. Only occasionally did she experience a flash of thought through her brain, like a shaft of sunlight, and she would feel she was on the edge of recalling something. The next moment it was gone and she would be remembering running up from the lake again, chasing Elizabeth, hoping to be the one to tell her parents about the kingfisher.

7

At that moment, Alf and Lucy Pearson were enjoying their Sunday lunch in the warm kitchen. Mrs Pearson was busy relating the telephone call with Martha Bracken and subsequent conversation she had had with Edwina.

"I'm sure there's something strange going on," she said. "It's very odd that her cousin had never heard of her. You can understand the old man not telling us." She emphasised the 'us'. "I'm sure he wanted to keep it a secret, but you would think his own relatives would know all about it."

"He probably had his own reasons for keeping it quiet," Alf suggested.

"And there's another thing! When did she arrive? Her taxi had to drive in past our house, but I never heard anything. Did you?"

"No. And I'm usually a light sleeper," he said. "She must have flown in."

8

Monday 15th February

When she woke on the following morning Edwina felt totally refreshed. She leapt out of bed and donned the pink dressing gown she found in the wardrobe. It fitted her perfectly, as she expected it would, and slipping her feet into the slippers beside her bed she set off down the corridor to her former bedroom, where there was an en suite bathroom.

Putting on the shower, she slipped off her dressing gown and silk nightdress. Before stepping into the shower she glimpsed her reflection in the long mirror on the tiled wall. Once again she was amazed at the slim lovely figure confronting her. She put her hand on her breast and could hardly believe how soft the flesh was, like a newborn baby. She stepped into the shower and delighted in the warm caress of the streams of water.

Wrapping herself in a large white towel she returned to Edward's bedroom and sat on the edge of the double bed while she towelled herself dry. It was then she noticed the case and handbag placed in the corner where they would be out of the way.

She gave a shriek of joy and jumped off the bed, letting the towel drop from her body. Grasping the case she hauled it onto the bed, flipped up the catches and lifted the lid. The case was filled with female clothing, a wash bag, containing toothbrush and toothpaste, a highly scented soap, various creams and lotions and a soft face flannel. There was also a vanity bag containing a hairbrush and comb, lipsticks, nail scissors and a nail file.

This had to be her case, even though none of the contents were familiar to her. Examining a few of the items of clothing she found them to be her size and similar in style and colour to those she had found in the wardrobe. She had felt comfortable in everything she had put on so far and it was a relief not to have to go out to buy anything to wear.

Abandoning the case she brought the handbag over to the bed. It was made of soft blue leather, like pigskin, and inside she found a purse, a black pen, a small hairbrush and comb, a lipstick and some nail clippers. Opening the purse she found a selection of coins and notes, both sterling and Euros. Without counting it she could see there was a large sum of money. There were no credit cards or any other plastic cards and no cheque book either. Disappointed she turned her attention back to the handbag, where she discovered a pocket closed with a zipper Opening it she found what she had been looking for; a passport and tucked into the pages, a birth certificate.

The passport was burgundy coloured and engraved in gold letters, 'Unione Europea Republica Italiana' above the Italian Coat of Arms, and at the bottom 'Passaporto' also in gold letters. Opening the cover she found her own photograph staring back at her, with just the slightest trace of a smile. Her date of birth was stated as the thirteenth of February, so she was just twenty years old and had arrived on her twentieth birthday. The place of birth was stated as Castelfranco Veneto. Unfolding the birth certificate she found confirmation of her date of birth, mother's name Anna Cabrossi, mother's maiden name Anna Cabrossi, father's name not stated.

Carefully refolding the birth certificate she placed it back in the passport and returned both documents to where she had found them in the handbag. She put on her gown and slippers and carried the suitcase and handbag back to her own bedroom.

At least I have definite proof of who I am, she thought, but only really half of who I am. Edward named me as his daughter in his will and power of attorney, so that is who I must maintain that I am, she decided, no matter what difficulties lie ahead.

9

It was soon after breakfast that the telephone rang for the first time. She was seated in the living room, staring across the lawn, deep in thought. She picked up the phone and simply said, "hello."

"Is that Edwina?"

She recognised Robert Skefford's voice. He sounded excited.

"Yes. How are you this morning, Robert?" She felt so relieved to hear a friendly voice.

"I'm great, and I hope you are too."

Without waiting for a reply he blurted out his invitation. "I've had a word with my mother and we would all love you to come for lunch on Thursday. Would Mr Grangelove like to come too, of course?"

"Thank you for inviting me and I would love to come, but I'm afraid my father won't be able to. He has gone to Italy for health reasons."

"Oh, well. Nothing serious I hope," Robert said, genuine concern in his voice.

"I don't think so," she said.

"Would you like me to pick you up?"

"Yes, please. Although I can see your house from the wood, I'm sure it's a long way to walk."

"It is," he said, with a laugh. "I will call to pick you up at twelve o'clock, if that's convenient?"

"Why don't you come a little earlier and bring your sister with you. I think you said her name is Margaret. I would love to get to know her."

"Of course," he said happily. "I'm sure Margaret would love to come, and I can't wait to see you again."

She laughed and whispered, "goodbye."

The second phone call came about an hour later. Edwina was reclining in her favourite armchair, contemplating with pleasure the forthcoming meeting with her neighbours. She had not set foot in the Skefford house for over twenty years and realised now that Edward had made a great mistake in cutting himself off from his neighbours and friends. She could visualise the farmhouse as it had been before, the entrance through the side of the building, straight into the large warm kitchen, that was always filled with the delicious aromas of baking bread or roasting meats. One or other of the dogs would be lying on the floor near to the door, waiting for any movement from their master, Robinson Skefford, to indicate a foray into the fields. The slightest shuffle of his feet was enough to make the ears twitch or the tails wag, while they kept their chins on the floor, their eyes constantly watching him. And then, realising Robinson was not about to move, they would close their eyes and snooze again. The two cats, in their separate beds, would not even blink an eye.

Edwina picked up the phone. "Hello," she said.

"Is that Edwina Grangelove?" a female voice demanded. It sounded as though she had great trouble even mentioning the name.

"No. It's Edwina Cabrossi," she replied.

There seemed to be an immediate release of tension at the other end of the wire.

"Oh," she said, in a less strident tone. "I was told you were Edward's daughter."

"That's correct," Edwina said. "And who might you be?"

"I'm Martha Bracken, Edward's niece."

"Oh, I'm so pleased to speak to you. I meant to phone you back yesterday. Please forgive me. I'm anxious to contact all my relations and especially my two cousins, yourself and your sister, Kathleen."

There was quite a lengthy pause and Edwina could hear the intake of breath.

"Are you inferring that you are related in any way to Kathleen and me?"

"If you are both Edward Grangelove's nieces, then you are both definitely related to me, since I am his daughter."

"That cannot be," Martha screeched, "since uncle Edward never married. I wish to speak to him straight away. Please put him on the line."

"I'm afraid I can't do that," Edwina said. "He's gone abroad, for health reasons."

"How very convenient," Martha said sarcastically. "I suppose you had nothing to do with that." There was no longer any attempt to disguise the animosity in her voice.

Edwina could understand the way she felt. From her point of view a complete stranger had taken over her wealthy uncle's house and possibly his fortune, while he had disappeared abroad. In her shoes Edwina knew she would be suspicious, but she wanted to avoid falling out with her cousins before she had even met them.

"I can assure you that I had nothing to do with my father's decision to go abroad at this particular time. Why don't we meet," she suggested.

"I don't think that would be a good idea," Martha replied. "I intend to get to the bottom of this, Miss Cabrossi," she spat out. "I shall be consulting my solicitor and probably the police." With that the line went dead.

After staring at the telephone for a minute Edwina replaced the instrument. It was clear that Martha Bracken intended to make trouble and Edwina felt very vulnerable. She would find it difficult to account for her existence if called upon to prove herself Edward's daughter in a court of law. She decided that it was time she had someone on her side and the obvious choice would be Bruce Collinridge, Edward's solicitor, who had drawn up the power of attorney and the new will. He might be able to tell her the circumstances surrounding the creation of those two documents and possibly throw some light on the supposed whereabouts of Edward, although Edwina knew perfectly well that Edward had ceased to exist from the moment she had come into being. It was as though she had come into an entirely new world on the night of the thirteenth, and indeed that was the only explanation that made any sense. While many things were the same and others seemed familiar, there were many anomalies.

10

The offices of Collinridge, Edmunds & Partners were situated in the High Street in the town of Stokesborough, which was about ten miles from Highfields. Mr Collinridge agreed to meet her that afternoon and according to his secretary, Annette Hyde-White, would relish the opportunity of making her acquaintance.

Although she knew she could drive perfectly well and had checked that the Rolls Royce was parked in the garage, she decided to order a taxi. She had not found a driving licence among her documents and it was quite possible that she did not possess one. She was not prepared to take a chance on being stopped by the police for driving without a licence or insurance.

On the journey to Stokesborough Edwina studied the countryside intently, but she could not notice any changes; it was as familiar to her as it had always been. The day had turned dull, with grey clouds scudding across the sky. Suddenly the rain began to lash against the windscreen and the driver hurriedly turned on his windscreen wipers. "It never stops raining," the driver grumbled. The remark seemed to spark a memory of a distant hill, where the sunshine had disappeared in an instant, to be replaced by a downpour of warm summer rain. They were running then, hand in hand, she and a dark haired woman, with deep brown smiling eyes. They sought shelter in a large barn on the side of the hill and the woman shook out her hair and smiled down at her with those lovely eyes.

"Cara mia," she said. "In England it never stops raining, so they say. You may go there one day and you can find out if it's true."

And then she laughed, as though amused by a joke. Edwina was sure it was a memory from her childhood, yet how could that be, unless there was a real Edwina, with a real mother in Italy.

The taxi dropped her off in the High Street and she walked the hundred yards to the hallway, at the side of the Nat West Bank. There was a glass panel above the doorway, which, in large black letters, proclaimed this to be the Nat West Chambers. A flight of stone steps led up to the first floor, where glass swing doors led into the offices of Collinridge, Edmunds & Partners. The steps continued upwards to the second floor, which housed the offices of Edward's accountants, Messrs. Reid, Haligan & Morgan. Edward had found it very convenient to have his bank, his accountant and his solicitor all in the same building.

Pushing the swing doors open, Edwina stepped into the waiting room and reception area. Immediately a pretty blonde girl rose from her desk and approached the counter, but before she reached it an older woman stepped through a door from the inner office. She was wearing a smart business suit and had her grey hair tied into a neat bun.

"It's all right, Jennifer, I'll attend to this," she called out to the blonde girl, who immediately turned about and sat down again.

Edwina had to suppress a giggle. As always, Ms Hyde-White looked and was the height of efficiency. She almost said, how are you Annette? It was obvious she had been lurking in the background, while keeping a watchful eye on the front entrance. Edwina could imagine she had hardly been able to curb her curiosity, while waiting for her to arrive.

After introducing herself, Edwina was quickly ushered into the office of Bruce Collinridge. He rose from behind his ancient leather-topped desk to greet Edwina cordially. He was a tall man, several inches above six feet, and now his shoulders were noticeably stooped with too much sitting and writing, but it was a relief to see the old familiar genial smile. Bruce and Edward had been friends since their schooldays, and Bruce's father, who started the practice, had also been a great friend of Edward's father. After shaking her hand, Bruce smoothed back the few hairs that still clung to his scalp and dropped into his leather armchair.

"I'm so pleased to meet you, Miss Cabrossi," he said. "I have been looking forward to it. I did ask Edward to let me know when you arrived, so that I could arrange a meeting. I would have willingly called out to see you, if that would have been easier for you."

"It's quite all right," Edwina said. "I'm sure you are a busy man. However, I thought I should make your acquaintance as soon as possible, as I know that you and father have been friends and business colleagues for many years."

"Indeed we have," Bruce said.

Fumbling in her handbag Edwina produced her passport and handed it over the desk.

"As we haven't met before I thought you might like to see this."

He took it and examined it minutely. She had deliberately left the birth certificate in her handbag, as she was not sure how much Bruce knew about her or how much Edward would have been able to tell him. Bruce took his pen and copied some details from the passport before handing it back to her.

"That's excellent," he said. "I need to obtain your signature on a couple of forms. Although your father made a power of attorney in your favour and the bank and your accountants have been informed, I need to send them specimens of your signature, and we will require some specimens for our own file."

He pulled out a drawer and took out some forms.

"This first one," he said, "is to enable you to sign cheques and other instructions on your father's bank account."

He passed the form across the desk and she took up the pen he handed her and placed three specimen signatures in the appropriate boxes. Without thinking, she had signed with her left hand. Is this just another indication of being totally opposite now, she wondered?

"The next one," Bruce said, "is for your accountants. They do all your father's tax returns and they manage his property investments. I am sure you are aware that he owns a large number of properties. A few years ago he decided to give up controlling the management himself and placed the whole portfolio in the hands of Reid, Haligan & Morgan, who are a prestigious accountancy firm. They manage everything; let the properties, collect the rents, organise repairs, pay the bills, and after deducting their charges, pay a monthly figure into Edward's account. The total value of the properties now is about twenty five million pounds."

Edwina did not have to fake the look of shocked surprise on her face. She had considered the portfolio to be worth nearer twelve million, but that was possibly ten years ago.

Bruce Collinridge looked up with a satisfied smile.

"And this final set of signatures is for us."

She signed and handed the form back to him.

He studied her face and could see that there was something else troubling her.

"Was there anything else you wished to discuss with me?" he asked gently.

"There is," she said. "I don't know whether my father mentioned to you that he was going abroad."

Bruce's brow furrowed, as he concentrated his thoughts.

"I don't recall anything," he said. "Why? Has he gone away?"

"Yes. In fact he left on the day I arrived, the thirteenth."

Bruce shook his head slowly. "He never said anything to me."

"Not even when he asked you to draw up the power of attorney and the new will."

"No," Bruce said, looking puzzled. "It seems strange that he should go away just when you are about to arrive. He must have been dying to see you."

Not a great choice of phrases, Edwina thought.

"I'm sure he will get in touch with you, knowing you are here now."

"I hope so," Edwina said, "but it has created difficulties for me."

She recounted the telephone conversation she had had with Martha and explained the family relationship and the difficulty this was obviously causing.

"I can understand the problem," Bruce said. "It must be very difficult to accept that their uncle has suddenly produced an heir, like a conjurer producing a rabbit out of a hat."

"It isn't as if they are poor," Edwina said. "In fact they are very well off, but of course it alters their expectations with regard to my father."

"Do you know they are well off?" Bruce asked.

"According to my father, his sister married a very wealthy man and the daughters also married into money."

"I see," Bruce said, rubbing his chin. "Well, it isn't as though your father is dead. That would be the time to start kicking up a fuss. I would suggest that, as soon as your father comes home, he should get in touch with both of your cousins and put their minds at rest. It should be a simple matter to explain the position to them. After all, they have no right to influence the wishes of your father with regard to his will, and if necessary, that needs to be made clear to them."

"But suppose he doesn't come home?" Edwina said, and added, "at least for a considerable time. In the meantime they could carry out their threats against me."

"I'm sure you are worrying more than you need," Bruce reassured her. "After all, your father expressed his wishes clearly to me, and here you are. I can vouch for you and for your father's actions regarding you. As you suggest, it may be that he will have a lengthy stay abroad, but surely he has covered that eventuality by signing the power of attorney in your favour. By that very act, he made it clear to me that you stood first in his regard and that he trusted you implicitly."

Edwina smiled in relief. "I'm sure you are right," she said, rising to depart. "Thank you for all your help."

"Don't forget, contact me if there is anything I can help you with."

11

Tuesday 16th February

Martha and Kathleen met at Kathleen's house at ten o'clock. Martha lived about twenty miles from Kathleen and she had quite enjoyed the drive through the wintry lanes, although the low sun dazzled her, as it slanted through the leafless branches. Externally she appeared to be calm, but inwardly she was seething with an uncontrollable anger. How dare she? How dare she! That was the phrase she kept repeating silently. Something had to be done and she needed Kathleen to be a party to whatever action was decided upon. She pulled into the tarmac drive and cruised past the huge front lawn, with its beds of rhododendrons and acacias, before pulling up opposite the front porch.

Kathleen must have been looking out for her, because the front door opened as Martha approached, and there was Kathleen, a smile on her lips and arms outspread to greet her. They exchanged pecks on the cheek and went inside. Martha was forty eight years old and her sister was three years younger, but Martha considered herself to be much older, wiser and more mature than her sister, whom she had always dominated since they were children. Martha had met her husband, Harvey Pinsent Bracken when she was twenty-five. It was not an earth-shattering experience for her, but she felt Harvey had all the right qualities to make a suitable husband, particularly the ability to provide the quality of life she aspired to. And besides, she was not getting any younger. They married a year after they met and lived a reasonably contented life. Harvey was the only son of George Pinsent Bracken and his wife, Ruby. George owned an engineering factory, which covered several acres and which prospered from government armaments contracts. Martha and Harvey had not produced any children, which caused a constant sense of loss to Harvey, but was a cause for secret relief to Martha. She had grown plump and self-satisfied in her middle age. Most of her spare time she spent in shopping. There were frequent trips to all the shopping areas within the locality, and many to London. Money was no object, but none of the exclusive expensive clothes she bought did anything to enhance her figure. Her face clearly showed the discontent she felt, the thin lips turning down at the corners and the wrinkles on her forehead setting into a permanent frown.

Kathleen, on the other hand, was still quite slim and attractive. She had a pleasant smile and liked to think that she was everybody's friend, which in truth she was prepared to be. She made friends easily, and had no difficulty keeping them, as she was always ready to join any village organisation that asked her, and to work hard in their cause. Kathleen Hastings had married at twenty-one and she and her husband, Keith, had produced three children, two boys, aged twenty-two and twenty, and a girl aged seventeen. Keith was an accountant, specialising in corporate tax and worked for a large public company. His job sent him frequently to subsidiary companies in the USA, Canada and Europe. He and Kathleen were still very much in love.

After the tea had been made and they were both sitting comfortably in Kathleen's living room, Martha recounted the details of her telephone conversation with Edwina.

"She has a foreign accent," Martha said, "not very pronounced, but I could detect it. And her name, Cambrossi or Cadbrossi, I think she called herself, sounds Italian. How can an Italian, with a name like that, be related in any way to uncle Edward? She's obviously an impostor."

And what do you think has happened to poor uncle Edward?" Kathleen asked.

"I fear for his safety. He was getting on and she might have had others to help her dispose of him. She may even be part of one of these mafia families." That had been a theory propounded by Harvey, when they were discussing the matter, while seated in front of the fire on the previous evening.

It's too horrible to contemplate, Kathleen thought. They both sipped their tea in silence, imagining the most ghastly end for poor uncle Edward.

"If she is in one of these mafia gangs," Kathleen said, "it might be dangerous to approach her."

"What!" Martha exclaimed. "Are you suggesting we just sit back and do nothing? The longer she remains at "Highfields" the harder it will be to dislodge her. No, we have to act now, before it's too late."

"Yes," Kathleen agreed, as she always did. "So, what do we do? What can we do? We can't go over there and forcibly extract her, can we?"

"That's exactly what I feel like doing," Martha said, "but I'm sure we have the law on our side, so we need to go through the correct channels to get her out."

"So, what do you suggest we do?" Kathleen asked for the second time.

"Well, we must act as one. That is essential, as we are both his true next of kin. She says she is his daughter, so the first step is to get her to prove it."

"Excellent," Kathleen said, enthusiastically. "How do we do that?"

"To keep matters on a legal footing we must get our solicitor to write to her with certain demands. I'm sure our solicitor will know how to go about it. That's their job; to know how to ask awkward questions."

"Yes," Kathleen agreed. She was feeling very much better about the whole business now.

"That's settled then," Martha said. "I'll phone my solicitor this afternoon and make an appointment for us both to see him."

"Do I have to go?" Kathleen pleaded. She hated formal meetings with lawyers, bank managers or anyone else who sat behind a desk and spoke, in what to her, was a foreign language. "Couldn't you do it?"

"No," Martha snapped. "We have to show a united front. We must see the solicitor together."

So that was settled. Kathleen retired to make a fresh pot of tea.

12

Thursday 18th February

The last three days had passed like a pleasant dream for Edwina. It was wonderful to be active again. She had helped Mrs Pearson in the kitchen, anxious to learn all she could about cooking, in particular. She had also spent a lot of time with Alf in the garden. The daffodils, which she loved, were beginning to flower, but unfortunately there were not enough of them to give a good display. As she walked beside the lake with Alf she asked him if he would plant more bulbs on the margins, in particular on a raised bank on one side of the lake, where they would make a spectacular show against the dark woods in the background. At present the grassy bank was bare and needed something to brighten it up.

Alf was flattered and delighted with the interest she showed in the garden and her praise for his work. He realised she had a good understanding of gardening and appreciated the skill and hard work involved. When he returned to the house for his lunch, he was full of admiration for Edwina. It was gratifying to know that she noticed all his efforts.

"What a lovely girl that Edwina is," he said to his wife, as he sat down for lunch. "She takes such an active interest in what's going on. The old man didn't seem to know or care what I was doing."

"Yes. She's just as keen on the housekeeping, as well, especially the cooking," Mrs Pearson said. "She wants me to prepare a pasta dish, Italian she said it was. It sounds absolutely delicious. She wants to learn how to cook it."

13

After her walk round the garden, Edwina hurried upstairs to prepare for the lunch engagement at Greenblade Farm. Her heart was pounding with excitement and anticipation at the forthcoming meeting with the Skefford family. She knew it would be an ordeal, meeting Robinson and Emily again, having known them over twenty years before. They would be changed, so much older. It might be painful. But she was looking forward to seeing Robert again and meeting Rupert and Margaret for the first time.

Deciding what to wear was a problem. As a man she had always found it easy to dress for any occasion. If it was a formal engagement, all men wore a dinner jacket, white shirt and a bow tie. They didn't have to worry whether the dress would be the wrong colour, or the same one worn a year before, or the same one Mrs Jones was wearing now. If the function was smart casual, men wore a combination of jacket and trousers, with a patterned tie, and if it was completely informal, a pair of old jeans and a tee shirt would do fine, or anything else that felt comfortable. For a woman, it seemed there were no such clear dividing lines.

After a few moments of thought, she decided to dress the equivalent of smart casual. As it was her first meeting with her neighbours she wanted to make a good impression on them. After looking at a few possibilities she decided on a smart kingfisher blue dress. It had an attractive Greek pattern running round the V neck. She selected a pair of blue low-heeled shoes to match. Although she had practised in higher heels, she had still not mastered them. She looked in the long mirror and smoothed the dress down over her body and against her thighs. She was well satisfied with the result and decided to dispense with a sweater. However she took out a light grey coat to cover the dress for the journey, as it was very cold outside. She laid the coat on the bed.

The next problem was what make-up to wear. Young girls spent years experimenting with different cosmetics and by the time they reached the age of twenty knew exactly what cosmetics suited them. For Edwina this was the first time that she had contemplated wearing any make-up. She had tried a few of the items in her vanity case in the previous few days, but had always washed everything off before appearing in front of Mrs Pearson. She had decided that a little lipstick would suffice for her first sortie in public. Tentatively she applied some lipstick, staring into the mirror to check the results. She had decided on the one that she thought suited her best, but it did not seem to want to go on without smearing. Twice she had to wipe it off with a tissue, but on the third attempt she achieved a light brushing over her top lip, and pressed both lips together, as she had seen women do, and was quite pleased with the result.

As she came downstairs, she heard a car approaching down the drive. She could feel her heart beating as she went to open the door. Robert stood there smiling, and beside him, his sister Margaret. She was so pleased that Robert had kept his promise to bring Margaret. She embraced her like a sister and told her how glad she was to meet her, and then offered her hand to Robert. Taking it in his hand very gently he felt something akin to an electric shock. He was amazed at the softness of her skin, and was afraid of bruising it if he squeezed too tightly.

"I'm so glad to meet you both," Edwina said, "without a hedge separating us," she added, with a smile at Robert. After taking their coats, she led them along the corridor and into the living room.

"What a magnificent view," Robert enthused. "I never realised there was a lake behind the wood."

"It's such a shame you were not able to come over here to play when you were children, but I wasn't here then, either." They were all standing in front of the large French windows, through which the strange visitor had appeared only a few nights ago, but that seemed to be in the distant past now. The thought of him made Edwina shudder.

"Come and sit on the settee," Edwina said, taking Margaret's hand. "I want us to be the best of friends."

"I would love that too," Margaret said. She had a soft voice, full of sincerity, and Edwina knew instinctively that they would indeed become the best of friends. She was shorter than Edwina by about two inches; her hair was blonde and was quite striking above her cranberry-coloured dress. She was a very attractive girl. Edwina also noticed that she was wearing fairly high heels, which enhanced the slimness of her figure.

"It's so sad that your father is not here to be with you," Margaret said. "Is this the first time you have come to Highfields?"

"Yes, it is," Edwina replied.

"I thought it must be, or we would have met earlier. Strangers are soon noticed in this area. It's so sad that your father is not here to be with you on your first visit."

"He wanted to be with me, very much, but these things happen in life. Now, can I get you all a drink?" Edwina asked, wishing to change the subject.

"Father has put some champagne on ice," Robert said, "so I think it would be better if we saved ourselves for that. He would be so disappointed if we didn't help him drink it."

"Of course," Edwina said. "It's such a pity we haven't got time to walk down to the lake; it's such a pretty walk. There will be other opportunities though, and hopefully the weather will then be warmer than this."

On the short drive over to Greenblades Farm Edwina sat beside Margaret in the rear, while Robert drove. He was feeling left out of it, but kept glancing at Edwina in the mirror. He thought she was even more beautiful than he had imagined on their first meeting and vowed to get to know her better. Then he was pulling onto the short road, which led up to the farm, and stopping in the yard at the rear. As she climbed out Edwina could remember the scene clearly from her last visit, all those many years before. Away in the distance she could see her wood, but the house and the lake were completely hidden.

They hurried into the warm kitchen and, as in the past, her nostrils were assailed by the delicious smell of dinner cooking. Margaret took Edwina's coat away, while Robert introduced her to his parents, Robinson and Emily, who were delighted to meet her. Their faces were older, but she would have known them anywhere. It was sad to see how people aged.

"This is such a happy occasion for us, that I thought it would be appropriate to welcome you with a glass of champagne," Robinson said.

Edwina smiled her appreciation. "How very kind," she said.

"Show her into the living room," Emily said to Robert. "The glasses are laid out ready."

Edwina followed Robert and he seated her where he could face her. Robinson and Emily followed them and Robinson opened the champagne expertly. Margaret came in, leading the absent member of the family, Rupert, who was stockier than Robert. He looked very much like Robert, but his features were rougher and his face was weather-beaten by working constant hours in sun and wind.

"This is Rupert," Margaret said, by way of introduction. "He can't drag himself away from the fields."

Rupert took her hand and stared at her in amazement.

"For goodness sake, you will embarrass the girl," Emily said.

"Oh, sorry," Rupert said, letting go of her hand. "For once, Robert didn't exaggerate."

They all laughed and Rupert took a glass and slumped into an armchair.

Robinson raised his glass and said, "here's to Edwina," and they all sipped the champagne.

Seeing them all gathered there, Edwina felt so happy to be with them. Highfields could have been filled with happy smiling people too, she thought. It was so pleasant just to sit there, listening to their friendly banter, as they laughed and teased each other. It was apparent that Rupert was obsessed with farming, and although the help his father could give was diminishing, he was quite capable of running the farm on his own. He and Robinson chatted animatedly about work and how it was proceeding, the prices for lambs and wheat, fertiliser and oil. Robert and Margaret wanted to chat to Edwina as they were interested to know all about her, but Edwina skilfully avoided all their questions, only fuelling their curiosity about her.

Mrs Skefford was the perfect hostess and eventually ushered them all into the dining room. It was nowhere near as splendid as the huge room at Highfields, but it was cosy and they all fitted comfortably round the table. Emily had prepared roasted lamb and it looked and tasted really good. It brought back a memory of sitting at trestle tables, covered with white sheets, fifty people or more in a long line, while a whole sheep cooked on a spit. The people talked incessantly in a foreign language she could understand, and ate bread and drank red wine, while they waited for the women to serve the lamb. Why am I remembering this, she thought. The day had been warm. The women were dressed in light colourful dresses and the men in open-necked shirts and trousers. Children clung to their mothers or raced about playing games.

"Do have a glass of claret," Robinson said. "It's very good." His words brought her out of her reverie.

"I'm sure it's very good," Edwina said, pushing her glass forward. "Just one glass, then." She already felt a little light-headed from the glass of champagne. A week ago I could have drunk half the bottle, she thought, with a smile.

Edwina asked Margaret what she did, and learned that she had been to Teachers Training College and was at present undergoing her year's training on the job, in the local school, before getting a full-time teaching post in September.

"It's very difficult now," Margaret said. "Small local schools are closing and others are merging into bigger units. I'm hoping I will be able to get something not too far away."

"And what about you?" Robert asked, unable to contain his curiosity any longer. "What do you do?"

"Well, I haven't any University or College degrees," she said, "but I have a fairly good general knowledge. Father has left me in charge of his affairs and that is a large responsibility. I just hope I can cope with it."

"I'm sure you will," Robert said, admiring the way she spoke and her demure demeanour. He thought it was wonderful the way she had fitted in with the family and the way they were all treating her. Everyone was relaxed.

"How is it that all the men's names begin with an 'R'?" Edwina asked.

"That's Robinson's fault, Emily said, laughing. "He insisted that he would be able to remember them better if they all had the same initial."

"It's a wonder I'm not called Rose or Ruby," Margaret said.

"The trouble is, we are always opening each other's letters," Rupert said. "Every letter is addressed to Mr R Skefford."

"I shall put the Christian name in full if I ever write to any of you," she promised.

"Perhaps you could start by writing to me when I go back to Agricultural College," Robert suggested.

"When will that be?" she asked.

"Next week, but I'm not looking forward to it. I don't think I'm cut out to be a farmer, unlike Rupert, who flew through College with distinctions and loves every minute he spends on the land."

"He keeps on about this," Emily said, "but I keep telling him there isn't any money in art."

"Is that what you want to do?" Edwina asked.

"Yes, it is. There isn't enough money in farming to give me a good living, as well as Rupert, and I don't have the same interest in it as Rupert."

"That's true," Rupert chipped in. "There isn't enough work either, with father looking after the sheep. I can manage the rest of the farm comfortably."

"There you are," Robert said triumphantly to his mother. "I finish at college at Easter and then what do I do? I shall have to get a job as a farm labourer on somebody else's farm. That's if I can find one."

"And what do you want to do?" Edwina asked.

Robert stuck out his jaw determinedly. "Paint," he said. Just the one word, but Edwina could see that he meant it.

"He's always painting something," Emily said. "At school his art teacher said he had talent and that he should go to art school."

"At least I wouldn't have wasted two years learning about crop yields and agricultural economics."

"I think you spend more time at college painting than you do learning about farming," Emily said. "He brings a parcel of them home at the end of every term."

"And what do you do with them?" Emily asked.

Robert scowled but did not reply.

"They go to join the others in the attic," Emily said. Clearly she had no great faith in his artistic talent, but in truth she had never bothered to go up to the attic to look at any of them.

"Perhaps you would let me see them one day?" Edwina asked.

"I would love to show you." Robert's face was a picture of pleasure at the prospect. "You can see them today if you like."

As they had finished their lunch, Robinson and Rupert were in a hurry to return to their farming duties. "It was real nice to meet you Miss," Robinson said sincerely. "Next time I hope Edward will be able to come over with you."

"It was certainly a pleasure to meet you, Edwina," Rupert said. "I look forward to seeing you again soon." He followed Robinson out to the kitchen.

Emily and Margaret began to clear the table, but insisted Edwina should relax. "You're a guest," Margaret said. "We don't allow guests to work. Take her into the living room," she suggested to Robert, "or up to see your paintings if she's interested."

"That would be lovely," Edwina said. "I really meant it when I said I would like to see them."

Robert was obviously delighted by the suggestion. "It would be a great pleasure, but don't expect anything spectacular. I'm not a Constable or a Turner."

Edwina laughed. "I'm sure you are being modest."

"Come on then." He took her hand.

"Just be careful how you go up that rickety old ladder into the attic," Emily warned.

Robert led her into the front hall, which seemed quite small compared with the impressive dimensions of 'Highfields'. They climbed the staircase to the first floor landing and along the corridor, to where a wooden loft ladder ascended through a gap in the ceiling and disappeared into the attic. Robert led the way, keeping a firm hold of her hand. She was quite capable of climbing on her own, but she did not object. The ladder was not nearly as rickety as Margaret had suggested.

Robert stepped through the square opening and helped her through, pulling her towards him. For a moment their bodies were pressed close together and to her surprise Edwina felt a thrill in her body, which was quite unique in her experience. It was just for a fleeting moment and then she was able to step forward, as Robert made room for her. With a flourish he switched on a light to reveal the contents of the attic. There were rows of pictures, none of them hung, propped against the walls, from one end of the attic to the other and on both sides of the room. What struck her instantly was his use of colour. It was as though the sun had burst out of the clouds on a dull day, and suddenly everywhere was bathed in sunshine. Her eyes were dazzled by the abruptness of it. She stared in fascination and bewilderment as she walked the length of one wall. She was only able to see those pictures on the outside of the stacks, and suddenly she wanted to see them all. Robert watched her in silence for several minutes, hardly able to breathe, desperately seeking approval from her lips. He thought how beautiful she was, far more than any picture he could paint.

"Well?" he said at last, unable to contain himself any longer.

"They are wonderful," Edwina said. "It must have taken you years to paint all these."

"I've been painting since I was about fourteen, but those at the end of the attic are the most recent. Most of those were painted at college in the last two years, when I should have been studying farming," he added, with a laugh. "Do you really like them? You aren't just saying that to please me."

"Of course not. I would never tell you anything, but the truth. I think you have enough talent to consider making it your career, if that's what you want. Not everyone has a special gift."

Robert threw his arms around her and hugged her close to him. "You don't know how much it means to me to hear you like and praise my work. It matters more than anything else. I thought you were perfect the moment I saw you and now I know you are."

He could tell she was startled by his unexpected and enthusiastic reaction to her approval of his work.

"I'm sorry," he said, releasing her, "but I haven't received any encouragement from the family, apart from Margaret."

"And what does she say?"

"That I should forget farming."

"She's a sensible girl, your sister. It's such a shame though, that all these lovely pictures are shut away in a dusty attic."

"There is nowhere else, unfortunately. If I took them into one of the barns it would be too cold and damp."

"Would you bring them over to Highfields?" Edwina asked, on a sudden impulse. I want to display them properly for you."

Robert looked at her in astonishment. "Where would you ……? Do you have enough spare room?"

"It's time the dining room had a transformation. There will be room for lots of them in there."

"But I'm sure your father will have pictures on the walls already."

"He has, but I can store those. Let me do this for you, Robert, please. You have a few weeks back at college until Easter, and then I want you to bring your family over for lunch on Easter Sunday. I think it's time they all saw your paintings. And it will give me something to concentrate on until we meet again."

Robert smiled his thanks. "You really are the most remarkable person," he said. "I couldn't argue with you, even if I wanted to, but what about the expense? It means framing, and that will cost a small fortune for so many pictures."

"Don't worry about it. Father gave me a very generous allowance when he went away. I hardly know what to spend it on."

"I don't know how to thank you," he said, putting his hand on her waist and kissing her cheek.

"Then that's settled. Bring the pictures over tomorrow."

14

Friday 19th February

The following morning was bright but very cold, with a crisp coating of frost turning the ground white and clean. The bare black branches of the trees stood out starkly against the whiteness of the fields.

Robert knew he would be unable to display all of his pictures, so he had selected those he considered to be the best in his opinion. He then began the task of bringing them down from the attic, wrapping them in protective paper and loading them carefully into his car.

At the same time Edwina had enlisted the help of Mrs Pearson in taking down the pictures in the dining room. These were taken upstairs to one of the spare rooms, wrapped in material, and stored.

"I hope Mr Grangelove doesn't object to this," Mrs Pearson said. "Mind you, I always did think they were a bit gloomy."

"It's fine," Edwina assured her. "The pictures won't come to any harm and can be put back when necessary."

At about midday Robert arrived and, with Edwina's help, they carried all the pictures into the dining room.

"What a magnificent setting this is," Robert enthused, "I can hardly wait to see how they will look."

Edwina picked one up and held it against the oak panelling, above the sideboard. The background enhanced the colours, and the picture appeared to take on a three-dimensional effect. It was quite startling.

"Wow," Robert said. "I'm getting really excited about this."

When all the pictures had been brought in, Edwina took Robert's hand and led him out of the dining room, shutting the door after them.

"You aren't allowed to see them again until Easter," she said, with a twinkle in her eye. He thought she looked so beautiful when she teased him.

"Let's jump in that car of yours and have some lunch at 'The Farmer's Arms'. I believe they have a reputation for serving good food and traditional ales.

"How do you know about that place?" Robert asked.

"Father passed on a lot of useful information to me," she said, with a wink. "He liked a good pint of beer occasionally; none of this tasteless lager for him."

"I agree with him," Robert said, "and I can confirm that the beer is excellent."

Within minutes they had driven into the village and had selected their choice from a menu of tempting home-cooked dishes. They chatted over the meal as though they had known each other for years. Robert sipped his beer and Edwina sipped her beer shandy, and they were totally relaxed in each other's presence. Their eyes met frequently, drinking in each gesture, each facial expression and detail. It was like a dream, as though they were the only people in the room. They might just as well be two survivors from a shipwreck, afloat on a raft in mid ocean, but not caring or sensing any danger, blissfully gazing into each other's eyes, oblivious of the outcome. They were falling in love.

Robert had to return to college the next day, but they were both reluctant to part, knowing that it would be several weeks before they would meet again. When Robert drove her back to 'Highfields', Edwina suggested a stroll down to the lake and the wood. She wanted him to see it as she had seen it on the first day they had met.

"I know it's quite chilly today," she said, "but the daffodils look lovely. I'm going to plant lots more. And you haven't seen the lake or the wood yet."

"Then what are we waiting for," Robert said, climbing out of the car.

They ambled down towards the lake and on the way he took her hand. It seemed so natural to her and she felt a warm sensation throughout her body, like no other she had ever experienced.

Robert again felt something akin to an electric shock when she gave him her hand. He could only describe it as wonderful. He glanced at her shyly, and received a smile right from the depths of Edwina's heart.

They strolled on towards the lake, each of them wrapped in sheer happiness. The wind sent ripples gliding across the surface of the water, causing the swans and ducks to bob up and down like living corks. The grey clouds rushed overhead and there was a promise of snow on the horizon. They moved in closer to each other. Neither of them spoke; there was no need for words.

They passed round the margins of the lake and entered the wood, where they gained shelter from the wind. They followed the well-worn path, strewn now with the dead leaves and broken twigs from autumn and winter gales. As they reached a small clearing Robert stopped and turned to her. There was shelter here and silence too, with the boughs of the surrounding trees uplifted like a great cathedral, and their canopies touching and almost closing out the sky. The clearing was dappled with shafts of sunlight, which managed to break through the grey shadow of the canopy. Edwina knew she had been waiting for this moment, anticipating it, deeply desiring it. Robert took her gently in his arms, pulling her towards him. She turned her face up to his and he kissed those lovely lips. They both felt as though their bodies were bursting with love. They had never felt such happiness before. A single tear trickled down Edwina's cheek and Robert kissed it.

"Is anything the matter?" he asked.

"Nothing," she said softly, touching his cheek with her fingers to reassure him. "It's just that I feel so happy, but that tear reminds me that we have many obstacles to overcome."

He pulled her in to him and they resumed their walk. Neither had declared their love, but they both knew they did not have to.

15

Monday 22nd February

Edwina felt so alone after parting with Robert, but at the same time she was filled with a warm glow whenever she thought of him and remembered how it had felt to be held and kissed by him. She had never felt like that before. Or had she? Not as Edwina for sure, but as Edward there had been an occasion she knew, and Edward had always tried to suppress the memory, until he had almost wiped it out entirely, but there were some tantalising snap shots which flashed across her brain.

She was puzzled that in her present being she was an Italian girl, presumably with an English father, namely Edward. Yet, although she had some vague memories of a life in Italy before waking in Edward's bed, she could not understand why there was such a cloud over her earlier life. Am I the real Edwina Cabrossi and the daughter of Anna Cabrossi, she wondered, or is it a figment of my imagination? If they were just figments of her imagination, how could she explain the passport, with her photograph on it, and the will, naming her as Edward's heir. She wondered if there was a real Anna Cabrossi and Edwina Cabrossi living somewhere in Italy. If there was, how could she be here in England? She could not be in two places at the same time.

At the back of Edwina's mind a thought was taking shape, but she was reluctant to give it credence, even though it might give some of the answers to the mystery. She resolved to do something about it as soon as possible. For now though the puzzle would have to wait. Putting on her warmest coat, as the day was very cold, she set out on her now daily walk, to where she had first spoken to Robert, and to the clearing where they had kissed for the first time. On this particular morning her mind was troubled and the future seemed as shrouded in doubt, as the woods were in mist. She shivered and pulled her coat collar up. She could not account for her depression and sense of foreboding, except to rationalise that she was missing Robert terribly, but in her heart she knew it was more than that.

On returning to the house, she found a letter waiting for her; the first she had received addressed to her, although, strictly speaking, it was not addressed to her, but to a Miss E Cadbrossi, not Cabrossi. She opened it and noticed, from the expensive, embossed heading that it emanated from the firm of Cavanagh, Slattery & Saunders, Solicitors of 1186 Crookham Road, Winkton Stewart. They announced that they were representing the sisters, Mrs Martha Bracken and Mrs Kathleen Hastings, who were concerned at the disappearance of their uncle Edward Grangelove, and equally concerned by the appearance of an unknown stranger, namely Edwina Cadbrossi, who had taken up residence in their uncle's house and seemed to be masquerading as his daughter. There followed several paragraphs of suggestions relating to 'dear uncle Edward's fortune which was undoubtedly being siphoned off to some mysterious numbered bank account in Switzerland or Italy. Finally there were threats of the direst consequences should any fraudulent activity come to light.

After reading the letter for the second time, Edwina collapsed into her favourite armchair in the living room and tried to keep the tears from her eyes. What can I do, she thought. I can't produce Edward out of a hat. I just hope my solicitors are up for the fight, because there is surely going to be a fight now. It's up to dear old Bruce to fight them off. She telephoned him and read the letter she had just received.

"You thought something like this might happen, didn't you?" he said.

"Yes, I did. They aren't going to accept that someone who is a complete stranger to them is going to come in and ..and..."

"Do them out of their inheritance," Bruce concluded.

"Exactly," Edwina said. She was close to tears again.

"Let me have the letter," Bruce said. "I will put Messrs. Cavanagh, Slattey and Saunders in the picture regarding the relationship between you and your father. Edwina was amazed that Bruce had quoted the name of the other firm of solicitors precisely, although she had only said it once. It increased her confidence in him and eased her worries slightly.

"I'm sure that when I have explained the position and given them a copy of the power of attorney they will be able to calm down your cousins."

"I do hope so," Edwina said. "I want to be friends with them."

After he rang off, Edwina placed the letter in an envelope, addressed it to 'Mr. B. Collinridge at Collinridge, Edmunds & Partners' and sealed it. Then she looked through the Yellow Pages and found a company in Stokesborough advertising a picture-framing service. Before hiring them, she decided, it would be prudent to inspect their work, so she called a taxi and travelled into Stokesborough. This time she made the taxi wait, while she entered the offices of Collinridge Edmunds & Partners and left the envelope containing the letter she had received, with the pretty young blonde girl, who was not headed off on this occasion by Annette Hyde-White. Then she travelled on to A1 Framing. Again, she asked the taxi to wait.

Entering the shop, she inspected the various frames displayed on the walls, whilst being scrutinised herself just as closely by a middle-aged grey-haired lady, through a pair of thick-lensed glasses. At last, unable to contain herself any longer the lady asked her if she needed any help. By now

Edwina was satisfied that the quality of materials and the standard of workmanship was indeed A1 and she asked if she could speak to the proprietor, as she had a rather large job for him and needed to know if he would have sufficient time to complete it by Easter. The grey-haired lady scuttled away through a door at the back of the counter and reappeared a few moments later, followed by a grey-haired man of about the same age, whom it turned out was the lady's husband and joint proprietor. He introduced himself as Brian Jefferson.

Edwina explained that she had approximately thirty canvases and watercolours to frame, and he produced a large book from under the counter, which contained photographs and samples of the various patterns and designs and different woods that were available.

"That won't be necessary," Edwina said. "I can see that the standard of your work is very high. Could you come over to see the paintings and where they are going to hang and we will decide on the frames then. What I want is for the whole display to look good in the setting of the dining room and to enhance the individual pictures with suitable frames."

"That's exactly what I always aim to achieve," he said, "but you will appreciate that cost enters into the equation, and sometimes people choose the cheaper option and are disappointed as a result." He shook his head sadly.

"Cost is not a problem," Edwina assured him. "I want the presentation to be perfect. Could you come tomorrow and bring your specimen book. The address is Highfields...."

"Highfields, did you say," Jefferson interrupted her. "I know that property. I've been there before. Mr Grangelove has asked me to do some framing for him in the past. Is he keeping well these days?"

"Yes. He's my father." She could not remember having consulted Jefferson before. "So you have been to the house before and will remember where it is."

"I could hardly forget such a beautiful place. Will around ten thirty tomorrow morning be suitable? It will be a pleasure to see Mr Grangelove again."

"I'm afraid you will be disappointed in that," Edwina said. "He is abroad at the moment."

"What a pity, but I look forward to seeing the pictures and doing a good job for you."

16

Tuesday 9th March

The next two weeks passed happily, with Mr Jefferson assisting Edwina to achieve her objective of displaying Robert's pictures to the best advantage. She insisted that he should call her Edwina and she called him Brian. After a while they were discussing each picture like old friends and deciding on its merits. Each was discussed, measured and a suitable frame chosen, before Brain departed to carry out the work in his studio. Not only was he a superb craftsman, but he also had an artistic talent himself, being able to assemble the paintings and hang them on the dining room walls in such a way that the effect was stunning. Every day he arrived, he had four or five new frames ready to take more pictures. Edwina often gave her own opinion on the positioning of some of the pictures and Brian had to admit that she was often right. At last the final painting was hung and Edwina was able to view what she considered to be a fine exhibition of Robert's work.

"What do you think?" Edwina asked.

"I think your friend has a superb talent and a great career ahead of him and I think he has a lot to thank you for. As you can imagine, I have many friends in the art world, and some of them are dealers. In particular I have a friend who owns a gallery in Kensington who has a reputation for finding the best new artists. I'm sure I could persuade him to come down to view Robert's pictures, if you like."

"That would be wonderful," Edwina said.

"This is a superb setting for an exhibition," Brian said, surveying the length of the dining room, now hung from end to end with Robert's pictures. If my friend is keen on them and you would permit it, and the artist also, of course, I am sure I could persuade quite a few people to come along to an exhibition."

"Here?" Edwina asked.

"Yes. Of course! It would be a spectacular setting. You should see some of the halls used for exhibitions."

"Robert will be home for Easter and I'll mention it then. If he agrees, and I'm sure he will, I will telephone you."

"My friend's name is Siegfried Baxter," Brian said. "I will give him a call in any case, just to find out how busy he is going to be in the near future. He spends so much time travelling from town to town that I know his diary is pretty full."

"Splendid! You have been such a help and if we can get this exhibition off the ground you and your wife's names will be the first on the guest list."

She regarded Brian as a good friend, after their days of working together in the dining room and was sure he would not have commented so favourably, if he had not been sincere in his remarks. After she had paid him and he had left for the last time, she felt almost sorry that the work was completed and they would not be having any more animated discussions about the right frames or hanging positions on the panelling. After walking the length of the dining room, slowly examining each painting, Edwina felt satisfied. She went into the kitchen and brought Mrs Pearson into the dining room to show her what she had been engaged on for the last two weeks. Since helping to remove the previous pictures Mrs Pearson had avoided the dining room, so she was amazed at the transformation.

"My word," she cried, "they look wonderful. I always thought those other pictures were so gloomy," she said, "stags on mountains, half covered in cloud and snow. Not one, but all of them."

Edwina had to smile, remembering the thousands of pounds spent on acquiring some of those gloomy pictures.

"Now these are colourful and cheerful," Mrs Pearson continued. "They make you feel happy." Edwina could have kissed her. Surely that was the best recommendation any artist could have.

"On Easter Sunday I have invited the Skefford family here to lunch. I know it will be a lot of extra work, but I will help you to prepare as much as possible in advance."

"Bless you, it will be no trouble at all. It will be a real pleasure to me to have a challenge. Your father never had any guests. It will be enjoyable preparing a banquet for a change. I can promise you they won't go away complaining about the food."

"Or anything else, I'm sure," Edwina said.

"It's so good to have you here," Mrs Pearson said. "You have brought some life back into the house. It was such a dreary existence for your father. I just wish he could come home and enjoy the happiness you have brought."

Mrs Pearson quickly turned on her heel and left the dining room, obviously embarrassed by such an outspoken observation. Edwina was moved by her remark, but it made her realise that sooner or later questions would have to be answered about the whereabouts of Edward, and nobody was likely to believe the true explanation, even if she could ever dare reveal it. Mrs Pearson is right, she thought, my existence as Edward was dreary in the extreme, and had reached the point of depression, despondency and hopelessness. Suicidal thoughts had been uppermost in Edward's mind on the night when Michael had appeared. She had not given much thought to what had happened to her, but had been overjoyed at the transformation and delighted to accept it without hesitation, even though it had entailed a change of sex and having to learn a new way of living.

Edwina was roused from her thoughts by the jangling of the telephone. She ran to pick it up, hoping and believing that it would be Robert, as he spoke to her every day, but she recognised the voice of Bruce Collinridge. Had her thoughts of a few moments earlier foreboded some dire news? She slid into a chair.

"Are you there?" Bruce asked.

"Yes," she whispered. "I was just sitting down."

"After receiving the letter from you, I wrote to your cousins' solicitors and assured them that I was fully aware of your existence before you arrived and that Edward had acknowledged you as his daughter and had granted you a power of attorney. I didn't mention the will, because it's none of their business, but I did send a copy of the power of attorney. It seems their solicitor was prepared to accept the situation and advised them to do the same, but Martha Bracken wishes to pursue the matter. Her solicitor has asked to be informed when Edward returns and she wishes then to visit him and meet you."

"That seems to be satisfactory, but I have no idea of when he plans to return."

"Don't worry about it," Bruce said. "Just let me know when he does."

After putting down the telephone, Edwina heaved a sigh of relief, but she knew it was only a temporary reprieve. Sooner or later the truth would emerge that Edward was not coming back. Then she would have to face some really difficult questions, but in the meantime she resolved to enjoy life, and especially the forthcoming reunion with Robert. He would be home within a few weeks and soon after that it would be Easter Sunday, and she would have the pleasure of entertaining the whole Skefford family.

17

Thursday 25th March

The morning was cold, but bright, with the sun sending out some heat at last. Edwina had cast off the gloom of the previous days. The gardens cheered her, with the daffodils in full bloom and the tulips coming into flower, with their varied brilliance delighting her eyes. Perhaps I should have been an artist, she thought, and then laughed. "I still could be," she said aloud. "I could be anything I choose, with years still ahead of me and all the money I could ever wish for." She laughed again, but she knew there was a serious side to her speculation and decisions would have to be made in due course.

She was sure that she was in love with Robert and that he was in love with her, but the situation raised questions about marriage and having children. She could not decide on that issue at that time.

On her walk she decided to get to know Robert's sister Margaret a lot better. After all, she was about the same age as Edwina and must know how to face up to the same problems that were exercising Edwina's mind. As usual she found herself in the clearing where she and Robert had kissed for the first time. At least here, I don't have any doubts, she thought. I know we both feel torn asunder at present. The clearing still gave the impression of being a cathedral to Edwina, and her daily walks to it represented her church visits. She could worship at the altar of light and shadows and dream of the moment she experienced her first kiss.

After she returned to the house she collected the mail from the small table in the hall, where Mrs Pearson placed the letters every day, and took them into the study. Usually it was only routine statements from banks, reports from companies about shares owned and dividends paid. There was also the usual plethora of unsolicited mail regarding never-to-be-repeated offers from gas, electricity and car insurance companies. Edwina dropped the offers into the waste paper bin unread, as she did every day.

Edward had set up a system whereby he received the usual monthly statement from his bank simultaneously with a statement from Reid, Haligan & Morgan, his accountants, detailing the rents that had been received in the month, the expenses paid out and the net sum paid over to Edward's bank account. He would then contact his broker and invest surplus funds in shares or other investments that appealed to him. In this way he had accumulated a vast portfolio, which grew and brought in further income. Edwina knew that in recent months Edward had felt too ill and disinterested to bother about anything, as he had nothing to spend the money on. His greatest pleasure in life had always been living at 'Highfields', the house he loved above all else. He was not indifferent to the needy in society and had set up a Charitable Foundation through his solicitors, into which he had transferred a million pounds ten years previously. It paid out substantial amounts annually to all the charities whose work he supported.

It struck Edwina as odd that she had not been asked by her solicitor to sign a specimen signature form in relation to Edward's brokers. Perhaps Bruce Collinridge felt he was protecting her and Edward by keeping her away from making investment decisions that could prove to be costly mistakes. She had to smile, when she visualised the look on his face if he ever discovered that she and Edward were the same person. She decided not to press the matter of the specimen signature for the brokers, as under the terms of the power of attorney she could soon start issuing instructions to the brokers if she wished, but she did not want to spend her time investing and making deals; there were far more interesting things to do.

She began to file the documents that she had received and wished to keep, but paused as she clipped in the statement from her accountants. She knew that it had been several months since Edward had taken any interest in the figures, but even a casual glance revealed that there was something wrong. The amount paid over did not have a familiar look. Examining several months, the net rents from a warehouse in Adelphi Street in Stokesborough had dropped by exactly £2000 per month. Edward had always been keen to join in the rent negotiations with the estate agents and always had the final say, so he knew within a few hundred pounds the amount that should be paid over, after expenses had been deducted. Edwina decided to investigate, but it would have to wait, as she had invited Margaret over to lunch. She had some free periods from her teaching duties that afternoon and had been giving Edwina some driving lessons. Edwina could drive perfectly well, but she did not have a British driving licence and could not find her Italian licence, assuming she had one. She had therefore taken out a provisional licence and Margaret had agreed to sit with her, while she prepared for her test.

Margaret arrived promptly at twelve thirty and Edwina ran out to meet her. She had been waiting in keen anticipation for her arrival, as she loved being in her company and they had become the best of friends. After the initial greeting they went into the house arm-in-arm. Edwina led her into the sitting room, where Mrs Pearson had set up a small table for the two of them.

"This is just perfect," Margaret said, "we have a lovely view from here, across the terrace and down to the lake."

"And from the side window I can see anyone who comes down the drive into the parking area. So I have time to tell Mrs Pearson if I don't want to be disturbed."

They both laughed and at that moment Mrs Pearson came in with the first course of minestrone soup. They sat down at the small table that Mrs Pearson had covered with a brilliantly white tablecloth. She had laid out the best cutlery and the best dinner service was being used on Edwina's instructions.

"I hope you like fish," Edwina said, a short time later, when Mrs Pearson came in with the main course.

"I love fish," Margaret said. "This is quite a banquet, considering that you said we would have some light refreshment before the driving lesson."

"We can't concentrate on the driving if we are hungry, can we? This is a little recipe of my own," Edwina said. "It is mainly salmon, with some white fish added, in pasta and a delicious cream and oyster sauce. It's very light."

"And did you prepare it yourself?" Margaret asked.

"Yes, I did. I have been learning from Mrs Pearson, who is an excellent cook and now I have started experimenting on my own."

"It looks and smells wonderful," Margaret said.

"It really needs a glass of Italian dry white wine to bring out all the flavours," Edwina said, raising a bottle from the cooler.

"I don't know," Margaret said hesitantly, "we are going to have a driving lesson afterwards, aren't we?"

"Yes, but we will also have only one glass of wine."

"Alright then," Margaret said, and Edwina poured the clear liquid into the crystal glasses.

The two girls toasted each other, feeling happy and relaxed.

After they had finished the meal, Margaret congratulated Edwina.

"That was wonderful," she said. "It's easy to see that you were brought up with a knowledge of Italian cuisine. I love Italian food, but you have to go to a genuine Italian restaurant to find it. That was so simple and so good. It was lovely."

"Thank you," Edwina said. "It's a pleasure to cook for people who appreciate it. Let's hope you appreciate my driving just as much."

They went out to the parking area, where Edwina had already driven the car round from the garage. It was a Silver Cloud Rolls Royce, which Edward had bought two years before and she loved it, but had had to adjust the seat considerably to reach the peddles.

Margaret stood in amazement. "Are you seriously going to drive that?" she asked.

"Of course. I'm confident of handling it perfectly well." And so it proved, when she started it up and drove onto the lane. She drove around the area and even into Stokesborough and back.

"You know, I couldn't drive this car," Margaret said. "It's far too big for me, but you handle it as though you have been driving it all your life."

"Would you advise me to get a smaller car?" Edwina asked.

"Normally I would say definitely, but you handle it without any difficulties," Margaret replied.

At a small housing estate on the outskirts of the village Margaret took her through reversing and doing a three-point turn, not an easy exercise on such a narrow road, with such a large vehicle, but Edwina completed the manoeuvres with no difficulty.

As she was about to drive on Edwina was suddenly contorted in agony. There was wrenching pain in her midriff and she clutched her stomach and leant against the wheel.

"Whatever is the matter?" Margaret asked in alarm.

"I don't know," Edwina gasped. "It hit me so suddenly, but it is easing off slightly. There's a throbbing and oh." She clutched her stomach again.

"Could it be your period?" Margaret suggested.

Edwina nodded in despair. Her cheeks were burning with embarrassment. She had not given a thought to what every woman experiences every month and what inevitably she would have to experience.

"We are quite near to the farm," Margaret said. "I'll drive us there."

"No, it would be dangerous for you to drive this car. Give me the instructions and I will get us there, but please don't make a fuss when we arrive. I feel humiliated as it is."

"Nonsense," Margaret said and put her arm round Edwina's shoulders. "There's nothing to be worried about. It happens to us all. I thought you might have been on the pill, though."

"On the pill?" Edwina asked.

"Yes. It prevents periods as well as protecting against other unwanted events," Margaret said, with a mischievous smile.

"Oh, I see. Perhaps I should see a doctor."

"No need. Just go to the Family Planning Clinic." Margaret laughed. "You are a little innocent, aren't you?"

"I'm afraid I am," Edwina said.

Following Margaret's directions Edwina drove to Greenblade Farm and, to her relief, none of the family was at home. Margaret quickly made her comfortable and gave her some painkillers and a glass of water. Before long she was able to pull her hands away from her midriff and sit back in her armchair, but her face was still pale and drawn.

"Are you feeling better now?" Margaret asked. She had been so worried about her friend, but now a little colour was returning to her cheeks. "Do you always experience such acute pain?" Margaret asked.

"I've never experienced anything like that before," she said honestly, and smiled. "Thank God I was with you. I thought I was dying."

They both laughed.

"I'm fit enough now to drive you back to Highfields to pick up your car. You must think I'm a complete idiot."

"Not at all," Margaret said. "I think you are like a refreshing breeze."

After they drove back to Highfields, they embraced, before Margaret got into her own car. "Please go to the clinic," she urged Edwina. "I know you are in love with Robert and he is crazy about you, so you need to take precautions."

"We haven't become lovers," Edwina said.

"Not yet," Margaret said, "but just in case."

18

Friday 26th March

After her usual morning walk, Edwina settled herself once again in her study and went over the figures she had been looking at the day before. There was no doubt about it; since the previous December the rent received had been short by two thousand pounds per month. After the new rent for the Adelphi Street warehouse had been negotiated, Edward had monitored it carefully for several months, but then he had lost interest in monitoring the items passing through all his accounts. His depression had set in and grew steadily, like a cancer.

Reaching for the telephone Edwina dialled the number of Reid, Haligan & Morgan, the Accountants, and asked to speak to Mr Haligan, who dealt with Edward's affairs.

"Ah, Miss Cabrossi," Haligan said, in his clear authoritative voice. As always, the Midland accent was unmistakable, and, as always he sounded warm and friendly. Perhaps, on this occasion, even more cheerful than usual, as it was the first time he had spoken to Edwina, and wished to make the very best impression on her.

"I have been so looking forward to meeting you. I hope you are settling in well. My wife, Pauline and I are going to invite you over for dinner one evening, but we didn't want to rush you. It must be difficult for you just now, with trying to settle in a foreign country, especially with your father abroad."

"Yes, it has been a complete change," Edwina said, suppressing a wicked smile. "I would like to come over and have dinner with you sometime, as I am trying to form personal friendships with all of my father's friends and business colleagues."

Haligan was amazed at the clarity of her voice, the perfection of her English, although there was a slight Italian accent, but most of all that she came across as a very sexy young girl and Haligan had always been keen on very sexy young girls, to be admired from a distance, as he knew that his wife, Pauline would break every bone in his body if he admired any of them from closer quarters.

"I will speak to my wife, Pauline tonight," he said, "and arrange a dinner date."

"That would be lovely," Edwina said.

"Was there anything else you would like to discuss? I appreciate that you are holding the reins now, with Edward abroad, so please do not hesitate to confide in me. I will help you out with all the questions you might have regarding Edward's investments, his properties, rents and rent reviews. It must be a great difficulty for you and I am only too ready to assist."

"You are very kind," Edwina said, "but I wondered if you had one person who looked after father's accounts, monitored the income and sent out the monthly statements."

"Yes, we have," Haligan said. "It's Patrick Plockton. He's one of our bright young stars. He comes from a poor family background, but worked his way through university and obtained his accountant's degree. He controls all your father's financial accounts and ultimately prepares his tax return. What's more, his mother is Italian, but I have never heard him mention his father."

"Could I have a quick word with him?" Edwina asked. "I'm sure he will be able to answer my trivial queries."

"Of course," Haligan said. Is there anything the matter, that I can deal with?"

"No," Edwina assured him. "Please put me through to Patrick."

"Of course, and I will telephone you about the dinner date as soon as I have spoken to my wife, Pauline."

There were a few clicks and eventually a young man's voice came on the line.

"Hello," he said, nervously. "I believe that's Miss Cabrossi, who is handling Mr Grangelove's affairs while he's abroad."

"That's correct," Edwina said, speaking in her most young innocent, little-girl-lost voice, emphasising the Italian accent. Immediately Plockton's voice seemed to gain in confidence.

"What can I do for you, Miss?" he asked.

"I find all these statements so confusing," she said, and gave a little girlish giggle. "I would like you to come here and explain them to me."

"I would love to," Patrick said, imagining nothing more pleasant than explaining some figures to this wonderfully sounding Italian million heiress. "Unfortunately, I don't know whether I can get time off."

"I have just spoken with William," she said, referring to Haligan by his Christian name. "You only have to mention that you are coming to see me, at my request, and he will agree. Come on Monday afternoon at two o'clock." She put down the phone, without waiting for a reply.

Soon after Edwina had finished speaking to Plockton the telephone rang.

"Is that Edwina Grangelove?" a man's voice asked. It was very deep and there was no trace of an accent.

"Speaking," she said.

"My name's Siegfried Baxter. Brian Jefferson may have mentioned my name to you."

Edwina had been hoping to hear from him, as she knew that he was the one man who could launch Robert's career in the art world. "Of course, I remember Brian telling me about you."

"All good, I hope." He laughed heartily. "Brian has told me about your friend's pictures and he has certainly captured my interest. I would like to see them, if that's possible."

"It would be a pleasure to meet you and show you the pictures."

Baxter was intrigued by the sound of her voice, soft and sexy, with its slight trace of an Italian accent. His mind conjured up visions of the most desirable women in the world and suddenly he was desperate to meet her.

"No doubt Brian told you that I am a very busy man," Baxter said, oozing charm, "but I am sure it would be a great pleasure to visit you and see your friend's pictures. I seem to spend most of my life travelling, but that's the only way to discover new exciting talent."

"When would you like to come?" Edwina asked.

"Let me see," he said. There was a pause, as though he was checking his diary, but he had made up his mind to see Edwina as soon as possible, as his life was devoid of sexual excitement at present and he was in need of a new adventure. At length he said, "I could come soon after lunch next Tuesday."

"That would be lovely," Edwina said. She was thrilled at the prospect of his visit taking place so soon.

"I can't give you an exact time," he said, "as I have another call to make."

"That's fine. I can be free the whole afternoon."

"Good," Siegfried purred, "until next Tuesday, then." He ended the call, and sank back in satisfaction, as he contemplated the exquisite excitement awaiting him on the following Tuesday. He had a passion for the opposite sex, which three marriages and three divorces, plus many more conquests and affairs, had failed to satisfy. Now he viewed the coming meeting with Edwina as a tryst, in which she was playing an equal part. He interpreted every word of their recent conversation as an invitation and already the passion burned within him.

19

Margaret often went with some of her friends to the sole nightclub in Stokesborough and after many invitations she had managed to persuade Edwina to accompany her.

"I won't be any good at it," Edwina protested. "I never could get the hang of dancing."

"There's nothing to it," Margaret said. "Just stand in the circle with the rest of us and move in motion to the music. I'm sure you can do that. I think you are just being modest; you are probably a wonderful dancer."

Edwina felt less self-conscious when she realised there were quite a few in the party. There were three teachers who worked with Margaret, two of their boyfriends and Rupert, who had decided to accompany Margaret. Edwina found the atmosphere and the crowds of young people, the music and the flashing lights strangely exciting, not at all as she had expected. She threw herself energetically into the dancing, which she found to be exhilarating and it was so good to feel the energy of youth flowing through her. With Margaret's help she soon learned how to wriggle her body in time to the music, which, it seemed to her, was all that was required to pass for dancing, but she put even more into it, making her body move sensuously in time with the rhythm. This did not go unnoticed, particularly by the men in the nightclub, who could hardly take their eyes off this beautiful stranger. Both girls had received plenty of unwanted attention, but they were able to brush aside these advances fairly easily, particularly as they had Rupert in the party. His powerful figure, muscular arms and bronzed face were enough to deter anyone.

Edwina noticed that the only time Rupert got up to dance was when she went on to the dance floor and that he always managed to position himself alongside her. By the end of the evening she had the distinct impression that Rupert was not so much interested in the dancing as in her. Sometimes, while several of them were dancing together his hands would circle her waist and linger longer than necessary. Rupert was good fun though and obviously very popular with Margaret's friends, but she hoped that he was not getting interested in her. Afterwards, as they drove back, she decided that perhaps she was taking life too seriously and that she should just laugh it off as a joke, but she was missing Robert and longed for his return from college.

20

Monday 29th March

After lunch Edwina carried down the property files and rent statements to the dining room. She had spent most of the morning going through the figures again to make sure that she had not made a mistake. In fact she hoped she had made a mistake, but the evidence was conclusive. She laid the files and statements out in front of the seat at the head of the table. From that seat the long polished surface of the table seemed to stretch almost into infinity, especially for someone unfamiliar with such surroundings. Beyond was the large window, with a view onto the gravelled parking area, surrounded by shrubs and trees. Robert's recently hung pictures looked down colourfully and cheerfully on the scene Edwina had so carefully set up.

As she watched, a small blue car came into view, swinging round the corner of the drive and coming to a crunching halt in front of the house. A young man, aged about twenty four climbed out, clutching a black briefcase and strode confidently, out of Edwina's sight, over to the front door. The bell clanged and, after a short interval, she could hear Mrs Pearson talking to the stranger. Mrs Pearson had not been informed that Edwina expected a visitor, so she asked the young man to wait in the hall. From there he could look down the length of the downstairs corridor and upwards to the massive stairs, curving round and out of sight to the right. It was an impressive and at the same time daunting prospect.

"I'm sorry to interrupt," Mrs Pearson said, "but a Mr Plockton says he has an appointment with you at two o'clock."

"That's right," Edwina said. "You can show him in."

She rose to greet Plockton, who was a handsome young man with a shock of unruly dark hair, which he kept sweeping out of his eyes. He was only an inch or two taller than Edwina and suddenly confronted by such a beautiful girl, he felt his hands becoming sweaty and trembling as he shook hands with her. She seated him in the chair at the head of the table. He had felt completely confident at the prospect of meeting her, but that confidence was evaporating fast. He felt intimidated by her beauty and by the huge bare table, stretching out before him, like some great whale about to swallow him up. He fidgeted with his briefcase and took out some files of his own. He glanced sideways at Edwina. She was far younger than he had expected and he was sure she was the most beautiful girl he had ever seen. He noticed the pictures, covering the panelling on both sides of the room, the antique sideboard and the vases displayed on its top.

Edwina studied him closely. She knew that her silence increased his nervousness. He is a handsome young man, she decided. His features were very boyish, beneath his tangle of thick black curly hair. He had brown eyes and long black eye lashes. Looking at him, Edwina found it difficult to believe that he could be a criminal. His discomfort was obvious, and it was increasing by the second, but Edwina was determined to make him open the conversation, which eventually he did.

Picking up a file at random he asked, "what, in particular would you like me to explain?"

This was precisely the question Edwina had expected, so she asked the question she had prepared, which concerned a parade of shops in Stokesborough High Street, where the rents added up to a substantial amount. She could sense the relief as he began to explain the terms of the Leases and how much rent was paid and how expenses affected each, before the balance was paid over to Edward's account. The figures flowed from his tongue, without having to resort to the files, so that it was obvious he was on top of his job. It was also clear that he would hardly have made such an obvious mistake regarding the Adelphi Street warehouse. Edwina was intrigued to know why he had resorted to embezzlement.

"That's very clear," she said at last, interrupting him. "You explained everything very well. Can you explain though why the rents from the warehouse in Adelphi Street are well below the agreed amount?"

He closed his eyes, swayed slightly, so that Edwina thought for one moment he was going to collapse; and then he leaned forward and buried his head in his hands. Edwina was expecting him to give his excuses, but she saw his shoulders heave and heard his first sobs. Within a minute he was sobbing uncontrollably. She was disconcerted by the sudden turn of events. She had expected him to be outraged, denying there was anything amiss and abusive towards her, alleging that she was making false accusations against him. Instead, he wept openly and then, gathering himself, he wiped his eyes.

"I am so sorry," he said. "I know I have done you a great wrong and I will repay every penny, but I was desperate. I knew Mr Grangelove was going away, but I did not deliberately intend to take advantage of that situation. I swear to God it is the truth," he swore in Italian.

"Then explain it to me," she said, also in Italian. She had said it automatically and knew instantly, on hearing him speak in Italian, that it came as natural to her as speaking in English.

"The young man's face looked up in amazement. "You can speak Italian," he said.

"Of course. With a name like Cabrossi, what else would you expect?"

"I never even gave it a thought," he said.

"So tell me what is going on," Edwina said.

"I will tell you the truth," Plockton said. "My mother has been suffering from cancer for over a year, but last December it became worse and the specialist said she only had weeks to live. He mentioned that there was a drug, called Erbitux, which could extend her life expectancy by as much as six months, but it was not available on the National Health Service. The cost is four thousand pounds per month. I couldn't bear the thought of my mother slowly dying in front of my eyes, when I knew there was this drug, which could alleviate her suffering and extend her life. I thought long and hard about it.

"When my father died he left twelve thousand pounds, so I decided to use two thousand of that every month and took two thousand from the Adelphi Street rent. I calculated that at least she would have the drug for six months."

"And has it been beneficial?" Edwina asked.

"Since taking it my mother is so much better. I know the cancer is not being cured, but her whole demeanour is different. She can even hope again. She will die anyway when she hears what I have done. She will die from shame." Once again he buried his head in his hands.

For a while she let him cry in silence, while she came to a decision.

"Tell me," she said at last, "how is it that you can speak such fluent English and Italian?"

He raised his head and rubbed his reddened eyes. "I had an English father and an Italian mother. After marrying, my parents came to this country and I was brought up here. My mother could never learn English, so, as a baby, she spoke to me in Italian all the time, while my father always spoke to me in English. Eventually I became fluent in both languages."

"When did your father die?" she asked.

"While I was at University he had a heart attack. It was a complete shock because he had always been so fit and active. It may have caused my mother's illness. After his death, life became very difficult, but we were just picking up when my mother became ill." He looked earnestly into Edwina's face. "I beg your forgiveness," he said. "I know it will mean dismissal and disgrace and possibly prison for me, if my employers complain to the police. I could bear all that, but I feel sick inside that my mother could die within weeks through the lack of her drug." He hung his head in misery.

"Is your mother at home or in hospital?" Edwina asked.

"She's at home," he replied. "She hates hospitals, and although it is not a very comfortable existence, she is contented and more relaxed in her own home."

"Do you have any help?"

"No. I look after her, get her meals, shop and clean the house. I didn't use any of the money for anything, apart from the drugs she needs."

"I think I would like to meet your mother," Edwina said.

Plockton shrugged his shoulders submissively. "Of course," he said. "You have the right to tell her, as I have betrayed your trust."

"I don't intend to tell her anything," Edwina said. "Can we go straight away? You can drive me there."

She rose, and reluctantly, Plockton led her out to the small blue car. They drove in silence through the narrow country lanes to the outskirts of Stokesborough. On the way Edwina wondered what course of action she would take and why she had not exposed the embezzlement to William Haligan, when she spoke to him on the telephone. Now she knew that she had been curious to get to the bottom of the mystery herself. She felt committed to see the problem through to the end. There was something about Plockton, which evoked her sympathy, and now she had to take into account his mother and her terminal illness. If he was telling the truth, her life could pay the price for his exposure and she did not want to be responsible for that.

On the journey Plockton's mind was in turmoil, imagining his mother's reaction to the news that her son was a thief. He had decided it was pointless to make any further appeal to Miss Cabrossi, although she had said that she did not intend to tell his mother anything. That gave him some hope.

The car drew up outside a terraced house close to the centre of Stokesborough. It was a drab street, like many others in towns and cities throughout the land, built in the 1930's, each house a replica of the next. Originally there had been lime trees planted every few hundred yards, interspersed with smart metal lamp-posts, but when the trees became too large, at first they had been savagely pruned and then, when the roots began to push up through the pavement slabs, they had been felled. All that remained now was the old metal streetlights, painted an ugly shade of dark green.

Edwina followed Plockton into the house. They stood in a small hallway, with narrow stairs climbing steeply up to the bedrooms above. There was just room for them both to stand side be side. There was a slight smell of dampness and stale cooking odours. The sounds of a television came from a back room."

"Do you do all the cooking?" Edwina asked.

"Yes. I have breakfast with mother in the morning, before going to work, prepare some sandwiches or a quiche for her lunch, and cook our dinner when I come home."

They entered the first room downstairs. The sounds from the television became louder. They were coming from the back room.

"A neighbour, Mrs Crossley, does the washing and ironing," he said. "That's a great help."

"Where is your mother?"

"In there," he said pointing to the back room. She finds it difficult to get upstairs now, so I brought a bed down and she can watch the television while I'm at work."

"Go in and tell her that I want to speak to her."

"What shall I say?" he asked, desperately.

"Tell her I'm a friend. There's no need to upset her at this stage." He crossed the room and opened the door to the back room, closing it behind him. After a few seconds the television was turned off and Edwina could hear them conversing in low voices in Italian, but she could not hear what was said.

After a short time the door opened and Plockton came out.

"She would like to see you now."

"Did you tell her who I am?"

"Yes. I told her you were the daughter of one of the firm's best clients and that you said you would like to meet her. She has jumped to the wrong conclusion, I'm afraid. She thinks you are my girlfriend. She has been desperate to see me married before she dies. She can't stand the thought of leaving me behind alone. Can you refer to me as Patrick?"

"Alright, Patrick, I'll play along with the girlfriend idea for the sake of your mother, but don't get any ideas."

"Of course not," he said. "The thought never entered my head, I swear."

"No need to swear," she said, with a smile. "I'll go in now,"

Patrick opened the door and ushered her in. "Mother, this is Edwina Cabrossi," he said in Italian.

"My God, are you Italian?" she said, grasping Edwina's hand. She was a slight woman, with darkish wispy hair, streaked with grey. She was about fifty years old, clearly very ill; her cheeks were emaciated and hollow, her arms were thin and her hands were pale and wrinkled. Her blue eyes though were dancing with pleasure as she clasped Edwina's hand. She was seated in a comfortable armchair, facing a television set and her bed occupied nearly half of the room. "I'm so pleased to meet you," she said. "I longed for this day."

"It's a pleasure to meet you, too," Edwina said to her in Italian, which caused her face to illuminate with a smile of sheer delight.

"You can leave us now," Edwina said, turning to Plockton. "I would like to speak to your mother alone."

Patrick withdrew from the room, closing the door behind him. He slumped into the only armchair in the room and could hear the two women talking quietly. Occasionally there was the sound of laughter, which raised his spirits. He had not heard her laughing for such a long time, but he knew there would be no reprieve for him. Edwina was such a beautiful girl. If only he had a girl like her to love him, then he could face any hardship. He knew though that she was also in a position of trust. It was not her money; it was her father's, and she was duty-bound to see that restoration was made.

There was another sudden burst of laughter. He looked at his watch. They had been talking for over thirty minutes. What could they be finding to discuss that was absorbing them for so long, he wondered. He leaned back and closed his eyes. All he could see was that beautiful face, her lovely black hair and her deep flashing eyes. It made him almost stop breathing, just thinking about her.

At last there was movement. It had been almost a full hour and he had dozed off. The door to the back room opened and Edwina emerged, smiling happily.

"Your mother is a lovely woman," she said. "I have promised to call to see her again."

"That's very kind of you," Patrick said. "Shall I take you back to Highfields?"

"Yes please." Nothing further was said until they drove up to 'Highfields'. After Patrick had stopped the car, he jumped out and opened the door for Edwina, whose mind had been in turmoil since meeting Patrick's mother.

"I think your mother is a wonderful woman," she said. "She's very brave and reconciled to her eventual fate. I am not going to make a hasty decision. I want to think about this over the weekend. I will telephone you next week and ask you to come to see me again. I want to tell you my decision face to face, not over the telephone."

With that, Edwina ran into the house. After closing the outer door, she stood still in the hallway. All was quiet. She leant against the banister at the foot of the stairs and the tears ran slowly down her cheeks.

21

That evening a meeting of some significance was scheduled to take place at the Bracken residence. Martha had been fuming and fretting for over a month now, and her solicitor's efforts were less than impressive, so she had called her sister, Kathleen and her husband Keith, and invited them to a second council of war. This time the meeting had been arranged for the evening, because Martha had decided that the two husbands should be present. They were both successful businessmen and in her opinion should be able to offer some advice and suggestions.

Keith and Kathleen drove over to Martha's house as soon as they had finished dinner. Kathleen was relieved that she didn't have to drive. It gave her time to prepare for the meeting, but in truth, she had no ideas to offer. She hated controversy, even though, in this case she believed that she and Martha were in the right and Edwina was in the wrong.

Keith turned into the long drive and parked on the turning circle in front of the impressive mansion. The front of the house was ablaze with lights, as the movement sensors triggered the fluorescent beams.

Martha opened the large oak door and, after the usual salutations had been exchanged, Harvey poured the drinks and they all settled back in their comfortable armchairs, just as though it was a purely social visit, but Martha cut short the small talk.

"We have a crisis on our hands," she said dramatically, "and we will have to act decisively, if we are not to be robbed and cheated out of what is rightfully ours."

"That's true," Keith said, "but Slattery didn't get very far, did he?"

"No," Harvey agreed. "At the first rebuff he ran behind his desk, with his tail between his legs." He guffawed and took a large swig of his whiskey.

"What else can we do?" Keith asked. "Amazingly this girl has arrived from abroad; nobody has heard of her, and she seems to hold all the trump cards."

"And she seems to have a better solicitor than us," Martha spat out.

For a while they all sat in silence, sipping their drinks.

"How much is this going to cost?" Keith asked.

"An absolute packet," Harvey said, rising to fill his glass. "Oh, anybody else?" he asked, as he stood at the drinks cabinet, waving his empty glass towards them. Martha frowned and hoped he was not going to drink too much. The others shook their heads. Martha knew he could produce brilliant ideas occasionally, but not after he began to hit the bottle.

"I think you should concentrate on the problem, before celebrating its solution," Martha said, bitingly.

"It's only the second, old thing," Harvey said, laughing, "and it was a damn difficult day in the office."

"Why don't we beard the dragon in her den?" Keith suggested.

"Do you mean, go over there and throw the bitch out," Harvey said.

"Yes," Keith said, but not as violently as that; just repossess the place."

"That's the same thing," Harvey said. "We were never in possession, so couldn't claim to be repossessing. She's in possession and that's nine tenths of the law, old boy. She's got it on her side." He rose to pour another drink. "Anyone else?"

"Perhaps we should find another solicitor," Keith said. "After all, what one solicitor sees as a hopeless case another sees as a winner."

"That's a very good point," Harvey said. "They are always interested if the stakes are high. How much do you think is involved?"

"At least five million," Martha said, "but it could be much more. I know he has always invested very heavily in property."

"That's a big incentive for a solicitor," Harvey said.

"Yes, I'm sure there are hundreds who would take the case to earn a big fat fee," Kathleen said sarcastically, surprised at her own forthrightness, "but can any of them win it. I think we have to make a different move."

Everyone in the room was amazed to hear Kathleen speak at all, let alone with such confidence. They all looked at her expectantly.

"I think I know what we should do," she said.

22

Tuesday 30th March

When Siegfried had telephoned he had said he would call on Tuesday afternoon, but he had not given a specific time, so Edwina had set aside the whole afternoon, to be sure to be available when he came. He had said he was a busy man and she was sure that was true, and no doubt he had many other calls to make before visiting Highfields. She was surprised therefore to hear a car crunching into the car parking area outside the living room window, soon after she had settled down after lunch. Putting aside the book she had chosen to read to while away the time, she looked out of the window. A large black Mercedes had just come to rest and Siegfried Baxter was just climbing out. From a distance he seemed to be a plump man, of medium height, dressed in a loud black and white check suit. As he approached the front door, Siegfried speculated on what this Edwina might look like. Brian Jefferson had described her as a real beauty, but Brian didn't meet many young girls in his line of business, and probably would consider them all to be real beauties. Her voice on the telephone had excited him though, more than he would admit.

He rang the bell and could hear it echoing throughout the house. Almost immediately, Edwina, who had hurried into the hall, opened the door. Siegfried was surprised and delighted with what he saw, such a vision of loveliness. Brian had not exaggerated. His eager eyes took in every inch of her. His smile widened and his imagination began to fantasise about her.

"I presume you are Mr Baxter," Edwina said.

"At your service," he said with a flourish, as though doffing his imaginary hat. "And you must be Edwina Cabrossi." He offered his hand. "May I call you Edwina?"

"Of course," she said, retrieving her hand.

"And you must call me Siegfried," he said. He had a rounded face, long floppy brown hair and a goatee beard. He was wearing a yellow shirt, beneath the check jacket and a gaudy cravat at his throat. Quite the dandy, Edwina thought, as he walked past her into the hall.

"What a magnificent staircase," he commented.

"Would you like some tea?" Edwina asked.

"Later would be wonderful, but I'm dying to see the pictures first."

Edwina crossed the hall and opened the dining room door. He followed her in, admiring the rear view, and gave a cry of delight when he saw all the paintings hanging on the oak panelling. To him it was like a sudden flash of sunlight. He moved slowly down the left-hand side of the room, stopping in front of each picture to examine it minutely, before moving on. He had taken a notebook from his pocket and occasionally made notes in it. Edwina watched silently, but she could see from his manner, and little noises he was making, that he was utterly absorbed in his work. At the end of the room he crossed to the right-hand wall and began to work his way back towards her, slowly examining each picture, until he stood beside her again.

"Well," he said, putting away his notebook. "I am impressed. How old is the artist?"

"Twenty two," Edwina said.

"He shows remarkable maturity, and I can trace from his work how rapidly he is developing."

"Can you tell that, just by looking?"

"Oh yes. Come over here" He took her hand and led her over to stand in front of a landscape, with trees and cattle in the foreground. As he leaned against her he could smell the perfume in her hair, which was brushing against his face. He pressed against her as he pointed upwards.

"You can tell that's an early picture, well painted, but lacking maturity. He is already developing his unique colour sense though." His arm swept down, his hand brushing the outside of her thigh.

"Now, compare it with this," he said, quickly moving her on, by placing his left hand on her waist and guiding her to a picture half way down the room. Again he placed himself directly behind her and did not remove his hand from her waist. Edwina was beginning to feel uncomfortable, but was prepared to put it down to his artistic temperament. Robert needed this man's help and advice, so she did not want to create a scene.

"Now this one, I would guess, is one of his latest," Siegfried said, enthusiastically. "His technique and use of colour has improved considerably." It was a picture of Brixham harbour, with the sun low in the sky and the small gaily-painted boats dancing on the water. Edwina always felt she was there on the quay, when she looked at it and could almost feel the movement of the boats and the sea. She became aware that he had not removed his hand from her waist, but was moving it gently in a massaging motion. She quickly moved away from him to stand in front of the next picture.

"Ah, now this one is the best of them all," he said, as though nothing untoward had happened. Perhaps it's just his way, she thought, but she was becoming irritated by his intimate touches. He was standing behind her again, as they viewed one of Robert's largest canvasses. It was her special favourite; a beautiful mountain scene, with a rocky crag, surrounded by trees. Fingers of mist clung to the rocks and some figures stood at the base of the buttress, their ropes spread out as they prepared to climb.

"Isn't it wonderful?" he said, his lips close to her ear. His left hand circled her waist and rested on her belly, his fingers pushing her back into him.

This time there could be no doubt about his intentions. "Let go," she yelled, and rolled out of his embrace. "How dare you," she snapped, facing him now, her face red and hot with anger. Instantly he was full of apology.

"I think you should go," she said.

"No, please don't send me away. I know I can be a naughty boy at times, but I can't help it, especially when I come close to a girl as beautiful as you. I meant what I said about your friend though. He could be the greatest artist in England within a few years, with my help. Can we start again?"

In spite of everything Edwina found herself smiling. He was such a likeable rogue. "All right then," she said, "but the house rules say no pawing, touching or rubbing or any other contact. Is that clear? If you do, you will walk out of the door."

Baxter could see that she meant it and decided to abide by her rules, as he did not want to miss out on all the income that he knew Robert could generate. He knew that if everything went well, the money would begin to flow in, and Edwina might even change her attitude then, with Robert in constant demand. He needed to get a signed contract first.

"I think I would like that tea now," he said, demurely.

While they were having their tea Siegfried sang Robert's praises, and quite clearly, was genuinely impressed with his work.

"After we had hung the pictures, Brian Jefferson suggested that the setting here would be very suitable for an exhibition," Edwina said.

Siegfried scratched his chin for a few seconds, visualising it, and then he cried out in excitement. "That is an absolutely fabulous suggestion. In London we will be pushed into some pokey little hall, which will be mean and draughty, and will cost a small fortune. Here you have all the advantages. We can invite all the right people and they will be able to view everything at their leisure. There will have to be refreshments, of course. A decent buffet and wine; plenty of wine." He laughed and winked at her. "There's just one problem," he said.

"What's that?" she asked.

"The huge table. It will take up all the floor space. People need to be able to move around freely, to stand back and admire from a distance and communicate with other viewers."

"I think we could overcome that problem," Edwina said. "Robert's father is a farmer. I'm sure they will be able to store the table in a barn for a short time."

"Fabulous," Siegfried cried out again. "You are a genius. I shall have to leave you in charge of the refreshments. I shall be much too busy doing what I do best. It will be quite expensive and a lot of hard work. You would have to invite the local dignitaries and press. I would make sure the art intelligentsia and London press are here. I can see it now," he said enthusiastically, jumping off the settee and striding up and down the room. Edwina giggled, as he cut such a comic caricature in his check suit and yellow shirt.

And so it was agreed, subject to Robert's approval. It was arranged that Siegfried would call soon after Easter to meet Robert and agree a contract.

23

Thursday 1st April

It was two days later that the plan, surprisingly suggested by Kathleen Hastings, and even more surprisingly agreed to by her relatives, was initiated.

Edwina had spent a glorious morning, walking in the grounds and helping Alf with the gardening. It was one of those clear bright days in early spring, when the sun felt warm and gave promise of summer to follow. It would be only a few days before she would see Robert again, and she felt a tingle of excitement at the thought of feeling herself in his arms once more. They would have the whole summer to look forward to, all those days to feel lithe again, youthful again and especially, to be in love. Looking back on his former life she knew that love was the main thing lacking in Edward's existence. And yet, if he was her father, who he undoubtedly was, there had to be some love previously in his life. She had spent many hours trying to recall the memories, which Edward had shut away so successfully for years. There had been glimmers of memories, like a flash of sunlight breaking through grey clouds, but just as suddenly, the clouds closed the gap and the memory went blank.

But that morning she had sat in her favourite clearing, on a bank of new soft green grass, surrounded by a profusion of bluebells, and leant her back against an ancient oak. Within seconds she had been dozing, as the sun broke through the branches to warm her face. The memories began to take shape and once started, the trickle became a flood. She had suddenly recalled a summer when Edward had had gone to Venice with two friends. They had stayed at one of the best hotels, close to St Mark's Square. On the second night of their stay, there had been a carnival in the square and the surrounding streets. The gondolas, their lamps lit, plied along the canals, their passengers, disguised by masks to hide their true identities, as they kissed and caressed in the night. The square and the streets around were filled with noise and music and the bustle of jostling hordes of people, many of them too, masked, not so much to hide their identities, as to increase the mystery and romance of the occasion.

Edward, too, had been pressed into wearing a mask by his two companions, who had both been swept away from him early in the evening. He had wandered through the streets, enjoying the movement and the colour of the spectacle, until he had been jostled by a group of revellers into a girl, also masked. She might have fallen, but Edward turned in time to catch her and led her to the side of the street. She had long black hair and dark eyes, which gazed at him appreciatively. As he gazed at her, she laughed, and he realised he was still clasping her hard around the waist. He apologised, and to his surprise, she replied in English, with a strong Italian accent.

They spent the rest of the evening together, laughing and drinking. Eventually, as the crowds began to disperse, he had taken her to his hotel and after a short time, to his bedroom. Edward, the confirmed bachelor, at fifty-three years old, was in love for the first time, with a foreign girl, aged twenty, he had never even seen before that evening, but it was not long before he saw all of her. They fell into each other's arms with an overwhelming passion. They made love until they fell back on the bed exhausted, and then they made love again. He could not believe the softness of her skin and the loveliness of her face. Eventually he sank back on the pillow and slept. When he woke she was gone, and all he knew of her was that her name was Anna.

"Why didn't you look for her?" Edwina cried out, raising herself from her grassy couch. She knew the answer already; he had to leave two days later and did not know where to find her, she would be unaware that her one night of love would result in a child. He had returned home and grieved for his lost love, as though she was dead, knowing that he could never trace her. He pined for her for years, and then, to bring an end to his suffering he cast her completely from his mind. In time he could wake in the morning without longing for her, and eventually without even remembering her.

Edwina leant her back against the tree and closed her eyes. She felt so sad. If only Anna had not left in the morning, how different Edward's life would have been. Not for the first time Edwina felt that her present existence was overlapping another time and place, another life. She felt she had to find out the answers to so many questions.

As she strolled back to the house, across the lawn to the front door, she noticed a strange car parked alongside her new Honda Jazz, which she had found easier to drive than the unwieldy Rolls. She had had no trouble passing her test first time and could now enjoy full mobility again. The strange car was a fairly old Vauxhall, which had seen better days. Mrs Pearson must have a visitor, Edwina thought, as she entered the hallway, and was about to go into the sitting room on the right, when Mrs Pearson appeared from the kitchen and hastened down the corridor towards her. She could tell from her agitation that she was concerned about something.

"I'm glad I caught you," Mrs Pearson said, "there's a policeman who wants to speak to you. I've put him in the sitting room."

"I'm sure I haven't broken any speed limits in my new car," she said. At the same time she felt uneasy, as everyone does when a policeman knocks on the door.

"Perhaps you could bring us some tea in about five minutes," Edwina suggested, as she entered the sitting room.

"Of course," Mrs Pearson called, as she hurried back to the kitchen.

A tall broad-shouldered man stood at the back window looking out. He must have seen her, she thought, as she walked up from the lake, crossing the lawn and making her way through the flowerbeds.

He turned just then and smiled at her. "I'm Detective Constable Stanley," he said, waving his warrant card towards her.

"Is that 'Stanley', Christian name, or 'Stanley', surname?" she asked, a mischievous twinkle in her eye.

"Stanley surname, Miss," he said very formally. He was a handsome fellow, about thirty, Edwina guessed and he looked very powerful; the sort of man you would want on your side, if there was any fighting to be done.

"Please sit down," Edwina urged. "I have ordered some tea. Is that alright?"

"Yes, Miss. That will be great." He dropped onto the settee close to where he was standing, fumbled in his pocket and produced his notebook and pencil. He studied the page of his notebook for a while and Edwina guessed he had written some notes or questions he wanted to ask, to jog his memory. Since meeting Edwina however, he was not so sure about how to conduct the interview. She was nothing like the picture he had formed in his mind. At last he cleared his throat.

"Are you Miss Edwina Cabrossi?"

"Yes."

"Is your father Edward Grangelove?"

"Yes."

"How is it that you have a different surname to your father?"

"My father did not know of my existence until some time last year. My mother brought me up on her own and naturally I took her surname."

"So your parents were not married." Edwina was not sure whether that was a question or a statement and decided it was the latter.

"Is Mr Grangelove here at the moment?"

"No. He's somewhere in Italy."

"Do you know where?"

"No. He left shortly before I arrived."

"So you haven't seen him since the day you arrived?"

"No. As I said, he left before I came."

"And when did you arrive?"

"On the thirteenth of February."

"And when did he leave?"

"On the thirteenth of February, but earlier in the day."

DC Stanley thought this over for a minute.

"That was strange, wasn't it? If he hadn't seen you for a long while, wouldn't he have wanted to spend at least a short time with you, before departing."

"I think he had made his arrangements and either didn't want to, or couldn't change them."

Stanley shrugged his shoulders and decided to change tack again.

"I believe this house is owned by Mr Grangelove? Is that correct?"

"That's right," Edwina said. She believed she knew the line the questioning was going to take, and she knew who had instigated it.

"Have you heard from your father recently?"

"No. I told you, he left before I arrived."

"But that was some time ago; over six weeks ago, to be precise. Surely you would have heard from him by now?"

Just then there was a knock on the door and Mrs Pearson came in with a tray, containing the tea things. It was a welcome relief for Edwina, but also for DC Stanley. He could not see this girl harming a fly, but the behaviour of Grangelove and his daughter seemed very peculiar. Edwina pulled across the small coffee table and Mrs Pearson put the tray down on it.

"This is Mrs Pearson, my father's housekeeper," Edwina said. "She spoke to my father on the day he left."

"I would like to speak to you before I leave," Stanley said. Mrs Pearson looked towards Edwina.

"That will be all right," Edwina said. Mrs Pearson nodded and left the room. "How do you like your tea?" Edwina asked.

"Milk and two sugars, please," he said. He watched as Edwina poured the tea. She even did that with a natural grace, which convinced him more than ever that she would be incapable of harming anyone. Even so, he decided to take a more direct line.

"We have received a Missing Person Report relating to your father," he said seriously. "These matters have to be investigated."

The irony of the situation suddenly struck Edwina and she nearly laughed.

"I think you should speak to Mrs Pearson and especially to my father's solicitors. It seems they were aware of his plans to go abroad as far back as last November."

"Really," Stanley said in surprise.

"My father and Bruce Collinridge have been friends for years, so it isn't surprising that my father took him into his confidence. After I arrived I found that my father had appointed me under a power of attorney to act on his behalf in all matters."

"Could you give me the name and address of the firm of solicitors?"

Edwina gave him the details, which he wrote in his little book. Then he thanked her for her time and ambled down the corridor to speak to Mrs Pearson. She heaved a sigh of relief.

After DC Stanley had left, Edwina sat in the living room for a long time, deep in thought. She knew what a hunted animal felt like now and dreaded to think of what might happen if the hunt reached its inevitable conclusion. She knew she could not resurrect Edward, so everything hinged on being able to head off the chase. She had to convince everybody that all was well, so that they stopped looking. To do nothing now, she felt, would play into the hands of Martha and Kathleen, and encourage them to become ever more persistent in their demands on the police. Eventually, she decided on a course of action.

She went into her study and after much thought she composed three letters. Then she telephoned Patrick Plockton and asked him to call to see her, that afternoon, if possible. She wanted to tell him her decision, face to face, as she had promised. He said he would call on her at half past two.

PART 2

24

Friday 2nd April

Promptly, at two thirty, the small blue car pulled into the parking area and Plockton stepped out. He hoped for the best, but he feared the worst. How could she possibly reprieve him, he thought. I can't make up the deficit, or cover it up any longer. The strain of the last few days had been enormous, and unbearable. His mother had commented that he was not looking well and that he must not worry about her. What will be will be, she had said. That very morning he had been on the point of knocking on Mr Haligan's door and confessing everything, but then he had received Edwina's phone call and had decided that his confession could wait, at least for a few hours longer.

After Mrs Pearson had answered the bell, she led Patrick into the sitting room. Now that the moment had arrived he suddenly felt calm. Edwina seated him on the settee and sat in one of the armchairs, immediately opposite him.

"Well, Patrick, I hope you haven't been kept waiting for too long, but I had a difficult decision to make. I know you would not have taken the money if it had not been for the sake of your mother and it's because of that I have decided not to tell your employers." Patrick felt as though the air had been sucked out of his lungs and he gasped for breath. For a while Edwina was alarmed, but then he recovered and began to breathe normally.

"I realise that not telling your employers would be only a partial reprieve, as I am sure their auditors would probably discover the discrepancies in the rents, when they do their annual checks."

Patrick, who had felt the burden of a lifetime lifted from his shoulders a few minutes earlier, realised the significance of what Edwina was saying. He nodded his head in agreement. His mouth and throat were too dry and constricted to speak.

"I have decided therefore to give you a cheque to put the Adelphi rent account in order. It will be up to you to see that it gets into the account and that an adjusting entry is made, paying the money back to Mr Grangelove's account. Can you manage that?"

At last Patrick was able to speak. "That is so generous of you," he said. "I will pay you back, every penny, and with interest as well."

"That won't be necessary," Edwina said. "And it won't be necessary to stop your mother receiving her treatment. I was so impressed with her; she is a wonderful woman, and I want to help her as much as I can. I am giving you one cheque payable to Reid, Haligan and Morgan for six thousand pounds to put their account right, and another cheque payable to you for twelve thousand pounds, to cover the next three months of your mother's treatment." She picked up the cheques from the coffee table and handed them to him.

Patrick could not believe what he was hearing. "How can I ever thank you enough, or repay you sufficiently," he said, greatly moved by her generosity. "If there is anything I can ever do for you I will do it without hesitation."

"There is one thing," Edwina said and laughed, seeing the expression on his face. "I won't be asking you to murder anyone."

"Of course not," Patrick said. "I was just worried in case it was something I couldn't do. I don't want to let you down."

"I'm sure you won't, Patrick. When I was speaking to your mother, she mentioned that her dearest wish was to return to

Italy, to visit some of the places she holds close to her heart, while she still has sufficient strength."

"I know," Patrick said, "she keeps on about it, but we can't afford it. You know that."

"I know that," Edwina said, "but I can afford it, and I want you to take her. I will cover the costs of the trip."

Patrick leaned back against the settee, hardly believing what she was saying. The last hour had been a pleasant dream, while he had expected a nightmare.

"I can't let you do that. You have done so much already and in any case, I don't have any holiday arranged," Patrick said. "Mr Haligan is a stickler for having holiday dates agreed in advance."

"I think you should go as soon as possible," Edwina said. "Leave it to me to speak to Mr Haligan. As soon as I have his agreement I will let you know, and book the flight and a hotel for you to stay at on arrival. After that you will be free to travel wherever she wishes to go. I will arrange for a car to be picked up at the airport. I want you to have three weeks on holiday, so that your mother can visit all the places she was mentioning to me."

"I don't think Mr Haligan will agree to that."

"As I said, leave Mr Haligan to me."

"You never said what you want me to do for you," Patrick said. "That will be my first priority."

"Your mother must be your first priority, but you may be able to find time for my errand. Your mother mentioned that she came from a small village north of Venice."

"That's right, I have been there, but not since I was about twelve years old."

"There's a town, also north of Venice, called Castelfranco. I'm sure it will not be too far from where your mother wants to be. I would like you to visit the town and make some enquiries about my mother, Anna Cabrossi. I'm sure I don't need to tell you, that these enquiries are to be made discreetly and any information gathered, is to be kept strictly confidential. Will you do that for me?"

"Of course. It will give me the greatest of pleasure to be able to be of service to you."

"I would like you to write to me, in Italian, to keep it confidential, letting me know anything you have found out, or even if you have not discovered anything."

"You can be sure I will leave no stone unturned."

"One more thing," Edwina cautioned. "Your questions will raise great curiosity among the locals. They will be interested to know who is making these enquiries and on whose behalf. You must not disclose my name."

"I give you my word that your name will not be mentioned."

"Good," Edwina said with satisfaction. "There is just one other small thing. When you arrive at Treviso airport I want you to buy some Italian stamps and post three letters for me. I will give them to you before your departure but you must post them before leaving the airport. Is that understood?"

"Of course." Patrick's curiosity was aroused, but he knew he must carry out this small task for Edwina without question, as it appeared to be so important to her. After what she had done for him, and was about to do, it seemed a very small service indeed, by comparison.

As he drove back to the office he felt as though a huge burden had been lifted from his shoulders. He would ask Mr Haligan for three weeks compassionate leave, starting just after Easter, which was only a week away, but he would delay his request for a few hours, as Edwina had asked, to enable her to speak to Mr Haligan first.

When she phoned she was immediately put through to Mr Halligan.

"Ah, Miss Cabrossi," he said, oozing friendliness. "It's so good to hear from you again. Settling down well, I hope. I haven't forgotten that dinner date. My wife, Pauline, has been very busy though lately. She does a lot of charity work you know. What can I do for you?"

"Well, I have a special request to make. It concerns Mr Plockton."

"Did he help you to understand the rent accounts and how we look after your father's business?"

"Perfectly," Edwina said. "While I was talking to him he mentioned that his mother is very ill; in fact, she's dying."

"I knew she was very ill, but I didn't realise it was as serious as that," Haligan said, sounding concerned. "He should have told me."

"It's her dying wish to return to Italy, but Patrick doesn't know whether he can get the time off at such short notice. It would be the week after next, for three weeks."

There was the sound of papers being moved round on the desk. What a nuisance, Haligan thought, but at the same time he was well aware that the Grangelove connection was worth a lot of money annually. "I think we could manage that," Haligan said at last.

"That is so understanding of you," Edwina said. "Patrick will be asking you himself and I am sure he will be most grateful."

"Well, it never hurts to have a grateful employee, does it?" he said, with a little laugh. Her voice sounds so sexy, he thought, as she thanked him again for being so understanding. She had made his afternoon. I really must have another chat with my wife, Pauline, he promised himself.

25

At last Edwina felt satisfied that she had done all that she could to protect herself from her cousins. At least she had put a plan into motion. Now it was time to relax. In a few hour's time Robert would be home, his stint at college ended, his agricultural qualification obtained and his duty to his parents honoured. She longed to see him again and hoped he would be desperate to see her. Margaret had invited her over and said all the family were looking forward to seeing her.

She bathed and perfumed herself, enjoying the sensuous experience of pampering her body and the excitement of anticipation. She had had time in the last few weeks to expand her wardrobe and had purchased a whole range of clothing, from lingerie to trousers, skirts and dresses. Shopping for the various items had been a new and pleasant experience. She could understand now why women spent so much time and money on finding and buying clothes for themselves; the range and variety was endless, compared with what was on offer to men.

She chose an ivory-coloured skirt, which came to just below the knee and a cranberry-coloured silk tunic, which enhanced the beauty of her face and hair. She regarded herself in the mirror and felt satisfied with the result. She was slimmer now than when she had first looked at herself; she was better groomed, with every hair in place and her clothes seemed to caress her body, instead of just hanging on her. She looked sophisticated, intelligent and, above all, very attractive. She decided to dispense with a coat, as the day had been warm for early April and she hated to feel too wrapped up.

Edwina was a little nervous as she walked across the farmyard and entered, as usual, through the kitchen door. The cats slumbered in their beds and the dogs rose sleepily to greet her with friendly tails. By now, they knew her well enough to treat her as a friend.

Mrs Skefford was busy at the stove as usual and was the first to give Edwina an effusive welcome. She had become very fond of Edwina and was sorry that she had no relatives who cared about her. Margaret, who had heard them talking, burst into the kitchen, kissed Edwina on the cheek and, taking her hand, led her away.

"You look absolutely fantastic," she said. "Robert is here and is dying to see you. He's waiting in the sitting room."

She opened the sitting room door and waved Edwina inside, closing the door after her. Robert was standing by the window, his back to her, and suddenly all her nervousness disappeared. She just wanted to be near him again. As she took a step towards him, he heard the rustle of her skirt and turned towards her. In two strides he took her in his arms and kissed her lips. The relief was enormous; she just surrendered to his passion, feeling overwhelmed by the strength of his arms.

At last their lips separated. "I love you," he whispered. It was the first time he had said it, but she had known it from the time they had had lunch in the Farmer's Arms.

"I know," she said, "and I love you too. I missed you so much."

He led her to the settee and sat beside her, his arm around her waist. He could feel the warmth and softness of her skin through the silk material. He had never felt so happy in the whole of his life, but he knew that nothing remains the same in life. Everything is constantly changing and moving on, from one second to the next. He just hoped that they would always be together.

Margaret innocently broke the spell, by knocking gently on the door and entering the room. She smiled when she saw them so close together, so obviously in love. She longed for that experience herself, but wondered if it would ever happen.

"I think supper is ready," she said.

They followed her into the dining room, where they were joined by the rest of the family. The food was excellent, as always, but neither Edwina nor Robert seemed to have any appetite for it. They could hardly take their eyes off each other. As usual, the conversation was animated between the rest of the family and it made Edwina regret, even more, that she could not make contact with either of her two cousins.

"Have you made up your mind?" Robinson asked suddenly, looking at Robert. The table fell silent and all eyes turned on Robert, as he looked directly at his father.

"Yes, Dad. I'm sorry, but I have made up my mind. I want to be an artist."

"Then you've wasted the last three years."

"You wanted me to finish the course."

"Yes, I did. I thought then you would want to join Rupert and me on the farm. There's a good living here, and if you came in I planned to buy a lot more land to keep us all busy."

"I'm sorry, Dad. I have to give it a go."

Mrs Skefford interrupted the conversation at that moment, sensing that it could become an argument, knowing that Robinson could be stubborn and that Robert was not going to change his mind. She knew that after he had met Edwina, Robert had been fired by a new enthusiasm for painting. Perhaps it had been there all along and they had ignored it, but Edwina, she knew, had encouraged him and given him confidence. The only thing to do now was to give him his head and hope he would succeed. The conversation soon turned back to farming and while Rupert and his father discussed the cattle, Edwina said how much she was looking forward to entertaining them all for lunch on Easter Sunday. Secretly, she was hoping that when they saw Robert's pictures, properly displayed, they would begin to have more confidence in his talent.

When Edwina left, Robert accompanied her, as they walked out to her car. It was a clear starlit night, but there was a cool breeze. She shivered, missing the coat she had decided she didn't need. Robert detected the shiver and put his arms round her.

"Will you come over tomorrow?" she asked.

"Of course," he answered, and kissed her gently.

As she drove back to Highfields she felt happier than at any time in her life. There had been only one other occasion to compare with it, from her previous life, as she now thought of it. That was that night in Venice, with that beautiful stranger, and she knew that in some strange way that had led directly to her present existence. That relationship was totally different though, and did not excite her sensually when she thought about it. She knew it had been Edward's one and only sexual encounter and she regretted that he had then determined to forget it and live the rest of his life as a sexual hermit.

Edwina had been fearful of entering a relationship with a man, but she realised now that there was no question of homosexuality involved in her feelings, quite the opposite; her longings and desires were completely feminine. The moment she had seen Robert standing by the window, she had known that the transformation to female had been total and that she was utterly in love with him. Where it would lead she did not know, but was now committed to whatever fate had in store for her.

26

Saturday 3rd April

Patrick phoned shortly after nine o'clock, to tell Edwina that Mr Haligan had been very kind and had granted him thirteen days leave of absence from Wednesday. Edwina had made provisional bookings, through a travel agent, for their flight, hotel and a hire car, to be picked up at the airport, as she knew her request to Patrick would involve some extra travel. It would also enable Patrick's mother to visit the places she wanted to see in greater comfort.

"I don't know how I can ever thank you enough for what you have done for me," Patrick said.

"You must not neglect your concern for your mother, in order to carry out my request," Edwina cautioned him. "She must be your prime responsibility. If necessary, abandon my task altogether."

"Of course," he said. "I just hope I can find the answers to your questions."

"Did you manage to put the account in order?" Edwina asked.

"Yes. Everything is in order now."

She told Patrick the name of the travel agent she had made the arrangements through, so that he could pick up the tickets. What she didn't tell him was that she had arranged for currency and travellers cheques, more than sufficient for their holiday, to be picked up at the same time.

Shortly after speaking to Robert, Edwina received another call. This time it was Siegfried, enthusiastic and pompous as usual.

"Just a quick call to my favourite Italian girlfriend," he said mischievously, and laughed. Edwina had to smile. He was such a rogue, but she couldn't help liking him.

"I have some good news," he announced. "The idea of the exhibition in your splendid surroundings seems to have inspired enthusiasm in all and sundry. It's just a question of the date, dear girl, for this spectacular event, and it will be spectacular, I'm sure. How could it be otherwise with you organising it?"

Before she could speak, Siegfried sailed on. "I am proposing Saturday the twenty fourth of April, to commence at six thirty. Does that suit you and give you sufficient time to invite your local people and book the caterers and purchase the wine, etcetera, etcetera."

"That will give me enough time, I'm sure."

"Splendid. Then it's full speed ahead. I need to meet Robert in the next few days. Is he home yet?"

"Yes, he came home yesterday."

"Excellent. Now let me see." There was a familiar shuffling of papers as though he was checking his diary. "I'm totally tied up next week, but how does Tuesday the thirteenth fit in with your plans? We can also swap notes on progress then."

"That will be fine," Edwina said. "Will you come in the morning?"

"Yes, dear girl, anything to please you."

Before she could reply he had rung off.

Robert arrived half an hour later. Edwina had been looking out of the living room window, watching for his car. As soon as she saw it, she ran out to greet him. She could hardly wait for him to get out of the car. Her heart felt as though she was bursting with joy. He laughed as they embraced and kissed.

"I hardly had time to get out of the car," he said.

"I know. It's so wonderful to be together again. We had such little time, before you were whisked away to college."

"Well, that's behind us now."

Arm in arm they walked into the house and sat down together on the settee.

"I can't tell you how much I have missed you," Robert said, pressing her close to him. It felt so good to feel her body in his arms.

Edwina smiled up at him and he stroked her cheek and hair. "At least I have honoured my word to my parents. I have completed the course. They would never have forgiven me if I had chucked it all up in the final term."

"Is that it then?" Edwina asked. "Are you quite sure that is the end of your farming days?"

"Yes," Robert said, with conviction. "Of course, if father was taken ill. Or Rupert for that matter, I would always come and help them out, but that's all."

"So you are going ahead with painting," Edwina said, gazing into his eyes. She knew the answer before he replied.

"You have inspired a new ambition in me. I could think of nothing else while I was away. I know I have to give painting a chance. I tried to paint a picture of you while I was at college. It's in oils, on canvass and all the other students wanted to know who the girl is, but it was a very poor likeness." He took her face in his hands and studied her closely. "Now I see your face again I realise how poor my effort is."

"Have you still got the painting?"

"Yes, I have, but it's worthless. I shall destroy it."

"No," Edwina protested. "I will sit for you, if you like. You can paint over the other picture and make whatever alterations you like. That is the advantage of oils, I believe."

"That's a splendid idea," he said. "When I was painting the picture of you from memory I was longing to have you sitting for me."

"If you finish it in time we might be able to squeeze it into the exhibition."

"What exhibition?" Robert asked.

"I've been dying to tell you. So much has happened since you went away and I didn't want to tell you until you were back home." Robert was looking at her in amazement, anticipating what she was going to say, but hardly daring to think it.

"Do you mean you went ahead and framed my pictures and hung them in your dining room?"

She smiled at him. "Every one of them," she said. "I found a splendid man, called Brian Jefferson, who has done a first class job. The pictures look absolutely beautiful and what's more, he introduced me to an art expert and dealer in London, who specialises in finding new talented artists. He came here last week and thinks your work is great. He was so impressed with the paintings and the way they had been displayed, that he suggested we should have an exhibition and hold it here, as he thought the house and the setting would be perfect. He will invite all the top people and press from London. I will invite the local press and dignitaries, and organise a buffet for them."

"It sounds absolutely fantastic," Robert said, "but it will cost you the earth. I can't believe you have gone ahead and done all that for me. Who is this art expert?"

"His name is Siegfried Baxter and he is coming here on the thirteenth of April to meet you and discuss business. He mentioned something about a contract. He phoned me this morning and wants the exhibition to take place on Saturday the twenty-fourth of April."

Robert's head was spinning. He was excited at the prospect of showing his work and meeting all the important people who could launch him on his new career, but most of all he was astounded that this lovely girl he had met only recently was prepared to do all this for him.

"I can't believe you have done all this for me," he stammered.

He turned to Edwina and she could see that he had tears of gratitude in his eyes. She put her arms around his neck and pulled his head down on to her breasts. He clung to her for several minutes, feeling the rise and fall of her body as she breathed and the softness of her breast against his cheek. Eventually, reluctantly, he raised his head.

"It was my lucky day when I met you," he said.

"Mine too," she whispered.

"Now, you must show me the pictures," he said.

She pulled him down beside her and kissed him lightly on the cheek. "You will have to wait until next Sunday," she said. "You are all coming to lunch here on Easter Sunday. I want you and your family to share that first moment of revelation together. Will you indulge me?"

"Of course I will," he said. "I will be patient until then."

"Good," she said with a smile. "Now give me another kiss."

27

Monday 5th April

When Detective Sergeant Malcolm Webster climbed the stone stairs to his office on Monday morning, it was just like every other Monday morning for the last six years. His mind was still on the weekend and the time he had spent with his wife, Carol and their two children; Paul, aged eight and Julie, aged six. As usual they had had a great time together. There were no call-outs, and after two days of activities with the children and two nights of passionate lovemaking with Carol, here he was again, climbing the stairs to his office.

When he pushed open the glass-panelled door he noticed DC Stanley, already at his desk, head down, concentrating on some papers.

"Morning, Bill," Webster growled. "Anything interesting?"

"That Missing Persons case," Stanley replied. "I went to see the girl. What a cracker, she is. It's very odd though; that she should arrive on the very day the old man departs. He told the housekeeper, Mrs Pearson, that he was leaving and that his daughter would be arriving, but she never saw him go. And what's more, she and her husband live in the lodge at the entrance to the drive and they never heard his taxi depart or the daughter's taxi arrive. She was working, as usual, in the kitchen on the morning of the thirteenth of February, having heard nothing unusual all night, and in walks this strange girl, Miss Edwina Cabrossi, not Miss Grangelove, you notice."

"You have my full attention," Webster said, grabbing a chair and straddling it. He still felt tired after his weekend exertions.

I went to see Grangelove's solicitor, Bruce Collinridge, to see if he could throw any light on the situation."

"And could he?"

"Well, yes and no. Grangelove told him about his daughter, Edwina Cabrossi."

"Collinridge referred to her by that name?" Webster interrupted.

"Yes, he did. That was definitely the name given to him by Grangelove."

"Carry on," Webster said. "It gets more interesting by the second."

"Well, according to what Grangelove told him, this Edwina Cabrossi was coming over from Italy to live with him. That was last November and it was the first Collinridge had ever heard about a daughter. Everyone regarded old Grangelove as a confirmed bachelor."

"He never gave any hint about how he had suddenly acquired a daughter?"

"None at all, Sarge, and Collinridge was reluctant to press him, for fear of upsetting one of his wealthiest clients. But according to him there could be no doubt about her being his daughter. There's no way he would have given her such power if she had been an impostor."

"What power are you referring to?"

"I was just coming to that. Grangelove instructed him to prepare a power of attorney in her favour, as he was going abroad, to Italy, according to Collinridge. She was to have full powers to run the show while he was abroad."

"Did he make a new will?" Webster asked.

"Collinridge wouldn't say, but I bet he did. If he gave her all that power he wouldn't want the nieces kicking Edwina out if something happened to him while he was away."

"I bet that has something to do with the complaint from Bracken and Hastings."

"You think they assume that a new will has been made and that it affects their chances."

"To put it mildly," Webster said, glowering at the ceiling. "How would you feel if you were the only living relatives of a multi-millionaire, and you suddenly discovered he had a daughter hidden away, and not only that, she appears on the scene and is given total control of the ranch, so to speak."

"Yes. They would be fizzing," Stanley said.

"They can guess that if he has given her that power of attorney, he has also named her as his heir. He must have learned about her only last year," Webster said.

"Which would account for the different surname. And, maybe, the sudden trip to Italy. It's odd though that he took off on the day she arrived."

They were both silent for a while as they absorbed what had been said.

"So what do you suggest?" Stanley asked at last.

"For the moment we do nothing. I'm not having you chasing around Italy trying to find a needle in a haystack. If we wait long enough he will turn up."

Stanley scratched his head. "It's odd though, that the Pearson's never heard either of the two taxis. They seem to be very observant people to me. They could miss one, but two?" He put his head on one side to emphasise his doubt. "And they would have to miss them going up the drive and coming down again," he added. "That's four journeys past the lodge."

"It's all very odd," Webster said. "They could have had the television on too loud, of course, or they could be deep sleepers." He thought for a minute. "Alright. Check the local taxi firms. One of them must have been used."

"They might have used taxis from the airport," Stanley suggested.

"The girl almost certainly would," Webster said, "but the old man would use a local taxi to the airport."

"I'll check both ends," Stanley said.

"Yes, do that," Webster said, and crossed over to his own desk, to pick up his morning post.

28

Tuesday 6th April

On Tuesday morning Edwina had gone, on her own, to visit Patrick's mother. She was overjoyed to see Edwina and very excited about the forthcoming trip. She said she was feeling stronger by the day and was sorry that Edwina was not going to accompany them. She still thought Edwina and Patrick were almost on the point of getting married. This idea gave her such pleasure, that Edwina could not spoil her fantasy by denying it. Edwina stayed with her until she felt Mrs Plockton was getting tired and then wished her a happy holiday and left, hoping that it would indeed be a happy holiday.

When she returned to Highfields she found Robert waiting for her in the sitting room, sipping a cup of coffee provided by Mrs Pearson.

"That looks good," she said. "I think I will get one of those."

When she returned from the kitchen, she pulled the coffee table in front of them and laid out a chart she had prepared, specifying all the arrangements and invitations that had to be completed to ensure a successful exhibition on the twenty-fourth.

"You have gone to a lot of trouble to see that nothing is overlooked," Robert observed. He was very impressed by the meticulous detail in her plan.

"We can't afford to have anything go wrong on the day," she said. "After all, this could give you a really good start."

For the rest of that day and the next they worked their way through the plan, contacting those they wished to invite and ordering supplies for the buffet.

By mid-morning on Thursday Edwina and Robert were able to relax in the knowledge that they had done everything they could at their end to promote Robert's work at the exhibition on the twenty-fourth. The wine had been ordered, the caterers booked and invitations dispatched to those considered worthy enough to attend such a spectacular occasion, including all of Robert's family, of course, Brian Jefferson, Bruce Collinridge and William Haligan. To persuade the mayor of Stokesborough, Edwina had talked herself into his office, and after meeting her and learning what a huge talent they had in their midst and that the national press would be swarming all over the event, he was only too willing to take this lovely girl's hand and swear to be in attendance, providing the world was still turning on its axis. She had also squirmed her way into the office of the chief editor of the Stokesborough Chronicle. In the end he was so grateful, not only to be invited as a guest, but also to have his star reporter there, to ensure that the citizens of Stokesborough would see that their local paper could not be scooped by London press when it concerned a matter of local importance.

Edwina had telephoned Siegfried regularly to inform him of progress and try to learn the number of people he expected to bring. He was very pleased to hear how well she was doing, but less forthcoming when it came to putting her in the picture regarding expected guests.

"Don't trouble about that now," Siegfried said. "I have organised hundreds of these exhibitions. It will be alright on the night."

Edwina was beginning to have serious doubts about Siegfried, but was reassured when she rang Brian Jefferson.

"That's Siegfried all over," he said. "Don't worry about it. He won't let you down."

She decided he was right; it was no use worrying about the event.

"I think you are worrying too much," Robert said. "Why don't we go for a walk?" he suggested. "You have worked so hard for the last few days, on my behalf, that you deserve a reward."

"If this exhibition is a success, that will be my reward."

"Come on," he said, pulling her to her feet and giving her a hug. "It's such a warm day, we must make the most of it."

As they took the familiar path to the lake and entered the woods, the cares of the last few days disappeared. Edwina was at peace, holding Robert's hand, admiring the profusion of purple crocuses covering every space between the tree trunks, like pools of water, when seen from a distance. When the breeze swept across the ground the small flowers bent their heads in unison, like waves rippling across a lake. Robert and Edwina watched transfixed by the beauty of the scene, transported to a fairyland of childhood pleasure.

"This is a magical place," Robert said, as they entered the clearing, where the trees arched overhead and where they had kissed for the first time. The crocuses made it even more beautiful, laying down a delicate coloured carpet for them to walk along. Fresh green leaves were now beginning to emerge on the bare black branches of the trees and they glistened as they caught the shafts of sunlight streaking through the canopy.

"Let's sit over here for a while," Robert said and led Edwina over to the same bank she had lain on several days before, longing to have him by her side. They sat and then lay side by side. Edwina felt her wish had been granted. Robert leaned over and kissed her.

"I love you so much," he said.

His hand caressed her breast. She responded by putting her arms around his neck. His touch excited her and they kissed passionately for several minutes. When his hand strayed to her waist and began to pull out her blouse from her skirt, she restrained him and, standing up, they resumed their walk, arm in arm.

They walked in silence for a time. Then Robert said, "I'm sorry. I didn't mean to –"

Edwina stopped and looked up into his troubled eyes. "There's no need to say that," she said, tenderly brushing his lips with hers. "I want you just as much as you want me. That's what love is all about."

They stood now in the centre of the clearing and kissed with a new fervour and understanding, knowing where their love was leading them.

On the way back to the house Robert asked Edwina if she would sit for him, so that he could finish the picture he had begun at college. Since coming home, with his parents' consent, he had begun to convert the attic into a studio, or as near to a studio as he could afford. So, after lunch at Highfields, they drove over to the farm and Edwina was able to inspect the Spartan alterations. All the rubbish had been cleared and Margaret had helped in sweeping out and cleaning the room. An old settee had been manhandled up the stairs, with Rupert's help, and two cane chairs and a rickety table had made their appearance. Robert was clearly quite proud of his new studio and of the help he had received from Margaret and Rupert.

Edwina sat on the settee while Robert set up his easel and prepared his paints. Finally he produced the canvass he had painted from memory, but would not let Edwina see it. He placed it carefully on the easel.

"I'm ready now," he said.

"How do you want me?" she asked, innocently, and they both laughed. She tried taking up several poses, but it always ended in laughter.

"I need a light blue curtain behind you, to give you the right background," Robert said.

"Are you sure you aren't just thinking of the flowers?" Edwina asked.

"Of course," Robert said. Suddenly he knew just how he wanted her to sit. "Lie back slightly," he said. "Put your elbow on the armrest; chin resting on your hand, looking past me, as though you are deep in thought. That's it, that's great."

He began to paint, working very quickly, almost feverishly. She could tell from the sound of his brush strokes that he was completely engrossed in his work. After an hour he told her to relax, covered the painting on the easel with a cloth and joined her on the settee.

"Is it finished?" she asked.

He laughed. "No, my love, it will take a few sessions yet, but it can be exhausting, posing for a long time, and I don't want to tire you out or rush it. I want it to be perfect."

On Friday and Saturday Edwina sat for him for four hour-long sessions, and she knew from what Mrs Skefford told her that he had been putting in a lot of work on his own.

29

Sunday 11th April

At last the day arrived that Edwina had planned for and looked forward to for so long, the day when she could entertain Robert and his family, return the friendship and hospitality she had received in abundance from the Skefford family and show Robert especially, but also his family, what she had done with his pictures. She was particularly excited about the latter achievement.

Robert too had longed for this day to arrive. He had asked Edwina to show him the pictures several times just after his return from college, but had then stopped asking when he realised she was so looking forward to Easter Sunday and the grand revelation. He was familiar with all the paintings of course, but he knew that a picture only really came alive once it had been framed; it was enhanced by the choice of wood or metal surrounding the subject matter.

Mrs Pearson had worked hard to prepare the lunch and had really enjoyed the challenge. Alf had volunteered to wait at table, along with Edwina and Margaret.

The Skeffords arrived at twelve o'clock, and although they were all dying to see the pictures Edwina took them into the living room to serve pre-lunch drinks. It gave them an opportunity to relax and admire the views across the lawns and flowerbeds down to the lake, and beyond to the wood. This view was hidden to the outside world and it was so long since Robinson and Emily had seen it that they had forgotten how beautiful it was. Mrs Pearson came in to tell Edwina that lunch was ready, but she knew that she had to delay serving it, to give them all a chance to view the pictures. As arranged, Robert led the way into the dining room. He threw open the door, took one step forward and stopped in amazement. The table was beautifully prepared, covered with a pristine white table cloth, adorned with the best china dinner service, gleaming cutlery and crystal glasses, but it was the two flanks of pictures on either side of the room that had brought him to a standstill, and now brought an intake of breath from everyone else as they crowded past Robert.

"That is just stunning," Robinson said. "Well done lad."

"My God," Rupert said. "You really do have talent. I want to see them all before lunch if there's time."

"There is," Edwina said. "I advised Mrs Pearson that you would all want to see the pictures before sitting down to the meal."

Margaret, her mother and Edwina set off down the left hand side, while Robert, Rupert and their father explored the right hand side. Robert was overjoyed to see the expert way they had been framed and the care that had gone into hanging them to produce the most balanced effect.

"You have done a wonderful job for Robert," Margaret said. "I hope he appreciates how lucky he is."

"Yes, indeed," Mrs Skefford concurred. "It must have taken hours to organise this."

When everyone had completed their tour round the table Edwina seated them and Mrs Pearson served the first course. Robert poured the wine and conversation broke like a wave over the table, with everybody expressing their views about what they had seen and admired. Mrs Pearson, who was a wonderful cook, had excelled herself. The meal passed like a dream for Edwina; it was such a pleasure to see all these people seated round the table. Admittedly there was room for very many more, but this was a big improvement on her first day, when she had sat by herself, looking down the length of the massive table, feeling very alone and terribly lonely. From time to time she glanced at Robert and occasionally their eyes met and exchanged loving glances; at others he was deep in animated conversation with one or other member of his family. It was clear how much he was enjoying the occasion.

At the end of the meal Robert left the table and returned a few minutes later carrying a picture. By now the room was silent and expectant.

"There is one more picture," Robert said. "This one is a present from me to the girl I love." He handed the parcel to Edwina, who tore off the brown paper covering, to reveal a portrait of herself. Instead of lying back on the faded settee though, she was reclining on that grassy bank in the clearing, amid a purple sea of crocuses. Edwina thought it was the most beautiful thing she had ever seen and turned the picture to display it to the others. There was a gasp of amazement.

Robert could see that Edwina was close to tears. He put his arms round her.

"How can I ever repay you," Robert said.

"You already have," she said, squeezing his hand. "I will always treasure this picture and it will always remind me of this happy day with you and your family."

30

Tuesday 13th April

The day dawned bright and sunny. Edwina skipped downstairs, singing, as she felt so happy. She entered the breakfast room where Mrs Pearson was standing as usual in front of the sink.

"Somebody sounds cheerful," she said.

"This is going to be a wonderful day," she said, laughing. "I feel it in my bones."

"Laugh before breakfast, cry before tea, my mother used to say," but she smiled happily. She was very fond of Edwina and thought of her now like the daughter she had never had. She could remember how wonderful it was to be twenty years old and in love and could share that happiness with Edwina.

"Is Robert coming over today?" Mrs Pearson asked, placing the freshly made pot of tea on the table.

"Yes, he is," Edwina said, "but Mr Baxter, this very important art expert and dealer, is coming down from London to meet him and discuss business."

"I'm sure he will be impressed with Robert. I love that picture he painted of you. It's the best of them all."

"Yes, it is good. I love it and I will cherish it all my life."

"Would you like me to serve coffee and biscuits?" Mrs Pearson asked.

"Yes, please. Put them in the lounge. It will be quieter in there." The lounge was smaller than the sitting room, and had been Edward's study before he decided to move to a larger room, where he had felt he had more privacy and a better view.

While this conversation was in progress DS Webster and DC Stanley had seated themselves at Webster's desk, to carry out a review of the Missing Persons File on Edward Grangelove. Beside each of them was a steaming mug of tea.

"So, what progress have you made?" Webster asked, sipping tentatively at his tea.

"This is a baffling business, Sarge. It's like the man on the stair, who wasn't there."

"I know that one," Webster chimed in, "he wasn't there again today."

"Oh, how I wish he'd go away," Stanley finished. They both laughed, raising heads from elsewhere in the office.

"Seriously though," Stanley said, "this Edward Grangelove must be the original invisible man. One moment he was in his home. That was on the thirteenth of February. It was a cold and foggy night, and there's no way a seventy-four year old man could walk to a bus stop or railway station, even if there was one fairly close. So you have to come to the conclusion that he had to leave by car."

"That would seem to be the only logical supposition," Webster agreed.

"I checked all the local taxi companies to see if they had picked him up, but drew a blank. If he went by taxi, it wasn't from a local firm. It struck me that he may have gone away in the taxi that brought Miss Cabrossi to Highfields; that would have cut the number of cars passing Hollytree Cottage, where the Pearsons live, from two to one, and increased the likelihood that the Pearsons wouldn't have heard anything. So I decided to start checking airports to find out which flights they came in on or left by."

"That seems logical," Webster commented.

"I started at Heathrow and Gatwick, then Stansted and Luton. I worked my way north as far as Manchester. Nothing!" Stanley spread his hands.

"So where does that leave us?" Webster asked.

"I think we need Miss Cabrossi to explain just how and where she arrived in this country."

Webster thought for a moment, but then shook his head. "That isn't what we are investigating, Bill. It is certainly intriguing to know how Miss Cabrossi arrived in this country, but it doesn't do anything to explain why Mr Grangelove is apparently missing. We mustn't lose sight of the fact that this is a Missing Persons case and the missing person is Edward Grangelove, not his daughter Miss Cabrossi."

"You're right Sarge, but I don't think we'll find him until we know how she arrived in this country. She isn't on any of the manifests for that day. I haven't checked them all yet, but I have checked all the probables."

"She could have come as a passenger in someone's car, on the ferries or through the tunnel. We can't even trace people who have no passport and don't speak a word of English, so what hope have we got in tracing her. We just don't have the time for it."

"Still Sarge," Stanley said, "it would be interesting to know how she arrived."

"Yes, it would," Webster said and exchanged meaningful glances with Stanley.

"Leave it to me," Stanley said.

Almost at that very moment in time, Martha Bracken, who like Edwina was in a very cheerful mood, was picking up the post from the carpet inside her front door. She was puzzled to see an unfamiliar envelope with a strange foreign stamp on it. She put this on one side, while she opened and discarded five items of junk mail. Why are they wasting all this time and energy using up the earth's resources on pointless advertising, she thought. She had even filled out a form requesting that all junk mail should cease, but it was as though the post office had added her name to the list demanding to be bombarded with every conceivable kind of nonsense they could churn out.

After dispensing with the junk mail, Martha's mood was not quite as cheerful as it had been a few minutes earlier, but it was with interest that she turned her attention to the envelope with the Italian stamp. Something about it had looked familiar when she first picked it up. Before she could satisfy her curiosity however, the telephone rang.

It was Kathleen and she was obviously in an agitated state. She was spitting out words so fast that Martha could make no sense of what she was saying.

"Slow down," she commanded. "I can't understand what you are saying. Speak slowly. Take a deep breath and start again."

There was a pause and she could hear Kathleen breathing deeply.

"That's better," Kathleen said. "I have had a letter from Uncle Edward."

"What?" Martha queried. "Are you sure?" She knew she should feel relief, but she could only feel disappointment.

"There's no doubt about it. He says he has written to you as well."

Martha examined the envelope she had received more closely. There was a distinct similarity between the writing and that of uncle Edward. "It can't be," she said furiously, slashing open the envelope and, with trembling fingers, pulling out the letter. It was a single sheet, folded into four and hand written. Her heart leapt as she recognised uncle Edward's handwriting; there could be no doubting it, for he had a very distinctive style.

"I've got one too," she said into the phone.

"Have you read it?" Kathleen screeched.

"Give me a chance," Martha said, recovering her self-confidence. "I'm going to read it now. I'll read it out loud."

'My Dear Martha,

I am sure you will know by now that you have a long-lost cousin, Edwina, my own lovely daughter. I was unaware of her existence until a few months ago, but I am overjoyed to have found her. I hope you and your sister, Kathleen, will become good friends to her, as she will need friends, coming to live in a strange country, where she knows nobody.

Her mother and I met in Italy over twenty years ago and, without going into details, the result of our brief encounter was Edwina. I had no idea until last year that I had a daughter. If I had known, my whole life would have been changed and I could have had a loving family round me, instead of years of loneliness. The clock cannot be turned back, but I hope to return with Edwina's mother and live the rest of my life in a happy loving family.

I know this news may come as a shock to you, as you and your sister had great expectations. Naturally, I have made a new will, but I can assure you both that you will still benefit generously from my estate in due course. I hope you will not resent Edwina. It is only natural that a daughter should be regarded higher than a niece.

I look forward to seeing you both in the future.

Yours sincerely.'

The letter was signed '*Uncle Edward*' and it was clearly his signature.

As she read this letter, Martha's heart sank, just as Kathleen's had, fifteen minutes earlier.

"What have we done?" Kathleen screeched down the phone.

"What do you mean?" Martha asked, but she knew perfectly well what Kathleen meant.

"What do I mean?" Kathleen repeated, "only that we have hounded her ever since she arrived on the scene, and complained about her to the police."

"That was your bright idea," Martha said, spitefully.

"You went along with it. In fact you were the one who went to the police and told them uncle Edward was missing." Kathleen wiped the tears from her eyes. "That poor girl. What must she think of us? And what will her father say when he hears what we have done and how we have treated her. He'll make another new will I should imagine."

"My God," Martha yelped. "I will ring the police straight away, to call off the hounds."

"I just hope it isn't too late," Kathleen said. "And we must think of a way to apologise to Edwina and become her friend, as Edward requests."

"Leave that to me. I'll think of something, but first of all I must phone Stokesborough police."

While this conversation was taking place Robert arrived at 'Highfields'. He was in a highly nervous and excited state, wondering what Siegfried would ask him. Edwina sat with him in the sitting room and talked to him to calm him down. Eventually Siegfried's car crunched into the parking area.

"Don't let him bully you," Edwina cautioned, as they went out to greet him. "And don't sign up to anything until Bruce Collinridge has had time to vet it."

"All right," Robert said. "If he's all he's made out to be, I'm sure we will get along fine. I don't intend to enter into any contract in excess of one year, and I have consulted with Dad's solicitor."

"That's great," Edwina said, squeezing his hand. She opened the door and there was Siegfried, a smile on his face as dazzling as the sun that morning.

"How wonderful to see you again," he said.

"This is Robert," Edwina said, by way of introduction. Siegfried grasped Robert's hand in an enthusiastic session of hand shaking.

"I'm so pleased to meet you at last," Siegfried said. "We are going to become very good business partners."

Edwina led them down the corridor to the lounge and left them alone to discuss the new venture.

On the way back to the sitting room she noticed that Mrs Pearson had left the mail and she collected it as she passed by. Like Martha's post that morning, there appeared to be a preponderance of junk mail, but she too had a letter addressed to her personally, bearing an Italian stamp and postmark. Settling herself in her favourite armchair she opened the letter. As she already knew the contents, having written the letter herself with her right hand, in Edward's distinctive handwriting, she hoped it would put an end to the vendetta by her two cousins, particularly if they admitted to receiving letters themselves.

As she read the letter again tears welled in her eyes, even though she could recall the words she had written. It brought home to her the depth of her loneliness and isolation. Her cousins had decided to be enemies rather than friends, and due to their actions, she was now under investigation by the police and knew that ultimately it would be impossible to explain her appearance and Edward's disappearance. She knew that the letter she held in her hand had to be the key to release her from her fears, and free her to live in this parallel world and love Robert.

She settled back into the armchair, closed her eyes and fell asleep. The letter slipped from her lap and fell to the carpet. She had been worried about her situation for a long time, but now she relaxed, knowing she had done all in her power to allay the suspicions of her cousins. She had played her trump card. She slept peacefully for what seemed a long time, but was in fact only half an hour, but her slumber was shattered by the clanging of the front door bell.

She heard Mrs Pearson opening the front door and the subdued conversation that followed. Then she recognised the voice of DC Stanley. Mrs Pearson knocked on the sitting room door and entered, closely followed by Stanley, who did not wait for an invitation.

"As you can see, Miss," Mrs Pearson said in an irritated tone, "Mr Stanley is here to see you again."

Edwina had drawn her legs up into the chair as she had slept and her skirt had risen up to the top of her thighs, exposing her legs. Hastily she took her legs off the armchair and pulled her skirt down to her knees.

Stanley had watched, fascinated by what he had seen. He was convinced she was the most beautiful girl he had ever set eyes on, and it made it very difficult to suspect her of any criminal act. She looked the picture of innocence.

Having adjusted her skirt, Edwina invited him to sit down. Stanley chose the settee, where he had sat on his previous visit. From there he was sitting directly opposite Edwina and could watch her reactions to his questions.

"I'm sorry to disturb you again, Miss," he said.

"It's quite all right. I fell asleep; it's such a cosy chair."

"Yes, I'm sure Miss. What I wanted to ask you was about your movements on the night of the thirteenth of February. In particular I would like to know how you came into the country, which airport or seaport you used and whether you had a taxi or a private car to bring you here?"

"That's a whole lot of different questions," Edwina said. "I take it you are still investigating the apparent disappearance of my father?"

"Of course, Miss."

"Then you will be interested to see a letter I received today." She put her hand on the arm of the chair, where she had placed the letter after reading it, but felt some alarm when she discovered it was not there. "Oh," she said, "I'm sure I put it there."

"Yes, Miss, I'm sure you did." He rose and picked up the letter from where he could see it had dropped beneath her chair, and offered it to her, but she declined.

"You may read it if you wish," she said.

Stanley opened the envelope and carefully read the letter several times.

'*My Dearest Edwina,*

How I wish I could be with you at this time, but for the sake of my health, I know it would be foolish to return until my convalescence is completed. Also, as you know, I have another mission, which may take me a long while to fulfil, but I am determined to achieve success.

I know my affairs are in capable hands and if there are any problems, you have a team of professional advisers only a phone call away to assist you.

God bless you my darling daughter. I will see you again soon.

Your loving father,'

It was signed simply '*Edward*'.

A smile of satisfaction flitted across Stanley's lips. "You can vouch that this is his writing?"

"Undoubtedly. I would swear to it."

"Would you mind if I borrowed this letter?"

"Well, you must promise to let me have it back."

"You can rest assured that I will."

"Then you can take it," Edwina said.

DC Stanley placed the letter carefully back in the envelope and then into his jacket pocket.

"I'm really pleased everything has turned out fine," he said. "I never suspected anything different for one moment, but we have to look into these matters."

"Of course," Edwina said. "I understand fully."

As he walked out to his car Stanley wondered if he had detected a slight satisfied smile play across Edwina's lips as he bade her farewell.

After DC Stanley left, Edwina felt as though a great weight had been lifted from her shoulders. She had been transported into this known and yet foreign society where she had met some familiar characters and others unknown to her. She had struggled to justify her position in these surroundings and at last she felt she was on the verge of accomplishing that aim.

The telephone rang and she picked it up.

"Hello," she said.

"Is that Edwina?" a female voice asked, much softer and more subdued than the last time Martha had spoken to her.

"Martha?" Edwina asked.

"Yes," Martha said. "I just had to telephone you to let you know that Harvey and I are really looking forward to meeting you. It was, of course, a great surprise to hear that uncle Edward had any offspring and it took some time to get used to the idea, but I would like you to know that you can count on me as a friend." Without waiting for a response, she continued, "I would love to meet you, Harvey too, of course. Perhaps we could arrange a meeting, either here or at Highfields. We had such lovely times at Highfields, Kathleen and I, when we were children." Edwina could remember the delightful summer days, when Martha's mother, Elizabeth, had brought the children to spend a few days with his parents, their grandparents. As their uncle he had loved spending time with them, amusing them, and playing their childish games. There had been much laughter during their stay and much sadness after their departure.

"It was unfortunate that Kathleen thought to report your father as a missing person to the police, but that has all been cleared up. I phoned them this morning myself to explain that it was all a mistake. I hope it has not caused you any embarrassment, and as I said, I can't wait to meet you."

Edwina was not a vindictive person and was only too ready to forgive her cousins, but she was well aware that it was the threat of further financial sanctions that was motivating this conciliatory approach.

"I would like you to speak to Kathleen and let me know a suitable date when you can come together."

"That will be wonderful," Martha said, trying to sound convincing. "I will phone again after speaking to Kath."

Edwina replaced the phone, with a satisfied smile, the second she had allowed herself that morning, while Martha banged the instrument down at her end and almost screamed in frustration.

When Robert emerged from his discussion with Siegfried, soon after this conversation, he was clearly very excited.

"We have had such a wonderful meeting," Siegfried said, giving Edwina his broadest grin. She was not taken in by his effusiveness, however. She had seen another side to his character and would want to learn the detail in the contract before celebrating. Even so, she gave him a friendly smile, for the sake of Robert. She did not want to upset the man who could establish his career."

"The good news, my dear Edwina," Siegfried said, "is that I have managed to persuade the two most influential art experts to attend the exhibition. When I say experts, I mean people who can and do like to set a trend in art, to claim that they have made a new great discovery, a break-through to the promised land, the next great school of artists. What they really want is to discover the next Picasso before anybody else is aware of his existence, but what they usually hail as genius is more often mediocrity at best. However they do possess the means to support their hunches."

"But surely the art critics can detect talent," Edwina suggested.

Siegfried laughed. "Of course, but the critics want to go along with the herd. They don't want to be the one who tells the king that his new suit doesn't exist. When these 'experts' declare that an upturned dustbin lid is a great work, of equal importance with Michael Angelo's ceiling in the Sistine Chapel, they can create a price for it well in excess of a work of true artistic merit."

During the conversation, Robert had steered Siegfried towards the dining room, as Siegfried had asked to see Robert's paintings again before leaving. Having entered the room he stood quite still, in an attitude of great respect, reminiscent of someone who had entered a church.

"Beautiful," he said. "This time they will both have something worthwhile to fight over." Turning to Robert, he said, "I believe you have a truly great talent and will achieve success whichever road you follow, but if one of these two sponsors acclaims your work, you will be on the high road to success, instead of the low road. It just needs one of them to admire and to acquire. Collectors will rush to buy, while prices are still affordable."

Having walked the length of the room, Siegfried turned to walk towards the door and noticed for the first time the new addition, the portrait of Edwina reclining on the bank in the wood. Due to lack of space Edwina had hung it directly above the door, so that it was not visible on entering the room. Siegfried paced quickly towards the painting, his eyes fixed on it.

"Magnificent," he breathed. "Stunning. I would like to buy this picture for myself."

"Then you will have to ask Edwina," Robert said. "I painted it for her."

"And I shall never part with it," Edwina said.

"You are quite right. It is beautiful. One day you may sit for another picture. I would suggest the same pose, but without the clothes. That would be a real masterpiece." He chuckled and smiled cheekily at Edwina. "And now, I must leave you. We will meet again on the day of the exhibition. I am confident that you have organised it to perfection. I will be here soon after lunch to run through the programme with you both. There's no need to look so worried, Robert, your task is the easiest. Stay close by me, be very courteous and attentive to all the people I introduce you to and answer all their stupid questions as best you can. Edwina has the hardest task, keeping all those glasses charged, the plates filled with goodies and straying fingers off her bottom."

With a wave of his hand he let himself out. Robert and Edwina dissolved into laughter and then collapsed into each other's arms.

"You know, he might have a point," Edwina said.

"Oh, what's that?"

"When he said you should paint another picture of me." She watched his face intently to see his reaction and he looked directly into her eyes.

"Are you being serious?" he asked. "Siegfried was suggesting a nude portrait, in the same pose."

"I'm aware of that. Don't you want to paint me like that?"

"Of course I do. I love you, every inch of you, but I don't want to expose you to other eyes. I'm jealous."

"But you're an artist and when people look at your paintings, they are only seeing your interpretation of what you see at that particular moment in time, They would not be seeing me, only how you see me at this time in our lives. You gave me a lovely portrait, and I will always keep and cherish it. I would like to give you something in return, to keep and always remind you of this time, and of how much I love you."

Robert put his arms round her. "You are so dear to me," he said. "Your face and form are constantly in my mind."

"In a way it's a selfish request," Edwina persisted, "because I want to preserve an image of myself, in youth and beauty, before the ravages of time reduce me to an old ugly wreck."

Robert laughed, but he could see she was in earnest, and there were tears in her eyes. Looking into her lovely face he said, "you will always be beautiful in my eyes."

"I know," she assured him, "but I want you to have a picture, just as I have one. You don't need to show it to anyone. You can keep it locked away, if you wish, but I know that one day you will want to display it. Perhaps it will be a comfort to you in a time when I am gone."

Robert kissed her lips gently; they were warm and soft, and her perfume seemed to overpower him with desire for her. "We could start work tomorrow," he said.

Her eyes smiled up into his.

31

Wednesday 14*th* April

Edwina saw the pale light of dawn slowly illuminate the curtains of her bedroom. She almost threw herself from the left hand side of the bed to the right side, and knew she had failed in her attempt to close her eyes long enough to induce sleep. The reason for her insomnia, as she knew, was the prospect of posing nude for the painting in front of Robert, and yet she had volunteered to do it and had in fact convinced Robert that she had to do it, and secretly was looking forward to it. So why am I worrying about it, she asked herself? She stretched her legs to the end of the bed and fell into a deep sleep.

Amazingly, when she awoke later, she felt thoroughly refreshed. She rose and took longer than usual in the bath, and in perfuming her body afterwards. Now that the day had arrived, when she would expose herself for the portrait, she still felt nervous and apprehensive, but also strangely excited. This would be a great test, she knew, that would define her commitment as a woman and her love for Robert. She did not have any doubts about it, but there were still times when she felt the influence of Edward on her thought processes. This was a situation though where she could only think as Edwina, as it was entirely foreign to Edward's experience.

She put on the minimum of underclothing, just pants and bra, and covered them with a warm tweed skirt and jacket. She placed her dressing gown in a small case, which she carried down to the hallway, before entering the kitchen. Mrs Pearson was bustling about as usual and after Edwina had sat down she made the tea and brought it over to the table.

"Is anything the matter?" she asked. "You look very pale."

"I'm fine," Edwina said, but she was feeling anything but fine. She had begun to have misgivings. Her stomach was churning and she began to shake. Mrs Pearson was alarmed.

"Are you ill, my dear? You are shaking like a leaf. Why don't you go back to bed and I'll call the doctor."

"No, it's all right, I assure you," Edwina said. "It just seems a little colder this morning."

She poured herself a cup of tea and managed to force herself to eat something, knowing that Mrs Pearson would insist on ordering her back to bed if she did not. Then she drank her tea and fled from the dining room, while Mrs Pearson's back was turned, snatched up her small case from the hall and raced out to her car. When she had driven away from the house, she felt calm and her resolve returned. She knew she had to go ahead for the sake of Robert and she knew also that it would prove to herself that she had completed the transition from male to female.

When she arrived at the farm Robert came out to greet her. He seemed nervous too.

"Are you sure about this?" he asked.

"Yes," she replied simply.

He took the small case from her and, taking her hand, led her through the kitchen and up the stairs to the attic. They met nobody on the way. The whole house seemed deserted. Robert noticed how cold her hand felt. Taking a key from his pocket he unlocked the attic door.

"I thought you might feel more comfortable if we could ensure privacy while you are here, and after we finish the work we can lock it away. I have made one or two other improvements since you were here last time," he said.

She noticed that the floor was now carpeted and an electric fire had been installed. Robert switched it on. "This warms the room very quickly."

He had covered the floor beneath and around the settee with a rich green cloth and had spread a light gold-coloured silk cloth over the settee. He knew that the addition of this material would enhance the quality and tone of her skin. His easel had been set up and a new prepared canvass sat ready on it. In the corner of the room he had rigged up a series of curtains to act as a changing room for her.

"Is everything ready?" she asked.

"Sit on the settee for a minute. I want to change your pose. To start with take up the same pose as last time."

She did as he asked. "I want you to rest your left arm along the top of the settee and, slightly turning and looking to the right, lean your right elbow on the arm of the settee. Open your right hand slightly and hold this piece of folded material. That's it. I will drape it across your right breast and lay it loosely on the top of your right thigh and let it cascade down, across your legs to the floor." He stood back to view the result. "I think that's excellent. Do you think you will be able to hold that pose for me?"

"Yes," she said.

"Good." He snatched up his sketchbook and quickly sketched an outline of her pose. Then he made some slight adjustments to the way she was sitting, always keeping her as comfortable as possible. After the third sketch he seemed satisfied. "We can begin now," he said. "I will make some more sketches when you have undressed and then I shall be able to start work on the painting."

She rose from the settee, picked up the small case and stepped behind the curtain cubicle. Slowly she removed her clothing and put on her dressing gown. Stepping out she walked over to the settee and removed her dressing gown before taking up the last of the three poses. All this time, Robert had his back to her, making some marks on his canvass. Finally, he turned to look at her and the sight almost took his breath away.

"You are even more beautiful than I could imagine," he said. He placed the folded cloth in her hand, draped it across her naked right breast and placed it in position on the top of her right thigh and draped it down her legs. Taking up his sketchbook again he worked feverishly for the next two hours, firstly on the sketches and then with the paintbrushes.

At last he relaxed and handed the dressing gown to her. "I think you have earned a break," he said. "We'll get some lunch at the Farmer's Arms, and afterwards we'll go for a walk."

"Don't you want me to keep sitting for you?"

"One session every morning will be sufficient," Robert said. "Then I can work on my own throughout the afternoon, or we can go for a walk, together to enable us both to relax."

"That sounds wonderful," Edwina said, slipping her hand into his.

After lunch at the Farmer's Arms they returned to Highfields. Edwina wanted to change before going on their walk. As they came into the hall she saw a letter waiting for her on the small table, where Mrs Pearson left the mail every day. It had an Italian stamp on it and she guessed it would be from Patrick. She felt excited at the prospect of knowing whether he had succeeded in his quest. She picked up the letter and examined it, before dropping it back down onto the table.

"Is that from your Italian boyfriend?" Robert asked.

"No, it isn't, but I'm hoping it will contain some good news about my family. I will only be a few minutes," Edwina said, and skipped up the stairs to her bedroom to change.

It was only after they had finished their walk and Robert had returned to the farm, to put in some more work on the painting, that Edwina collected the letter, carried it into the living room, settled herself in her cosy armchair and slit the envelope. As she expected, the letter was from Patrick. She unfolded the sheets and read:

Dear Miss Cabrossi,
I am sorry to have taken so long to report back to you, but mother was not very well for the first two days after we arrived. Now she is really enjoying herself and we have visited many of the places and people she wished to see. Unfortunately some of her old friends have either died or moved away. In the course of our travels, I have tried to spend time searching for your mother. As you had lived in Castelfranco, we spent a whole day there. We seemed to be met by a wall of silence. None of the local people wanted to discuss anything with us, but in the end I had to explain to mother what I was doing to assist you. It was really useful having her with me, as it seemed more natural to the people there that she should be the one looking for an old friend.
We learned that you had left the town to take a job in Venice, in one of the large hotels, as receptionist, it was thought, but nobody really knew, as you had not returned to the town since then. Your mother had left Castelfranco a year after you, and most people thought she had gone to join you, but I knew from what you had told me, that she did not join you in Venice. Two people in Castelfranco, who had known your family, suggested that your mother was now living in a small village about half way between Venice and Castelfranco. It's called Bassano del Marostica. I intend to go there tomorrow. The time seems to pass so quickly and I have to see that mother visits all the places on her list. Her health has improved since we came, and the warmer climate seems to suit her. I thank you again for giving us this opportunity to spend some of her last days together. We will be returning on the twenty-first. Hopefully, I will have some better news for you by then, as I do

not want to let you down. I will continue the search until the last moment.
Regards,
Patrick

Edwina folded the letter and placed it in the envelope. So that's that, she thought. If I ever go there, people might greet me on the street, and I will have no idea who they are.

It seemed as though her past was buried forever.

32

Saturday 24th April

Edwina woke early and raced downstairs, excited that the day of the exhibition had arrived at last. The past few days, since Siegfried's visit had passed like a pleasant dream. Every day she and Robert had spent hours together, talking, planning and dreaming, as young lovers do. She had spent an hour each morning, sitting for the picture, but Robert had not let her see it yet. After each session he covered it with the cloth, which hung down the back of the canvass, while Edwina donned her dressing gown. She still felt shy about exposing her body, but Robert was full of praise for her, and never tried to touch her or even to kiss her, while she was sitting. In the afternoons they had usually walked in 'their wood' and through 'their glade' and there had been time for many embraces and many kisses. Edwina felt as though she was in heaven, her happiness was so complete.

With the help of Robinson and Rupert, the large dining table had been dismantled and removed, along with the rest of the dining room furniture, to storage in one of the barns at Greenblade farm. The oak floor had been cleaned and polished, until it had been restored to its pristine former glory. The ornaments, some of which were extremely valuable, had been packed away carefully upstairs. The dining room seemed to be longer than ever and had been transformed into a gallery. The pictures now dominated the room entirely and with the empty floor space, Edwina was sure the room would be able to accommodate the numbers invited and provide them with enough space to mingle and view in relative comfort. It was important that people should feel at ease, but it was essential to have enough people to show it was a popular and well-attended evening.

As Edwina ate her breakfast Mrs Pearson kept up an incessant chatter. She seemed to be as excited as a schoolgirl going on her first school trip. She had desperately wanted to be involved in the evening, so Edwina had asked the caterers to let her help with serving the drinks. They had agreed, on condition she wore the same uniform as their own staff. She had been provided with a smart waitress dress, and she was eagerly anticipating the time when she could put it on. Margaret and Mrs Skefford were looking forward to attending, but Robinson and Rupert had declined the invitation, much to Robert's relief. Edwina was glad that she would have Margaret to talk to, if she found the proceedings dragging and had decided she could always get rid of the occasional bore by speaking to them in Italian.

The caterers arrived at midday and began to organise the buffet and the bar. Robert came over soon afterwards and had a snack lunch in the kitchen with Edwina. He was very keyed up, but looking forward to the day. No sooner had the pair finished their lunch than the front door bell clanged to announce the entrance of the local press, a reporter and a cameraman, who began to take photographs of Robert in the dining room, with the picture-covered walls as background. After he was satisfied, the reporter took Robert aside and began to interview him. He thought a farmer's boy, who had just obtained his farming degree, and had given up farming to paint, was quite a good human-interest story. Edwina crept away at that point and went up to her room, to change into her dress. She had searched a long time to find something suitable and had eventually settled on a dress designed by one of the leading

London fashion houses. It was a black cocktail dress, that had a narrow waist, and a low cut bodice, with a built-in bra. A narrow shoulder strap and the perfection of Edwina's figure kept the dress in place and revealed the immaculate beauty of her naked shoulders. She looked at herself in the mirror and decided that it suited her. A week earlier she would have felt self-conscious about wearing it, but after a week of posing for Robert, she had become more daring.

As she descended the broad staircase the local press photographer saw her and recognised her as the girl in the picture over the doorway in the dining room.

"I must have a picture of you in front of your portrait," he said. "It will be the perfect advertisement for Robert's pictures."

Edwina had been on the point of waving him away, but when he said that, she decided to let him take his picture. She went with him into the dining room and stood beneath the doorway, feeling totally relaxed and smiling confidently. As the photographer focussed on her, he realised what a great picture this was going to be. The flash blinded her momentarily. That's the first photograph I have had taken in this new life, Edwina thought. The cameraman took two more shots in quick succession, but then Edwina waved him away. He thanked her and, taking a small notebook from his pocket, asked for her name.

"The editor will insist on a name if we are to publish it," he said.

She told him and then wrote it in the book for him, as he seemed to be having trouble with the spelling.

"Are you Mr Skefford's fiancée," he asked.

She smiled and showed him the fingers of her left hand, and shook her head.

"Are you his girlfriend?" he asked.

"You must ask Mr Skefford that," she said, teasingly.

At that moment the doorbell clanged again, announcing the arrival of Siegfried. He strode into the hall with his usual self-confident swagger, wearing one of his bizarre outfits, green corduroy jacket and trousers, yellow silk shirt and a green and yellow spotted cravat. One thing was certain; that everyone would remember who Siegfried was by the end of the evening, and Edwina was sure that it was a deliberate ploy on his part and the secret of his success.

Some of the London press were next to arrive and Siegfried quickly took Robert in tow and introduced him, with his usual witty remarks. Poor Robert had to undergo a barrage of flashing cameras and Edwina hoped that at least one of the photographs would make it into the morning editions. Only four of the more serious daily papers had been contacted and they had all accepted the invitation.

While Robert was receiving the film star treatment, Siegfried sidled up to Edwina.

"You look absolutely seductive in that dress," he said. "I hope you are wearing it just for me." He laughed, as he didn't expect a reply. "When this session of photographs has finished, take these hungry hounds off for some refreshment. We want to get them out of the way before the really important people arrive." He meant those with the money and influence in artistic circles of course, but his remark disgusted Edwina, as it showed the shallowness of his character. Even so, she stepped in when the cameras stopped flashing, to lead the photographers into the kitchen, where a separate buffet had been laid out on the kitchen table especially for the press. Mrs Pearson, proudly attired in her waitress dress served the drinks, a choice of either beer or wine, while a young girl from the caterer's staff served the food. Edwina almost laughed aloud as she heard Mrs Pearson cautioning them against drinking too much, which had caused an outburst of laughter.

"As if reporters ever drink too much," one shouted, in an assumed thick Irish accent, which brought about a great shout of laughter.

Returning to the dining room she found that Siegfried was just finishing his briefing of the reporters. When he had finished they followed one of the waitresses down to the kitchen for refreshments.

"They will be gone before the guests arrive," Siegfried said. "They need to file their copy if it is to appear in tomorrow's paper." He looked at her critically. "You must relax and smile all the time," he said. "Did I tell you how lovely you look in that gorgeous dress? Why don't we run away together, to the Caribbean or the Seychelles? They say it's very nice in Hawaii at this time of the year."

Edwina had to laugh, no matter how hard she tried to keep a straight face.

"That's better," Siegfried said, "that's what the customers want to see." He went off to talk to one of the waitresses.

Robert, who was finding the experience difficult, came over to talk to Edwina.

"You look fabulous," he said. "I'm so glad you are here. Whenever I feel like running, I just look at you and see how cool you are."

She smiled. "How did the interviews go?"

"Better than I expected. Siegfried had briefed me very well and has proved that he knows what he is talking about. I hope he is just as good when it comes to the next part of the evening."

"I'm sure he will. Did you remember to tell your mother you would be sleeping here tonight? It's going to be a long night and I'm sure you will drink a fair quantity of wine, so I don't want you driving under the influence."

"You are right, I'm sure. I could murder a pint right now."

"I've put you in Edward's room. It's very comfortable and has an en-suite bathroom."

The doorbell clanged again.

"This is it," Edwina said. She took his hand and gave it a squeeze.

Then Siegfried led him off into the hall.

It was amazing how quickly the room filled with people. The caterers cleverly released waitresses to serve drinks as required, to meet the demand. Margaret and Robert's mother arrived and were astounded by the transformation of the dining room since the Easter Sunday lunch. After talking to them for a few minutes, Edwina had to leave them to talk to Brian Jefferson and his wife.

"This is wonderful," Brian said. A girl arrived with a tray-full of drinks and he and his wife helped themselves. "Where did you put your portrait?" Brian asked.

"If you turn round, you will see it," Edwina said. Both he and his wife turned towards the door.

"Excellent! That's the one place that was still available, and the place of honour, where it deserves to be. Now, I must renew acquaintance with these old friends," Brian said.

As Brian and his wife went off to view the pictures Edwina stepped forward to greet the Mayor and his wife. After they had accepted drinks Edwina started them on a tour of the pictures and quickly introduced them to Robert and Siegfried. The waitresses were now offering plates, filled with tempting morsels of food, and as the volume of wine drunk increased, so did the noise of conversation. Just by looking around Edwina could now see that everyone was having a good time.

She returned to the door in time to greet William Haligan and his wife, Pauline. He was surprised that she had been able to pick him out amongst the crowd, but delighted that she had. "I'm so pleased to meet you at last," he said, "And this is my wife, Pauline. I can't say that either of us is an art expert, but these seem to be the kind of paintings that anyone can enjoy." It was a simple statement, but a profound one, Edwina thought, and gave him one of her special smiles, which almost made his knees tremble. Edwina thought they were a very pleasant couple and were easy to talk to.

"I haven't thanked you properly," Edwina said. Haligan looked puzzled. "For giving Patrick all that time off."

"Patrick is the brightest young man in the office and I know he will make it up to the firm. He already works harder than any of his colleagues, even though he has a sick mother to look after. One day he will be sitting in my chair."

"Come along," his wife whispered. "I want to see the paintings."

"All right, Pauline. It was so nice to meet you," Haligan said and they disappeared into the crowd. It was only a few days later that he wondered how Edwina had known him on sight, when he was sure they had never actually met.

One of the last to arrive was Bruce Collinridge, accompanied by his secretary, Annette Hyde-White.

"I was afraid you were not going to make it," Edwina said.

"Wouldn't have missed it for the world, would we Annie," he said. They both accepted drinks and chatted to her about Robert and his paintings. Edwina had wondered in the past if there was a more intimate relationship between the two, than just boss and secretary. The familiar way they looked at each other and were so relaxed together seemed to answer that question. Before moving off, Bruce lowered his voice and said, "by the way, I have heard from Detective Sergeant Webster that the inquiry into the whereabouts of Edward Grangelove has been closed. The police are convinced that the complaint was malicious, but understandable in the extraordinary circumstances."

"I'm so pleased," Edwina said. "I have spoken to Martha and invited her and Kathleen to come here so that we can get to know each other. Thank you so much for helping me at a time when I knew nobody. I won't forget your kindness."

"Think nothing of it, my dear, and now, Annie, we must view these wonderful paintings."

By now all the guests had arrived, including the VIP's, who were being shepherded around the hall by Siegfried, with Robert in close attendance. Poor Robert seemed to be out of his depth, so Edwina decided to join him and give him some support in talking to the honoured guests. She collected a glass of wine on her way to join them. Siegfried seemed relieved to see her.

"And this is Edwina, Robert's beautiful young fiancée," he said. "Let me introduce you to Boris Andraev Barlinski and Sir Rudolph Watson-Shepperton.

The Russian billionaire, a swarthy black-haired man in his late thirties, almost devoured her with his eyes as he took her hand and kissed it. "Enchanted," he said.

Sir Rudolph, a man in his sixties, who was famous for setting up his own museum and art collection held her hand and gazed at her for so long that Edwina thought he might be contemplating adding her to one of his collections. She smiled and retrieved her hand. Siegfried insisted later that Edwina's intervention in their conversation influenced the outcome in Robert's favour. They all engaged in polite conversation for the next half hour and, relaxed in the company of a pretty girl, had another glass of wine. Then, quite suddenly, the four men had disappeared into the sitting room, which had been kept closed from the guests, in case Siegfried needed somewhere apart to talk business.

The numbers in the room were dropping significantly as people made their way home. It had been a good party, with good food and good conversation, but like any host or hostess, Edwina felt a little sad to see the guests depart. She had planned for such a long time, it seemed, for this one evening, and time had moved slowly until the day had eventually arrived. And now, the party was ending, almost before she had time to participate, leaving her feeling a little empty inside. Margaret had seen her standing alone, and came over to her, with Mrs Skefford.

"It has been very successful," Margaret said. "If I ever want to organise anything on this scale I'll call on you." She gave Edwina a hug.

"Where's Robert?" Mrs Skefford asked.

"Locked away with the powers that be," Edwina said. "The real business of the evening is just taking place in the sitting room."

"Thank you for being such a good friend to Robert," Mrs Skefford said, taking Edwina's hand. Leaning forward she kissed her on the cheek. "We all love you," she whispered.

It was so sudden and unexpected that Edwina did not have time to react. Mrs Skefford had taken Margaret's hand and they were already on their way out to the car.

Looking round Edwina realised that everyone had gone. Mrs Pearson came over, looking prim in her waitress outfit.

"You have had nothing to eat all evening," she said, "and the same is true for Robert. I have saved food for you both in the kitchen."

"Thank you so much," Edwina said. "When you are the hostess, you never eat anything yourself, because you are so concerned to see that your guests are well catered for."

"I know," Mrs Pearson said, "but you can rest assured that everybody has been well catered for this evening. You are such a generous person. I'm so glad I was able to help." With that, she darted off to the kitchen. I seem to be receiving a lot of compliments tonight, Edwina thought.

At that moment the door to the living room was thrown open and the four men emerged, laughing and in high spirits.

Edwina watched as they all shook hands and departed, leaving Robert standing alone. She flew to his side.

"How did it go?" she asked.

"Wonderful," he said, pulling her to him. "I can't believe the prices they were talking about. They both wanted to back me, so in the end it was agreed that they would both get half of my paintings for two years. Siegfried is meeting them again tomorrow in London to thrash out the details. I'm starving."

"Wonderful," Edwina said, and threw her arms around his neck. "And now we will have something to eat. Mrs Pearson has left us food in the kitchen, probably enough to feed an army, if I'm not mistaken."

They helped themselves to the food, which was superb, and they drank some more wine. Robert tried to remember everything that had happened in the meeting, but could not remember everything. He knew that in the end an agreement had been reached. Barlinski and Sir Rudolph had both wanted exclusive rights and the argument had become heated, according to Robert, but fortunately Siegfried had stepped in and arranged a compromise. It will mean that all the pictures, with the exception of your portrait, of course, will be transported to London and exhibited as a joint show in Sir Rudolph's art gallery. Just showing the pictures there will increase their value enormously, according to Siegfried. I will be tied though to selling all my pictures to the two of them for the next twelve months. I will receive five hundred pounds for every picture in the dining room now, and the same price per painting in the next year."

"That's wonderful, Robert."

"Isn't it just," he cried out, laughing, "and I owe it all to you."

He took her in his arms and kissed her. She put her arms around his neck and continued the embrace.

"I think it's time I went to bed," Robert said, letting go of her. "I feel so elated, but tired out."

Taking his hand, Edwina led him out of the dining room, up the stairs and along the corridor to Edward's room. She opened the door and put on the light. "I've put your overnight bag in the bathroom," she said.

Robert put his arm around her again and kissed her. She closed her eyes and felt his hand caressing her bare shoulder. He lifted the strap of her dress, and she made no attempt to stop it, as it slipped off her shoulder. He bent over and kissed the naked skin.

"You are so beautiful," he murmured. She could feel herself trembling, but lifted her willing lips towards his. As they met, he lifted the other strap and the dress fell away, revealing her naked to the waist. While his hands sought her breasts, she stooped and pulled her panties over her hips and with one tug sent them sliding down her legs to the floor.

Edwina surrendered her body to him, delighting in every touch and every caress. His hands sought to examine every hidden inch of her and she held nothing back, opening her thighs when his fingers endeavoured to explore her. They kissed without pause and their kisses were intoxicating. Then he caught her up in his arms, lifted her up, lovingly, and carried her to the bed. He laid his precious burden on the coverlet, gazed at her in awe, his eyes taking in every detail of her naked beauty. Then he leant down over her, kissed her breasts, her belly, her thighs and between her legs. Edwina squirmed with pleasure at every kiss. He reached down and removed her shoes and then slowly rolled down her thigh-length tights, his fingers tantalizingly creeping over every inch of her skin. As he finally pulled them off her toes she sank back on the bed in an attitude of complete surrender. She felt, rather than saw him remove his clothes, and then his naked body was next to her. It felt hard against her softness and inflamed her desire even more. As he pressed against her she could feel his excitement and her hand reached out and held him, causing him to cry out in ecstasy.

Neither of them had ever experienced anything like that moment, when he rolled towards her, lifted himself up, and their bodies joined. She threw her legs around him and thought she would faint with joy, but after the rapture, they both sank back on the bed, momentarily exhausted. Edwina pulled back the covers and they both wriggled between the sheets and sank into each other's arms. They felt as though they had been transported to another world, or was it heaven. They kissed and cuddled until eventually they fell asleep.

33

Sunday 25th April

Edwina was the first to wake. At first she could not remember why she was in Edward's bed, but then she became aware of Robert lying beside her, and the delightful experiences of the night before came back to her. Being careful not to disturb him, she let her hand stray shyly over his body, which felt so different from her own. Then she slipped quietly out of the bed, into Edward's bathroom and into the shower. When she had finished, she wrapped herself in an enormous bath towel and, picking up her dress and shoes, went off to her own room.

Mrs Pearson always had Saturday and Sunday off, but was prepared to come in if Edwina wanted her. This morning the kitchen was deserted when Edwina came downstairs and began to prepare breakfast. Robert joined her and they had their first breakfast together.

"This is such a large house," Robert said. "When I woke up I wondered where you had gone. I looked into a whole corridor of rooms, before I discovered your cosy little hideaway at the end of the corridor. Why are you tucked away there, instead of having one of the much bigger rooms?"

"It's because my father chose it for me and prepared it, and the moment I saw it, I loved it, and didn't want anywhere else."

"You are a lovely person and I know why I love you so much. Now, what are we going to do on this lovely morning?"

"I want to be taken out somewhere, to where there is a large park, a beautiful garden or a majestic house, and I want lunch somewhere noted for the excellence of its cuisine and the fame of its chef." She laughed mischievously.

Looking serious, Robert said, "I think I can meet all your requirements, but top chefs and top restaurants tend to be booked up early on a Sunday."

"Then it's just as well that I took the precaution to book in advance." Robert looked puzzled. "I knew we would be spending the day together, so I booked a table at the White Swan, on the river. I hear it's very good."

"Are you joking? It's one of the best restaurants in the country. I've never been there, but I think you need a fortune to eat there."

"You seem to be forgetting. You have something to celebrate after yesterday and I can afford to treat you. It won't be long before you will be able to afford the White Swan every week if you wish."

"I have more than one thing to celebrate," Robert said, placing his hand on Edwina's.

"Well, there's that, too," Edwina said, colouring, but smiling at him.

The restaurant was approximately twenty miles away, but en route there was a famous country house, with beautiful gardens. It was a National Trust property, superbly maintained, where the public could wander at will and Edwina had wanted to visit it for many years, but had never had the right companion to accompany her. She and Robert sauntered along the gravelled paths, arm in arm, between the flowerbeds and colourful borders. In truth, they did not take in their surroundings in any detail, because their eyes were focused mainly on the other's face, but everything was beautiful and unforgettable that morning. Occasionally, when they reached a deserted corner, they stopped and exchanged a kiss. Reluctantly they had to leave, to drive the remaining miles to the restaurant.

They were shown to a table, looking out onto the river, which was a hive of activity that Sunday morning. Boats of all sizes and descriptions seemed to be sailing or chugging on the water. Edwina was so happy that she felt as though she was floating on a cushion of air. The meal, when it was served, was excellent and they both thought the chef's reputation was well deserved. They went to a table on the lawn, at the edge of the water, when they had finished eating, and coffee was served to them there. They were able to take as long as they desired, relaxing in the beautiful surroundings and enjoying the warm sunshine. Afterwards they drove back through the leafy lanes. Everywhere was green and fresh with new growth. Edwina's body seemed to be tingling with expectation and she found herself longing for Robert's touch.

As they came to a stop in front of 'Highfields', he reached over and drew her to him. She seemed to melt into his arms, her whole body becoming limp and he was aware that she was ready to make love to him again, if he desired it, and he did desire it, but his duty to his family beckoned him. They had not seen him since the previous evening, and had not heard about the successful outcome of the exhibition.

"I love you so much," he said, kissing her passionately, "but I must go home now. After all their support, I need to tell the family about the contract. Then I want to spend the rest of the day working on your portrait. I want you to come over and have lunch with us at the farm and then sit for me in the afternoon. I think I will be able to finish, apart from the final touches, and you will be able to see the finished painting."

"That's wonderful," Edwina said. "I'm dying to see it."

They kissed again and she went into the house, feeling sad, even though she had had a really memorable day. As it was Sunday, the house was deserted, so she went into the kitchen to make herself some tea. As she sat at the pine breakfast table, she suddenly felt very alone. Having fallen in love and after giving herself to her lover, and experiencing the joy of being in his arms, she did not expect to feel so lonely. She speculated on the future. In her previous existence, as Edward, she had spent years on her own and could not bear the thought of being abandoned again. Robert was set on a glittering career, with a triumphal progression, from success to success, in front of him. They would probably marry and have children. That was what most people who were in love did, but the thought of having children scared her; it seemed so alien to her memories. Marriage and children might be wonderful, she thought. She had a picture in her mind of a happy family scene on the lawn in front of the house, on a hot summer's day, and one of the children rushing up from the lake, closely followed by another child, who was younger and could not run as fast. The first child, almost breathless, blurted out that she had seen a kingfisher down at the lake, and attempted to describe the glorious colours of the bird. 'I seed it too,' said the little boy behind.

Edwina laid her head on the table and silent tears ran down her cheeks.

34

Monday 26th April

The morning was bright and sunny and Edwina felt happy and cheerful. She had cast off her despondency of the previous evening, which she put down to missing Robert. After Saturday night she just wanted to be with him all the time. After showering she put on a pretty summer frock with a light green and brown leafy pattern that matched her mood. Already she could feel the warmth building and knew it was going to be just like a hot summer's day, without a breath of breeze. She skipped downstairs and was so pleased to find Mrs Pearson in the kitchen. As Edwina ate her breakfast they chatted about the exhibition on Saturday evening. Mrs Pearson had enjoyed herself thoroughly and she had been such a help to Edwina.

She had just finished breakfast when the first of the telephone calls came. Edwina took the phone and headed off to the living room, where she curled up in her favourite armchair. It was Brian Jefferson, thanking her for inviting him and his wife.

"We had a lovely time," he said, "and it was so good to see you again, and the paintings, of course. I thought the one of you was excellent and it was great to meet the artist at last."

"I want to thank you again, Brian, for introducing us to Siegfried. He's a strange character, but he seems to know what he's doing."

"I noticed he had a couple of big names in tow. If one of them could get interested in Robert, his future would be assured."

"Well, apparently, they are both interested in him and agreed to sponsor him jointly."

"Amazing!" Brian exclaimed. "All I can say is that your Robert will fly high very quickly, but he will also have to work very hard."

After Brian had rung off, the phone rang again almost instantly and it continued to ring throughout the morning. Edwina spoke to many people she knew and some she had met for the first time on Saturday, but they all conveyed the same message. They had enjoyed the party and loved the pictures. In a pause in the telephone calls the caterers arrived to pick up their supplies and present their bill. Edwina wrote their cheque and congratulated them on their efficiency. Everything had gone smoothly and their waitresses had been courteous and efficient; the proof of that was that nobody had noticed them, moving about through the throng, handing out drinks and food, and everybody had received whatever they required. As they disappeared through the front door she looked at her watch and could hardly believe the time. She had promised to have lunch at Greenblade Farm and was due there in ten minutes.

Snatching up her keys she raced out to her car and, opening the front windows, allowed the warm breeze, created by the forward motion of the car, to blow through her hair. It gave her a sense of complete freedom and excitement. She drove faster than usual, to feel the wind whipping at her face and blowing the skirt of her dress up around her thighs. At last she calmed herself, smoothed back her hair and pulled her dress down. She laughed.

"It's so good to be alive," she shouted out loud.

Robert was waiting for her in the farmyard and stepped forward as she got out of the car.

"I was wondering where you had got to," he said. The phone has never stopped ringing since I had breakfast, and I have only just got rid of the caterers."

Robert put his arm round her waist and kissed her.

"You look beautifully dishevelled," he said, laughing.

She started to open her bag for mirror and comb.

"No need for that," he said, "You look great. Everybody is ready to eat."

They went through to the dining room, where she was greeted like one of the family, and treated like one of the family too. Robert's father and Rupert were in from the fields. Edwina knew it was a mark of special favour for her and Robert, as they would probably normally have stayed out almost till darkness before coming in for their main meal. Margaret was there, as it was Easter and she would be on holiday for the rest of the week. Mrs Skefford had prepared everything in her usual efficient manner and Edwina gave her a special smile as she heaped food onto her plate.

"That's far too much," she protested.

"You're so thin. I'm sure you aren't being fed properly in that big house of yours."

"When do you want us to bring back the furniture?" Mr Skefford asked.

"Do you know when they will be moving the paintings?" Edwina asked.

"No," Robert said. "Siegfried said it would take a few weeks before Sir Rudolph would have an exhibition room free. Can they stay where they are until then?"

"Of course they can. I love looking at them, and I'll miss them when they go to London. As the pictures are staying you can bring back the furniture whenever you three strong men are all free."

"How about Thursday?" Rupert suggested. So that was agreed upon.

"I think Dad and I missed out when we turned down the invite to your party. Mum and Margaret said it was a great night."

"It was," Edwina said, "but there was plenty of booze left over after the night. Perhaps we should have our own party to celebrate getting the furniture back. Even taken apart that table weighs a ton."

Soon afterwards the family split up. Robert and Edwina went upstairs to the attic. As they cleared the dishes away, Mrs Skefford laid a hand on Margaret's arm.

"I hope Robert's treating her all right," she said, a worried frown on her forehead.

"You don't have to worry about that. You can see they are both madly in love."

"I know," Mrs Skefford said, "but Edwina is such an innocent. And why does he carry her off to the attic every time she comes, and now he keeps the door locked."

"Mum, you are the innocent. He's an artist. That is his studio, and if I'm not mistaken, Edwina is his model. Naturally, she will be shy about letting anyone see her while she is posing, or even seeing the picture until it is finished."

"I understand. Of course I do, really, but I'm still getting used to the idea of him being an artist."

"After he's finished with Edwina, it will be your turn next," Margaret said, laughing and skipping away from the mock smack aimed at her rear.

"Get away with you," Mrs Skefford said.

Upstairs Edwina was just taking off her dressing gown and settling into her pose. On this occasion Robert watched and marvelled at the perfection of her figure. Edwina was aware of his admiring gaze, but did not object.

"My God, you are beautiful," Robert said. Then he picked up a brush, studied her face and began to paint. On the previous day he had worked on the painting long into the evening, unable to capture the expression he wanted, but now, seeing her before him, he knew exactly what he wanted, and soon captured her on the canvass. His hand worked feverishly, with brush after brush. Edwina had learnt that Robert did not like her to talk during their sessions, so she kept silent and watched him work with complete concentration. He seemed to be in another world, inspired, as though he was seeing her for the first time. She kept perfectly still, hardly daring to breathe and so the afternoon wore on. Not once did Robert speak, until, after a sigh, he laid down his bush with an air of satisfaction and sank to his knees as though he was worshipping the image he had just created.

"I know that's it," he said. "Do you want to see it?"

"Can I?"

"Of course."

She gathered up her dressing gown and ran forward to look at the picture. It was truly amazing, stunning, dazzling her eyes with colour and the beauty of her body and his portrayal of her.

Robert stood up beside her and put his arm around her. Because she had not spoken, Robert thought she was disappointed.

"You don't like it, do you?" he said.

She turned to him, took his face in her hands and kissed him solemnly on the lips.

"It's wonderful," she said. "It's the best you have ever done. You must enter it for the Royal Academy exhibition."

"That comes a bit later in my career, I think," he said. "In any case you posed for me to give me a picture, as I had done one for you. I don't think you will want everybody looking at you naked."

"But I'm not bothered about that," Edwina said. "As you said yourself, it's just a painting, not the real me. The picture needs to be exhibited. It's a masterpiece and will enhance your reputation. Promise me you will exhibit it and not just lock it up somewhere."

"All right," Robert said, drawing her to him and kissing her cheek. "But whatever happens I will never sell this picture."

"What about your contract with this Sir Rudolph and the Russian multi-millionaire?"

"That has not been signed yet. This painting belongs to us."

"To you, Robert," Edwina corrected. "Now, let's get away from the smell of oil paint and into the sunshine, before it has all vanished." She sprinted across the room, ducked behind the curtain and emerged a minute later, ready to go.

They drove over to Highfields and ambled across the terrace and down the steps leading to the rose garden. Some roses were already in full bloom and they admired the variety of colours. Their steps led them inevitably down the lawn to the lake. It was like a day in mid summer, it was so hot. It was a relief to enter the wood and gain the shade of the trees. Their steps led them eventually to their clearing, where they had kissed for the first time. The bank where she had lain was covered now with soft fresh grass, but the crocuses had all gone. Edwina sat down and Robert noticed how her light summer dress blended in with the spring colours of the leaves and the browns of the branches. Robert lay down beside her and held her in his arms. She had longed for this. He kissed her and explored her body. There was no hurry; they had all the time in the world. This was their very own enchanted world, in their own enchanted wood. They made love tenderly, and after they had disentangled their bodies, they lay naked in each other's arms, while the sun moved across the clearing. At last, reluctantly, they rose, dressed and walked slowly arm-in-arm back towards the house.

Mrs Pearson had prepared tea for them of cold meats and a salad. They sat at the kitchen table and chatted, while they ate. Edwina opened a bottle of wine left over from the party and poured them both a glass of Chablis. They were both excited by the events of the last two days and were both ravenously hungry. They could not remember when they had had such a satisfying meal. After Edwina had poured them both a second glass of wine they went into the living room. Robert was so buoyed up that he talked at length about his ambitions.

"None of this would have happened without you," he said. "What a glorious chance it was, when I spoke to you when we met on the edge of the wood. And now, I love you so much and I want to spend the whole of the rest of my life with you."

Edwina was close to tears of happiness when she heard his declaration. It was the first time there had been mention of spending their lives together, but then they had always had a sixth sense when it came to understanding what the other was thinking or feeling.

"Are you sure our meeting was just by chance?" Edwina asked, wistfully.

"What else could it be?" Robert asked.

They talked for another hour and then, because Robert had come over in her car, she gave him her car keys and kissed him goodnight.

"Sleep well and dream of me," he said, as he departed. "I'll bring your car back about ten o'clock."

After he had left Edwina locked up and was walking back along the hall to the staircase to go to bed, when she noticed a letter on the hall table, where Mrs Pearson had left it. She had been too busy throughout the day to notice it earlier, and now she felt too tired to read it. Picking it up though, she could tell from the Italian stamp and the writing on the envelope, that it was from Patrick. Taking it into the living room she put on the light, settled herself in her armchair and slit the envelope with her finger. There was just a single sheet of paper, dated four days earlier.

Padua
Dear Edwina,
I'm afraid I have some terrible news.
Mother died yesterday afternoon, after being admitted to the local hospital in the morning. She was very quiet and peaceful during the last few days and never complained once. I was convinced she was improving and I know how much she treasured these last days in her homeland.

At the end she asked to be buried here, in the town where she was born, and with almost her last words she sent you her blessing and her love.

I have made all the arrangements for the funeral, which will take place next Monday morning.

I will return next Wednesday, as planned, and would like to come and see you after I return. From information I have received I am now convinced that your mother is living in the village of Bassano del Marostica.

God bless you for your kindness.
Patrick

Edwina felt numb. She folded the letter, put it back in the envelope and left it on the arm of her chair. Then she climbed the broad oak staircase to the landing above. There she turned towards Edward's room. Throwing off all of her clothes she scrambled beneath the covers. Only then did the tears start. She buried her head in the pillow and longed for Robert to be beside her.

PART THREE

35

Sunday 14th February

Edward groaned as he turned in the bed. The grey light of dawn was just filtering through the curtains into the room. He lay for a little while, wondering why his body ached so badly; then, as realisation came to him, he sat up and pushed his legs out of the bed. The bottle he had drunk the potion from lay on the carpet. He rose stiffly and went into the bathroom to look into the mirror. The beautiful body of Edwina had disappeared and in its place he recognised himself, just as he recognised all the old familiar aches and pains. Had it all been a dream then, he wondered.

"No!" he said out loud. He could remember all of it. He had lived and, yes, loved as Edwina, in that other world, that was so familiar, yet foreign. He had heard talk of parallel universes and thought that perhaps he had been transported into one. If so, now he had been transported back.

He went back into his bedroom, donned his dressing gown and pulled back the curtains. The fog still clung to the lawn and obliterated the view of the grounds. He slipped his feet into his slippers and went downstairs. According to the clock in the kitchen, the time was eight o'clock. He put the kettle on and made himself some breakfast. Sitting alone, while he ate in silence, he felt as though his heart was breaking. He had reached a low point when Mrs Blakewell left, but it was nothing compared with what he was suffering now. It was as though Edwina had died and he had been left alone, to mourn her.

After breakfast, he showered, shaved and dressed in a smart blue suit. It was as though he was expecting visitors, but there were no appointments in his diary. The morning paper had been delivered while he was dressing. He picked it up and anxiously scanned the date. It was the fourteenth of February. According to that he had gone to bed the previous night, the thirteenth of February, but he knew that in reality he had gone to bed on the twenty-sixth of April, after spending one of the happiest days of his life.

As he walked into the living room the telephone rang.

"Hello, is that Mr Grangelove?" a woman asked. There was a certain familiarity to the sound of her voice.

"Yes, speaking," he said, tentatively, while searching his brain to recall why the voice sounded so familiar.

"I saw your advertisement for a housekeeper in the Stokesborough Gazette. Is the position still available?"

"Yes, it is," Edward said, hope rising.

"I know it's a Sunday, but would it be possible to see me today. I'm in Stokesborough at the moment and believe it is not too far away."

"Do you have a car?"

"Yes. And incidentally, there was another advertisement in the same paper for a gardener. My husband is an extremely experienced gardener."

"That position is still vacant as well," Edward said. "Why don't you both come over straight away." He gave her directions. "What name is it?"

"Mr and Mrs Pearson," she replied.

Edward's heart leapt in his chest. Could it be possible, he wondered? After putting down the phone he sat back in his armchair and speculated on what had just occurred. He had recognised the voice, but it was too crazy to believe it would be the same Alf and Lucy Pearson. He waited with growing impatience and mounting excitement, until at last he heard the car coming along the drive. He ran to the window, impatient to glimpse the arrival of his visitors, but as soon as the car door opened he recognised them. There could be no doubt about it.

'How can this be,' he wondered, as he went to open the front door.

He had to restrain himself from embracing them, he was so happy to see them. He greeted them like old friends, which he felt they were, but which surprised his visitors. Then he showed them into the kitchen and they all had a cup of coffee while they sat around the kitchen table and he explained what their duties would be.

"We have a problem," Mrs Pearson said. "We left our previous employment last Friday, and as it included living accommodation, we have nowhere to live at the moment. We are staying in a small hotel in Stokesborough, but can't afford to stay there too long."

"My previous housekeeper had a small suite of rooms on the first floor," Edward said. "There's a lounge, a bedroom and a bathroom. She used the kitchen as her dining room and you can do the same for your meals, and, apart from breakfast, I will eat in the dining room or the living room. As you came into the drive, did you notice the gatehouse? It's very dilapidated at the moment, but if you like the job and we get on well, which I'm sure we will, I will have it refurbished, and you can move in there. I have been intending to do something about it for some time. It will give me something to organise."

"That would be wonderful," Mrs Pearson said, "as long as the rent isn't too high."

"Goodness! I wouldn't dream of charging you any rent for it," Edward said.

"That is so wonderful," Mrs Pearson said. "I can't believe we have been so lucky."

Edward showed them the rooms on the first floor and they were delighted with what they saw. He took them then to show them Hollytree Cottage and explained that, as he owned many other properties in the area, he employed his own builders, so he could set them to work on the cottage as soon as they had finished their current job.

"As for the gardens, the grounds are quite extensive and will keep you fully occupied," Edward said to Alf. "You can't see them very well at the moment because of the mist, but you can have a walk round now, if you like or leave it until after you have moved in."

"I would love to have a walk round now," Alf said, enthusiastically, rising from the table. "There's no need to show me the way. I can explore for myself." He hurried out, eager to see what, at close quarters, the mist had hidden on the drive in.

"This will be ideal," Mrs Pearson said. "Alf had to find extra work previously, because the garden only kept him busy a couple of days a week."

"We had a lovely rose garden here when I was a child and I would like to restore it. There was also a tennis court at the side of the house, opposite the parking area. If the site could be cleared I would like to build a new hard court. But there's no rush with any of this. I'm just saying there will be plenty to keep him occupied."

"That's the way Alf likes it," Mrs Pearson said, "and I know he appreciates a boss who takes an interest in the garden. You must tell him exactly what you want and he will make sure it's done."

Edward smiled knowingly. "Do you want to take the jobs?" he asked.

He detected hesitation and then realised there had been no mention of wages.

"Bless me," he said, "we haven't discussed pay. I don't expect you to work for nothing. I will pay each of you a hundred pounds per month more than you were receiving in your last jobs. In addition you will live in the house rent-free and you will have a housekeeping account, sufficient to meet the needs of all of us. When the cottage is ready you can move in and live there, and as I said, it will be rent free, but from then on you will need to cover your own housekeeping, but Alf will be welcome to come in every day and have his lunch in the kitchen."

"That sounds just wonderful."

At that moment Alf came in from the garden. "There's plenty to do," he said, rubbing his hands together, "I just can't wait to get started."

Mrs Pearson explained the financial details to Alf, but Edward could tell he was more enthusiastic about the work than the pay. "We're so grateful to you," Mrs Pearson said. "When shall we start?"

"Move in tomorrow morning," Edward suggested. "I'll get Luke Middledew to come over and you can go through the cottage together, to see how you would like it."

And so it was settled. Edward could not believe what had happened, but it felt as though it was all part of the same dream, or was it a plan? For the first time in months he was experiencing what he could only describe as hope.

After the Pearsons had left he went to the Farmers Arms for his lunch and spent a contented afternoon reading the Sunday paper in his favourite armchair. That evening he went to bed wondering what new surprises lay in store for him. If the Pearsons could turn up, then it must be possible for other people he had known in that previous existence to appear. 'I await the future with interest,' he murmured to himself, before he fell asleep.

36

Monday 15th February

On the following morning there were no further surprises. Edward telephoned Luke Middledew and asked him to call round, as he had an urgent job for him. Luke knew better than to keep Edward waiting, especially if he said it was an urgent job, so he told his secretary to put off any meetings until the afternoon. Then he drove over to Highfields.

Luke Middledrew was a lean man in his mid-forties and was several inches shorter than Edward. He had wispy sandy hair and spoke with a distinct Durham accent. He invariably wore a brown suit and a tie, beneath khaki overalls, to distinguish him from the tradesmen who worked for him. After taking over the business from his father, Edward had advertised for a man capable of carrying out most, if not all of the jobs in the building trade. Luke had answered the advertisement and had proved himself to be indispensable, so much so, that when Edward had decided to expand his property interests he had formed his own building company and made Luke managing director. The choice had proved to be inspired and Luke loved his work and the challenge of running his own business.

When Luke arrived Edward took him upstairs.

"I've got a new housekeeper and gardener arriving today," Edward explained. "They are going to live here to start with, but I want you to completely refurbish Hollytree Cottage, so they can move into it as soon as possible."

"I wondered when you were going to do up that old place," Luke said. "It's a fine cottage and shouldn't be left to rot."

"Well, it won't be now. Mr and Mrs Pearson will be moving in as soon as you complete the work. When they move in I want the suite of rooms they will be occupying here to be given a complete makeover and that small room at the end of the corridor is to be cleared out for a very special guest. I will be able to give you precise details of the colour scheme, carpet, furnishings and everything else when you are ready to start. I had not appreciated until recently what a very pleasant room that is, especially for a young lady." Luke was intrigued, especially at the mention of a young lady, as he knew Edward had always seemed to be a contented and confirmed bachelor.

At that moment Mrs Pearson rang the front door bell.

"Ah, that will be Mr and Mrs Pearson now. I would like you to meet them."

After introducing them, they all helped to bring their meagre possessions into the hall. Then Edward explained that Luke would be renovating the cottage for them, that they could leave everything in his capable hands, but if there was any particular requirement he would try to fulfil it.

"As to colour scheme, I will leave that entirely to you. Luke will provide paint and wallpaper charts. Just pick out the papers and colour schemes you want."

Edward could see how excited Mrs Pearson was. He decided to leave them in the capable hands of Luke, while he went into his study to deal with the day's post. As he sat at the old familiar desk, looking at the pile of mail waiting to be dealt with, he realised how much he had been letting everything slip, but suddenly he felt a renewed enthusiasm and set about dealing with the backlog. He wondered why he had told Luke why he wanted to renovate the suite of rooms the Pearsons would be occupying, after they had moved out, and particularly why he had asked him to work on the corner bedroom that he could think of only as Edwina's room.

After lunch at The Farmers Arms, Edward decided to telephone his old friends, Robinson and Emily Skefford. Mrs Skefford answered the phone and was most surprised when she learned who her caller was.

"I've decided that I have lived the life of a hermit for long enough," Edward said. "It's time I came back into the land of the living. So I'm starting with my nearest neighbours, and oldest friends, if possible. I would like to call over to see you if I can."

"We would love to see you," Mrs Skefford said. "Robinson is out on the farm, with Rupert, at the moment, but at this time of the year they come in about four o'clock. Why don't you call over about five, that will give them time to clean up."

"That would be most satisfactory," Edward said. "I look forward to seeing you."

And so, promptly at five o'clock, for the first time in over twenty years, Edward called at Greenblade Farm. As he parked in the yard the back door opened and Robinson came out to greet him. He looked exactly as Edward expected him to look, exactly as he had looked when he and his sons brought back the dining table and the rest of the furniture from storage in one of his barns. That had been the last time he had seen him, only three days ago, in that other existence. Time had not dealt too kindly with his old friend, but he could see Robinson scrutinising him closely. He knew there were many changes, but after a few seconds examination, Robinson grasped his hand and shook it warmly.

"You haven't changed much," Robinson said, with a broad grin. "Come on in and have a drink." He led the way into the kitchen, where Mrs Skefford was bustling about as usual. She gave Edward a warm welcome, as though she had seen him every day for the last twenty years.

"Come through to the living room," Robinson said. "You too, Emily. Are all the children at home?"

"Rupert and Robert are, but Margaret isn't back from school yet, but she won't be long." Edward felt disappointed that she was not there; he was so looking forward to seeing her again.

Robinson poured a glass of beer each for himself and Edward and a glass of white wine for Emily. Then he called up the stairs to summon his two sons, who had obviously both been briefed, as they appeared dutifully within seconds. They both seemed to be nervous, to be meeting at last the eccentric millionaire recluse who lived next door. Edward smiled at them and shook their hands warmly, to such an extent that they were quite alarmed, but the cause of his enthusiasm was that he recognised them both straight away. He was so relieved to find that the people he had met in the other world, as he now thought of it, were exactly the same as the people in his world. He gazed at Robert to see if there was any special feeling of affection for him, but there was not. Edward wondered if he was interested in art and becoming a painter.

Both boys chatted away freely and revealed that Rupert had completed his farming degree and was destined to take over the farm. Robert was still at college, but Edward could not bring himself to enquire whether he was painting. It was clear though, from his remarks, that he was not very enthusiastic about a farming career. All the time Edward found himself growing more and more impatient to see Margaret.

At last the door burst open and Margaret swept into the room. One thing Edward was able to appreciate was how attractive she was. She was also very extrovert, as he had expected. Margaret was very pleased to meet her neighbour after such a long time, and after accepting a glass of wine, collapsed into an armchair and described an incident that had happened in the classroom that morning. Edward was fascinated. His heart rejoiced that he had found these friends and he determined to cement his relationship with them. He could not take his eyes off them; he looked from one to the other and wondered how the miracle had happened. Fortunately he did not have to add much to the conversation as they were all full of their own tales of what was going on in their lives, but far from feeling shut out, Edward drank in their words and delighted in their enthusiasm.

"What do you find to occupy your time?" Robinson asked during a lull in the conversation.

"Well, at the moment I'm about to start doing up Hollytree Cottage. I have just engaged a couple as housekeeper and gardener, and I want to do everything I can to hold on to them. So the cottage will be their home for as long as they wish."

"When did you take them on?" Robinson asked.

"Yesterday."

"Then you are taking quite a risk in spending so much money, before you even know what kind of a job they can do."

Edward smiled. "I think I know what a good job they will do. I would like you all to come over and have a meal with me, when the Pearsons have settled in. In the meantime though, if any of you have some free time, why don't you drive over and have a walk round the lake and through the woods."

"I didn't know you had a lake," Robert said. "If it's okay with you, I'll drive over tomorrow morning. I'll bring my sketch pad."

Edward noticed the look of disapproval on the faces of his parents and Rupert. Margaret though smiled encouragingly. So, nothing is different, Edward thought.

Soon after, he made his excuses and drove back to Highfields. As he drove into the drive it struck him how gloomy the whole place seemed to be. Hollytree Cottage was in complete darkness and looked as if it was neglected and deserted. Once past the cottage the road ran though some trees and opened up a view to the main house, which was also in total darkness. It looks like the set for a nineteen fifties horror film, he thought. I will change that image in the next few weeks, he resolved.

37

Tuesday 16th February

After breakfast Edward was relaxing in the sitting room when he heard the sound of a car engine and saw Robert's car sweeping round the curve in the drive and pulling up, with a crunch of tyres on gravel, in the car parking area. He watched as Robert stepped from the car. He was holding what appeared to be a sketchpad and he hesitated for a moment, glancing towards the house, as though he was unsure whether to take off on his walk or whether to knock on the door and ask for permission first. But he recalled that Edward had been most insistent that any of the family could explore the grounds and wander in the woods at any time and would be most welcome. So Robert set off on a voyage of discovery that was to delight his eye and excite the artist within him.

Edward wished that he had been able to accompany the young man on his first walk through the grounds and especially through the woods, but Robert was glad to be alone. He felt released from the burden that was weighing him down. He had confided only in Margaret that he wished to become an artist and had spent most of his time at agricultural college studying art in preference to agriculture. He had done enough work on the course to ensure that he would achieve his agricultural qualification, but not enough to come anywhere near matching Rupert's outstanding results. That was just as well. It might give Robert some reason to convince his parents that he was not destined to be a farmer. He was sure that his mother knew that already. He sensed it in her remarks to him when she saw his poor results, but he had still felt unable to confide in her about his true ambitions.

When he started the course at the agricultural college he had persuaded his parents to let him have the attic as a workroom for what they considered to be his hobby. He was always sketching and both of his parents thought that he could "draw a good picture."

At College though, freed from parental shackles, as he described them, he had been able to break out and found himself spending more and more time on painting and less and less on farming practice. Each time he came home he brought with him a new collection of sketches, watercolours, pastels and latterly, even oil paintings, which he smuggled into the house and stored in the attic. Margaret knew what was happening and even helped him occasionally to carry the pictures up the stairs. She was full of praise for his efforts and could see that there was definite progress in his work.

Edward spent the next two hours reading the newspaper and the novel he had picked up in the second hand bookshop in Stokesborough. Then, glancing out of the window, he could see Robert just climbing the steps from the lawn to the terrace. Moving as quickly as he could he opened the front door in time to head off Robert before he reached his car.

"You must be ready for a coffee, after such a long time out in the cold," Edward called. Robert hesitated. "I'm just about to have one myself," he added.

"Then I'll join you gladly," Robert said, turning towards the house. "You don't realise how cold it is when you get engrossed in a sketch."

After poking his head into the kitchen and asking Mrs Pearson to provide two cups of coffee, Edward led Robert, still clutching his sketchpad, into the sitting room.

"Did you find anything to sketch?" Edward asked.

"Oh, yes. I could spend weeks out there and still find fresh subjects, and then spring, summer and autumn would come along and each season would change the whole outlook. I never realised these magnificent grounds were here. You are entirely hidden from the road by the lodge and the trees surrounding the drive, leading up to the house. It's all so private and beautiful, like having your own private park." He sounded so enthusiastic.

Edward smiled. "Yes," he agreed, "but perhaps it's time to share my private park. As I said, when I called on you yesterday, you are very welcome to come in and enjoy the grounds whenever you like, and I am very pleased to see that you have accepted the invitation."

Mrs Pearson knocked and brought in a tray, which she placed on the small table in front of Edward. "This is Robert, from Greenblade Farm," Edward said, by way of introduction. "And this is my new housekeeper Mrs Pearson," he said to Robert. "Her husband, Alf, will be looking after the grounds for me, so you will see many improvements in the months ahead."

"Do you want me to pour?" Mrs Pearson asked.

"No, that's quite all right," Edward said. After Mrs Pearson left, Edward set out the cups, poured the coffee and handed a cup to Robert who was looking at him quizzically.

"That's very strange," Robert said. "You must be psychic. You added one spoonful of sugar and just a small amount of milk. It's just the way I like it."

Edward laughed. "Then I must be psychic. I did it without thinking." But he knew he did not have to think; he knew exactly how Robert liked his coffee, from pouring many cups for him in that other world. It proved that everything was the same, but in a parallel universe. He knew he would have to be careful not to reveal the extent of his knowledge, acquired in that other existence.

"Would you mind if I sketched you?" Robert asked suddenly.

"Not at all," Edward said. "Do I have to pose?"

"No. It's fine, as long as I can see your face." Robert opened his sketchpad and immediately began to draw. He seemed to work very quickly, as he had when he had painted Edwina's portrait; the strokes of his pencil were strong and confident. Studying him while he worked Edward could not detect any point of difference with the Robert that Edwina had fallen in love with. After about ten minutes Robert laid aside his pencil, with a sigh of satisfaction.

"Can I see?" Edward asked.

"Of course." He handed over the sketchpad and Edward gazed in astonishment at the masterly sketch of himself. Every detail of his face seemed to have been captured. It was a great accomplishment.

"You don't like it," Robert suggested, seeing how long and carefully Edward was studying the picture.

"On the contrary, I think it's wonderful," Edward said. "Clearly, you have a great talent."

"Would you like the sketch?" Robert asked, preparing to remove it from his sketchpad.

Edward restrained him with a gesture of his hand. "Please keep the sketch, but I would like you to paint my portrait when you come home at Easter, after finishing your course at the college. I always intended to have one done, but like many things in life, never seemed to have time for it. I shall pay of course, and pay you well. It will be your first commission; the first of many, I'm sure." Robert was delighted. He had been dreading the examinations and the end of his spell at college, for he knew that then his parents would get to know how poorly he had done. Now, at least he would have something to look forward to.

"Did you find the woods interesting?" Edward asked. "I'm sure there must be some subjects in there worthy of your skills."

"I'm sure there are many, but I never got beyond the lake. It's like a bird sanctuary down there. I could spend days sketching the scene."

"Then you will have the pleasure of exploring the wood on a future visit."

"Indeed I will. Would you like to see the sketches I did?"

"Yes, but I would like to defer the pleasure until after your first walk through the wood. Then I can see what has caught your eye in each part of the grounds."

"That will be tomorrow," Robert said, rising to depart.

"Don't forget to come in for a coffee after you finish your walk."

Edward watched as Robert drove away slowly. The merest hint of an idea was forming in his mind, which was to grow into a plan in the following weeks.

Later that day Edward received a surprising telephone call.

"You won't know me, sir," the young man said, but in that he was mistaken. Edward recognised immediately the voice of Patrick Plockton. "My name's Patrick Plockton, and I work for Reid, Haligan and Morgan. I look after your accounts with them. I'm the person who sees that all the rents are paid on time and I send out your monthly statements."

"Oh, yes," Edward said, dreading what he thought was coming next. "There isn't any problem, is there?"

"Well, there is, actually. Checking through, I have found that the rent for the Adelphi Warehouse did not get paid in for January. "I've chased it up, of course, and it seems it was an oversight on the part of the Adelphi's bank. They say they are putting it through to-day, but I thought I ought to let you know as your statement from me is due to go out today."

"That's very thoughtful of you," Edward said, feeling relieved. "By the way, how is your mother?"

"My mother?" a bewildered Plockton replied.

"I thought she had been very ill."

"No, she's in good health, I am pleased to say."

"Oh. Perhaps I got confused when I was speaking to Mr Haligan recently." Edward felt like kicking himself. "Anyway, thanks again for letting me know."

He rang off quickly and sat back in his chair, with a sigh of relief and then he laughed. He was greatly relieved to know that, at least on this planet, Mrs Plockton was not in imminent danger of dying, and that Patrick was not being forced into embezzlement to pay for cancer drugs.

38

Monday 5th April

As Easter approached Edward felt a sense of relief and achievement that his plans were taking shape. Mrs Pearson had taken charge of the household chores including the cooking, as he knew she would, and husband Alf had made great changes in the garden, which could be appreciated as the weather improved. The lawns were mown, the flowerbeds weeded and the spring flowers were in bloom. The new rose garden had been planted with a huge number of different varieties and was being tended daily. The old tennis court had been marked out with tapes and in spare moments Alf was removing the top layer of grass and weeds. A specialist contractor had been hired and the new hard court would be in place within the next two weeks,

The refurbishment of Hollytree Cottage had been completed and the Pearsons had moved in ten days ago. They were overjoyed with their new home and Mrs Pearson wept unashamedly when she made her first tour of the cottage. Edward was equally delighted with the work and by the look of pleasure on the Pearsons' faces.

Immediately Edward had set Luke Middleton to work on the corner bedroom he referred to in his thoughts as 'Edwina's room.' He explained in great detail what he had in mind, to convert it into a replica of that other room he had been happy to occupy as Edwina. Strangely he could remember every detail of the colour scheme and the furnishings, but was unable to find exactly the same wallpaper, although he found one that was a fairly close match. He hoped that Edwina would like it, if she ever occupied the room. That wish had become an obsession now and Edward spent hours planning how he could trace her, as he was convinced that if she existed in reality in that other world, then she should exist in this world. If she did exist he had determined to find her, but all his preparations had to be completed first.

Each morning, after breakfast, he had enjoyed hours contemplating how he was going to find Edwina and how that would lead inevitably to finding Anna, if she was still alive. His life had suddenly been filled with a purpose, thanks to the strange visit by Michael. If he had admitted the visitation to anyone, he knew they would have considered him to be mad or at least on the verge of madness, but he knew he had lived every one of those days as Edwina.

The ringing telephone brought a halt to his reverie. He assumed it would be Luke, checking on some detail, but it was a woman's voice that spoke, without waiting for him to answer the phone.

"Is that uncle Edward?" Martha Bracken demanded. She sounded just as strident as on that first morning when she had phoned to discover that Edward had gone away and that Edwina had arrived.

"It is," Edward replied calmly.

"Oh, that's a relief. I thought something dreadful might have happened, as I hadn't heard from you."

"I would hardly have been able to tell you if something dreadful had happened."

"I know," Martha said, giving her best imitation of a girlish giggle. "Kathleen and I have been very worried about you."

Not enough to try to contact me though, Edward thought. "That was two months ago," he said. "I was hardly at the top of your priority list."

There was a moment's silence while Martha digested the implications of this remark.

She and Kathleen had discussed his predicament after his appeal to them in February and although they had expressed the uttermost sympathy for him, it had not included leaving their homes to minister to his needs. 'I can't possibly go,' Martha had said, 'Harvey couldn't manage for a day without me.' 'And Keith couldn't cope with all the demands of the children,' Kathleen had countered. She had three young adults to cook and clean for, as well as her husband. She felt that Martha was the one who should go, but she knew any appeal she made would fall on deaf ears, so she kept silent.

"How are you now?" Martha asked. Edward could detect a note of irritation in her voice. Clearly she did not expect to be rebuked.

"I'm fine," Edward replied simply.

"Did you get a new housekeeper?" Martha asked, conversationally.

"Yes, I did. She's a marvellous woman and an excellent cook. Her husband looks after the gardens and acts as my chauffeur if I want."

"So the house will be quite full?"

"It was good to have their company for a time, but I had Hollytree Cottage renovated and they have moved in there now."

"Was that wise?" Martha asked. "If something happened to you we could have a problem getting them out." She was already visualising herself and Harvey living in the luxurious surroundings of 'Highfields' and the cottage would be a useful source of income. Kathleen would have to be pacified in some way, but that should not be too difficult. She had always been able to bully her younger sibling into submission.

Edward had the greatest difficulty in containing himself. Clearly Martha had assumed that she and Kathleen would inherit the house and his fortune. Perhaps she had been disappointed to hear him answering the phone.

"That won't be your problem," Edward said casually.

This time there was no lengthy pause while Martha considered the implications of the remark. She recognised the hidden meaning instantly.

"Oh, you mean the executors would get them out," she said, hopefully.

"No. I mean they can live in the property for as long as they like. My daughter will see to that."

"What!" Martha shrieked. "You don't have a daughter."

"I believe that I do, and I intend to find her and bring her back here to live."

"Are you sure you are feeling well, uncle?" Martha asked. "I am really concerned about you. Can I come up and see you. I could be there tomorrow."

"No," Edward said firmly. "That will not be convenient. I have too much to do."

"You must get over this delusion," Martha said, convinced that Edward had had a nervous breakdown or even worse.

"I will be in touch when my daughter arrives," Edward said. "Goodbye for now." He put down the phone.

***

Robert had returned from college on the previous Friday and was looking forward to visiting Highfields, and renewing his friendship with 'Mr Edward', as he referred to him. Also, he was hoping that Edward would still want him to paint his portrait. He had bought all the materials, including a canvas, which had exhausted the last of his schooling allowance, but he didn't care. He just wanted to get to work, so on that Monday morning, he drove over to Highfields.

After parking in his usual spot, he set off towards the lake, carrying his sketchpad and pencils. He had dreamed of this moment for the last few weeks, and felt a glow of pleasure inside him in anticipation of renewing acquaintance with those glorious grounds. The weather was completely different from his last visit; there was heat in the sun and not the slightest breeze. He marvelled at the improvements made by the new gardener, lingered for a time to study the colourful display of spring flowers and explored the new rose garden. Alf had laid out a pattern of red shingle-covered paths, so that each rose, when it bloomed, could be studied close at hand. Robert could see that when all the bushes were in flower it would be a delight to amble along the paths. Each rose was clearly marked with its name.

Edward had seen Robert arrive and set off on his walk. He watched him, with a smile of satisfaction, until he was out of sight and then settled into his favourite armchair to wait for his return.

In the meantime Robert reached the lake, skirted it and entered the wood. He had not had time to explore it on his previous visits in February, but now he let the paths lead him on a voyage of discovery. He stopped whenever a particular view caught his attention and quickly sketched it, before moving on. At last he came to a large clearing in the centre of the wood, where the trees arched over. He discovered a grassy mound beneath a large oak tree, and began to sketch. Time seemed to pass so quickly and sketch followed sketch. Glancing at his watch he could hardly believe how long he had been there. He closed his sketchpad and set off for the house, where he rang the front doorbell without any hesitation.

Soon he was seated with Edward in the front sitting room, a steaming cup of coffee in front of him, while Edward studied his sketchpad, which was almost full. There was a wide range of subjects, from landscapes to seascapes, from town and city views, to numerous sketches of students at the college. Boys and girls alike had been glad to pose, knowing that Robert worked so quickly that they would not be inconvenienced for more than a few minutes. Edward could tell that Robert had caught the essential essence of the sitter in each case.

"I think they are all wonderful," he said at last. "I hope you are still prepared to paint my portrait."

"Of course I am," Robert said. "I have bought all the materials and can start on Monday, if you like? That will give us a whole week before Easter."

"Excellent. If it isn't too difficult I would like the painting to be in this room, with that window behind me, showing the view across the terrace and lawns, if that's possible?"

"I couldn't have suggested a better location," Robert said. "The light is particularly good in this room and that view will make an excellent backdrop, as long as it is not allowed to dominate. The light is at its best in the morning, particularly on this side of the house, so I would suggest we start work at ten o'clock."

"That will be fine," Edward said. "I'm really looking forward to it."

"It's quite hard work, posing for any length of time," Robert said, "even though you are sitting in a chair or on a settee. The maximum session will be from ten until midday, and we can take breaks for coffee or just to relax, whenever you want. You mustn't think you have to force yourself to go the full distance. In my case I won't need you to sit every day. Most of the work will be done when I am on my own."

And so that was settled.

After lunch Edward drove into Stokesborough and called at the offices of Collinridge Edmunds & Partners. Annette Hyde-White, Mr Collinridge's secretary, greeted him cheerily and, after a short wait, ushered him into Bruce's office. They exchanged the usual pleasantries and then Bruce settled back to await the purpose of the visit. Edward studied Bruce closely, aware that he was making comparison with the other Bruce. They were identical as far as he could make out, even to the small amount of hair that still managed to cling on to his nearly bald skull. It was uncanny.

"I've been thinking about my will," Edward said at last. "I have decided to change it."

"Oh," Bruce said, "I'll get my copy out of the safe."

"No need for that," Edward said, "I have the original in my safe at home and I have checked it out recently."

"As I recall, you only have two blood relatives alive, both girls and both nieces."

"That's right. They are both married and inherited substantially from their parents. In addition they both married wealthy men and want for nothing. The oldest niece has no children and the other has three, all adults now."

"I seem to remember you split the residue between the two of them."

"That's right, after making various gifts to charity. Now I want to reduce their share to ten thousand pounds each. The charity donations stay the same, but the residue I want to leave to my daughter."

Bruce, who had been writing down all these instructions, stopped with his pen in mid-air and stared at Edward, wondering if he had taken leave of his senses. He had known Edward since they were at school together and knew he had lived the life of a bachelor. He wondered momentarily whether his old friend was playing a practical joke on him, but studying his face he could see that Edward was in earnest. "I didn't know you had a daughter," he said.

"Neither did I, until a few months ago, but I'm sure of it and I intend to find her."

"You mean to say you don't even know who she is or where she is."

"I know who she is, but not definitely where she is," Edward said emphatically. He realised how crazy this must sound to Bruce, but the truth would sound even more insane. Her name is Edwina Cabrossi and I intend to find her."

"Is she married?" Bruce asked. Edward shook his head. "Only with a name like that I thought she must be married."

"No. That's her mother's surname. We didn't marry."

Bruce scribbled another note. "Is that everything?" he asked.

"There's one more thing. I want to leave fifty thousand pounds to Mr Alfred Pearson and his wife Mrs Lucy Pearson, who are my gardener and housekeeper. I also want them to continue to live in Hollytree Cottage for as long as they wish, rent-free. This right does not pass to their relatives or next of kin. When they die or decide to move out of their own accord the property reverts to the ownership of Edwina. This also applies if they cease to work for the estate until normal retirement age, unless of course they are struck down by illness."

"You seem to have thought it through very thoroughly."

"I have," Edward said, "but if you can think of any snags, you must let me know."

"I can think of one major snag right now," Bruce said. "If you can't find this daughter of yours and you die before you have found her, you are going to leave somebody with a mighty headache sorting out your estate. I can imagine your two nieces creating quite a fuss, as they will be the next of kin."

"Yes, I know you are right. In that case the residue, including my house and personal effects will go to the National Trust."

"Nothing more for the nieces?" Bruce asked.

"No. My mind is made up on that point, and with this alternative clause, there will be little point in their making a claim on the estate."

"Very well," Bruce said. "At least the will can be resolved one way or the other with that additional clause in it. I should have it ready to sign by early next week. It would help if you could find Edwina Cabrossi as quickly as possible."

"That's exactly what I intend to do," Edward said, with grim determination.

39

Saturday 8th May

Edward and Robert sat in the first class seats on board the British Airways flight bound for Florence. Edward had intended for some months to persuade Robert to accompany him on this trip and the opportunity had been taken, whilst Robert was painting his portrait, to motivate him by holding out the prospect of viewing the great art treasures of northern Italy. Edward had paid Robert very generously for the portrait, which was not yet completed, but in addition had agreed to cover all expenses of the trip, as Robert would be acting as his companion and chauffeur during the time that Edward felt it would be necessary to hire a car. The plane circled around the city, revealing views from time to time of the distant snow-capped mountains to the north and of the blue Mediterranean to the south. As the plane swooped lower on its final approach to the airport, the city came into view, the river Arno with its many bridges prominent, its waters glinting in the bright sunshine, and even at that height the great dome of the cathedral of Santa Maria del Fiori seemed to dominate the city. Then they were skimming across rooftops of houses and warehouses, the wings rising and falling, as the pilot lined up the aircraft with the runway. The plane shuddered as the wheels banged down and after a few seconds of silence the jets screamed, as the reverse thrust halted their headlong charge.

Two hours later Edward and Robert were ensconced in their separate rooms in the Borghese Palace Art Hotel in the via

Ghibellina. Edward had chosen it for its excellent reputation and for its location between the Piazza del Duomo and its proximity to some of the most prestigious museums and art galleries in Florence. After an excellent dinner in the hotel dining room they went for a stroll to the plaza del Duomo, the huge square, dominated by the cathedral of Santa Maria del Fiori. The square was fairly crowded, even so early in the season, but there was sufficient room to walk comfortably on the pavement without being jostled by throngs of sightseers and students. They were able to find a table at one of the pavement cafes and within seconds the waiter was hurrying off to fetch their drinks, while they sat back and admired the huge Duomo, floodlit now; it not only dominated the square, but also the whole of Florence. The street and roadside cafés and bars shed patches of yellow light into the street, in contrast to the stunningly bright white light of the floodlighting on the walls and dome of the great cathedral. There was constant noise from the people sitting at the tables around them and passing by on the pavement, and from the never-ending flow of traffic on the street. There seemed to be a constant pfut-pfut from the engines of the vespas, as they flitted around the square, with boys bent over the front of the machines, like TT riders and beautiful girls astride the back, quite indifferent to the danger of falling off. People called and waved to friends they recognised as they passed by; there were shouted conversations, followed by laughter and then they were swallowed up by the moving tapestry of figures. It reminded Edward of his University days in Cambridge, but then it had been a multiplicity of bicycles clogging the streets.

Edward was content to sip his cognac, and let the rest of the world go by, satisfied and excited too that, with luck, he might know the answers to his questions within the next few days, but Robert, determined not to waste a second of his time, had his sketchpad out and was making hasty drawings of the scenes in the square. Edward admired the quick fluency of his pencil strokes. And then, suddenly, amongst the throng, he thought he caught sight of someone he recognised. Dressed all in black, tall and thin, moving like a phantom, flitting through the throng on the far side of the square was a shadowy figure. Edward rose from his seat and stared in bewilderment, straining his eyes to keep track of the man, who had his back turned, and seemed to glide through the crowd, visible only for seconds at a time, as he bobbed and weaved, disappearing completely from sight and then reappearing, but always going further away. As he reached the far corner of the square he disappeared from view and did not reappear. Edward watched intently for some time, but there was nothing. Edward was convinced though that he had not been mistaken and that he had seen Michael.

Robert had become aware of Edward's odd demeanour and had stopped sketching.

"Is there something the matter?" he asked in alarm, afraid that his elderly companion might be suffering a stroke or a heart attack.

"No, it's quite alright," Edward reassured him. "It's probably nothing. You know how it is sometimes when you are watching a crowd of people. You see someone you think you know, but it's almost certain to be someone else, who looks like the person you know."

He sat down and took a good sip of his cognac.

"Did you happen to see the man in the dark suit, over there, a minute ago?" he asked. He was walking with his back to us and disappeared when he came to the corner of the square."

"I never noticed anybody in particular, I'm afraid. I was busy sketching the scene, trying to capture as many images as possible, as quickly as possible. I work too quickly to remember each image. Who was it you thought you had seen?"

"It doesn't matter," Edward said. "It was nobody you would know. In fact, I only met him once myself."

Edward was anxious to drop the subject, fearing he had imagined the whole incident, but then he thought of a way he might resolve the matter. "Were you sketching the people on the street?" he asked Robert.

"As a matter of fact I was, amongst other things."

"Let me see," Edward said eagerly.

Robert handed over the sketchbook and there on the last sketch he had been working on was the black figure, caught for a second by the skilful hand of Robert, partially obscured by other people, but outstanding in his black attire, which contrasted so much with the light coloured shirts of all the other men in the square.

"There," said Edward, stabbing his finger at the page. "That's the man."

"I drew him because he stood out like a sore thumb," Robert said, laughing. "He looks like an undertaker." Edward could not join in the laughter. He handed back the sketchbook, impressed by the detail Robert had been able to capture in so short a time, but concerned at the reappearance of Michael. He wondered if it boded ill for his expedition.

"At least I know I wasn't imaging it," Edward said.

After he had turned in for the night Edward could not help wondering if there was any significance in what he had seen in the square. There was no proof that it had indeed been Michael he had seen, and there seemed to be no reason to fear his reappearance. On reflection he had to admit that he had suffered no ill effects from their first encounter. On the contrary his life had changed completely for the better as a result. He fell asleep wondering where he would turn up next.

On the following morning Robert was filled with excitement at the prospect of visiting some of the great art exhibitions on display in Florence. In particular he wanted to visit the Uffizi Gallery and in view of its popularity he had made two reservations for himself and Edward, which might save several hours of waiting to get in. The gallery housed works by such famous Italian artists as Raphael, Caravaggio, Rubens, Titian, Giotto, Leonardo and Michelangelo. In addition they had a large collection of European art, mainly from Holland, Spain and Germany. After they had gained entrance Edward told Robert to set off on his own, so that he didn't hold him up.

"I will make my own way and meet you in the restaurant at one o'clock."

Robert had mapped out his own itinerary and set off with a confident step, while Edward sauntered at his leisure from room to room, impressed by the brilliance of the artists, but regretting that there were so many representations of religious subjects. Eventually, tired of walking, he made his way to the restaurant, ordered a coffee and waited for Robert to join him. While he waited he could not help wondering if he would see Michael again and found himself scrutinising everybody who entered the restaurant, but the only familiar face was that of Robert, when he came through the double doors to join him at his table. He was full of enthusiasm for everything he had seen and over lunch he described some of the highlights to Edward.

"I intend to look at some of the European Renaissance art this afternoon," Robert announced. "Do you feel up to some more viewing?"

"I'm looking forward to it," Edward said, "but I will plod along at my own pace. When I have had enough I will return to the square, where we were last night. I want to see it in daylight and pay a visit inside the cathedral. After that I will return to the hotel and prepare for dinner."

After spending some time viewing some of the masterpieces of renaissance art, Edward left the gallery and walked back towards the cathedral. As he entered the square the great bell was chiming the hour, to be quickly echoed by countless lesser chimes around the square. There were considerably more tourists present than on the previous evening, no doubt bussed in by numerous coaches and cars. They clogged the pavements with their slow perambulation, while individuals stopped to take photographs every few yards, it seemed. Eventually Edward found himself at the corner where Michael had disappeared the previous night. There was a narrow turning and Edward followed it until it broadened and joined a main highway leading to the east, out of Florence, signposted towards Venice. It seemed to be urging him to go in that direction and that was the way Edward intended to go when they left Florence.

He turned and headed back into the square and entered the Duomo. It too was crowded with tourists and Edward waited in the shadows while a large party, led by a courier jabbering in Italian, led them off down one of the side aisles. It was pleasantly cool inside the huge building, in contrast to the heat outside. He made his way over to a quiet Lady Chapel passing beneath the huge cupola and found a quiet pew. There were just a few people here, sitting or kneeling, in quiet contemplation or prayer. He sat and found the atmosphere completely restful after the hectic time in the art gallery. His feet ached, as he wasn't used to so much exercise in one day. His thoughts drifted and he found himself wondering if he would ever see Michael again. Could it be that Michael had been sending a veiled message, suggesting the way Edward should go on the next stage of his journey, but if it was, he was pointing in the direction Edward had always intended to go. The stay in Florence was for Robert's benefit, a chance to see some of the works of art he had dreamed about.

Suddenly Edward woke with a start. The mighty organ was playing the opening hymn of benediction. Many of the pews in the main body of the church had filled up and the people joined in with the organ, singing weakly. Edward looked at his watch. It was gone six o'clock and Robert would be wondering what had happened to him. He stirred himself and left the Duomo with the mournful sounds of the hymn echoing around him.

After he had showered and changed he knocked on Robert's door and found him ready for dinner.

"I tried your door several times," Robert said. "I thought you might have fallen asleep."

"I did," Edward admitted, "in the Duomo. I found it so cool and so restful. Did you have an exciting time in the gallery?"

"Yes. I met some foreign art students. It was so interesting talking to them and nearly all of them could speak English, at least, that is, well enough for me to understand them. I hope you don't mind, but I arranged to meet them for a drink after dinner. They were all very impressed that I was staying in this hotel. They are all in hostels and bed and breakfast places."

Edward laughed. "Of course you must meet up with your new friends. It will be a good experience for you and I am feeling the tiredness of the journey yesterday and all the walking this morning. I intend to have a good dinner and retire to bed early."

40

Monday 10th May

After an excellent night's sleep, Edward woke up, fully refreshed and ready to keep pace with Robert, whichever art gallery the young man chose to explore. As Robert had not appeared for breakfast, Edward had a very leisurely meal, but was beginning to get worried, until eventually Robert put in an appearance, looking rather bleary eyed.

"It looks as though you had a good night," Edward commented. "I would recommend some marvellous Italian tomato juice."

"A very good idea," Robert agreed. "It did turn out to be a late night, but I didn't have much to drink. It's just that I'm not used to wine. The students I was with met up with a crowd of other young people here on holiday, all Italians, and it became very exciting and totally incomprehensible. They were all chatting away non-stop and I couldn't understand a word. Even the students who could speak English could not be bothered to take the time to translate for me, but I didn't mind that. I had brought my sketchbook with me and, as I think I told you once, I used to impress my fellow students at agricultural college, by making rapid sketches of them. So, I began to sketch as many of them as I could, before they realised what was happening, but sure enough somebody discovered what I was doing and insisted on seeing my sketch. Then they all wanted to be sketched and, if I gave them the sketch, they insisted on buying me a glass of wine. I think I could make a reasonable living just by sketching people and selling the sketches, if I ever fall on hard times."

"I'm sure you are right," Edward agreed with a chuckle, knowing how brilliant Robert was in capturing an image in the flick of an eyelid.

"And then an extraordinary thing happened," Robert said. Edward could tell from the change in his demeanour that he was hesitant about sharing what had happened on the previous evening. It may have been because Edward was still a comparative stranger and he was a long way from his parents and Margaret who would be his normal confidantes. There was no one else in whom to confide, apart from Edward, so after a pause Robert continued, self-consciously.

"A beautiful dark-haired girl, one of the holiday crowd, came up and asked me in English if I would like to sketch her. I was amazed at the perfection of her English and I have to admit that I took longer than I normally take to sketch her, as I wanted to capture as much detail of her as I could, and just to keep her there, in front of me, for as long as possible. We became quite friendly then and have arranged to meet today."

Edward's heart sank. He knew it had always been a possibility that Robert, who was young and handsome, talented and attractive to girls, might meet and fall for a girl on such an exciting holiday, especially when it was to a part of the world he had only dreamed about visiting. It was inevitable, he thought.

"I said I would meet her on the steps of the cathedral at ten o'clock."

"Do you have the sketch of her?" Edward asked.

"No. She was so pleased with it that I gave it to her." He looked at his watch. "I must fly or I will be late. Can we meet back here later?"

"Why not invite her back for lunch," Edward suggested. "Let us say one o'clock."

"That would be wonderful. We'll meet in the bar. Now I must fly."

Edward watched as Robert hastened out of the restaurant. He recalled that he had had too few romantic meetings in his life, too few occasions when he had hurried, breathlessly, heart beating wildly towards a rendezvous with a girl, beautiful or not. And then there was that other occasion, which he had decided he could allow himself to recall now, when he had been swept off his feet for such a brief interlude. He had been so careless, allowing Anna to slip out of his life. Life could be so unfair. How was he to know at the time that there would never be anybody else?

"Will there be anything more, signor?" the waiter asked, startling Edward.

"No. Nothing," Edward said, with a shake of his head, as he rose and left the dining room.

Robert hurried towards the great doors at the front of the Duomo, scattering the pigeons beneath his feet as he ascended the steps. At the top he paused for breath and looked around, but he could not detect his companion of the previous evening. He was pleased that he had arrived first, as he would not have wished to keep her waiting, but as the minutes ticked by and the Cathedral clock chimed the quarters and all the other clocks in the square seemed to mock his vigil with their echoing chorus, his heart sank and he began to realise that she was not going to appear. He scanned the endless streams of visitors as they poured in and out of the cathedral, afraid that he might miss seeing her in such crowds. Eventually he gave up in despair and turning towards the cathedral allowed himself to be carried along by the throng beneath the great vaulted cupola. At once he experienced the shade and coolness that Edward had experienced on the previous afternoon. He wandered aimlessly up and down the aisles, not paying attention to anything, hurt and disappointed that he had been let down.

Eventually he found himself outside again, on the top step, in the full glare of the sun, wondering what to do next. He had no idea where she could be, or even which hotel or guesthouse she was staying in. As he pondered the situation he heard someone call his name. It was a female voice and at first he thought it might be her, but then he saw the group of students he had been with the previous evening and recognised Adriana, a pretty blonde who had been in the party. He ran down the steps, relieved that he had met up with them, hoping they would have some news of her.

"I'm so glad to have found you," she said. "Eddy and her friend, Bianca, received a message this morning. The mother of one of them is very ill and they have had to leave. Eddy asked me to meet you, but the other girls held me up. I'm so sorry."

"That's all right," Robert said, "but I must find her. Do you know where she comes from?"

Adriana shook her head. "We only met two days ago. We became friendly because I speak very good English and so does she."

"So you don't know where she has gone?"

"No. I'm sorry, but they may be able to tell you at our hostel. It's the Casa Rossa."

"Of course," Robert said, a sudden ray of sunshine illuminating his black cloud of depression. "Where is the Casa Rossa?"

The rest of Adriana's party had moved off and were calling to her. They were anxious to get on with the pleasures of the day. "It's down that narrow street at the corner of the square." She pointed to where the strange character, dressed all in black, had disappeared on the previous night. "Then it's the first turning right," she called over her shoulder, as her friends dragged her away. With that she was gone, amidst a crowd of colourful laughing girls. He watched as they disappeared raucously, shouting happily to each other.

Robert sauntered back to the hotel, where he was due to join Edward for lunch at one o'clock. As he was early, he went to his room, collected his sketchbook and settled himself in the comfort of the lounge on the first floor. Then, from memory, he began to reproduce the sketch he had drawn the previous night. After the first few lines it was as though Eddy was sitting in front of him, in exactly the same pose as on the previous evening. He could see the fine lines of her face, framed in her shoulder-length black hair and her dark eyes staring up at him. There was a trace of a smile on her red lips and he could recall his longing to kiss them. It was almost as though she knew the effect she was having on him and wanted to tease him for a while. As he sketched, further details of her came to him and translated into lines on the page. At last he was satisfied with the finished drawing. To bring her even more to life he coloured her lips red. Satisfied, he closed the book and went off to meet Edward in the bar, where he was having an aperitif.

After Robert had ordered a beer they made their way into the dining room, where the table had been laid for three on Edward's instructions, but he made no comment as Robert sat down opposite him. He could tell from the droop of his shoulders and his dejected expression that things had not gone well.

"She has had to go home," he said at last. "She sent word by one of the girls in her hostel, a family matter, I believe. One of the girls' mother was taken ill, but I'm not sure whether it was to do with her family or her friend Bianca's."

Edward could see how thoroughly miserable he was. "Do you know where she was staying?" he asked, sympathetically.

"Yes. At the Casa Rossa, but there doesn't seem to be any point in going there. She left early this morning, which was why she couldn't meet me. I have managed to reproduce a sketch of her though. Would you like to see it?"

"Of course." Edward reached across the table and, after opening the book at the right page, Robert handed the book to him. As he glanced at the picture Edward felt something like an electric shock. He was looking at a perfect replica of Edwina. A photograph could not have given a better likeness.

"What's the matter?" Robert asked, alarmed at the sudden change in Edward's demeanour. His cheeks were pale and his eyes seemed to be staring out from their sockets.

"It's nothing," Edward stammered, but his heart was racing. "She is very beautiful though. What did you say her name was?"

"I don't think I mentioned it, but her friend called her Eddy and that's what I called her."

Edward felt his excitement mounting. Eddy could be an abbreviation of Edwina and the picture was definite confirmation. It had to be her. No two girls could be so identical. What an amazing coincidence though, if it was Edwina; was that why he had seen Michael on the previous evening? Edward knew he had to follow up this opportunity.

"We will go to the Casa Rossa this afternoon, if you wish, but you may prefer to visit another gallery."

"No," Robert replied emphatically. "I want to find her if I can, but I can't expect you to go chasing after her. It will spoil your holiday."

"Not at all," Edward said. "It will add a little adventure to our holiday. Who knows where the trail may lead us." He smiled quietly to himself and Robert was relieved to see that he had recovered his composure and he felt elated at the thought that he may yet see Eddy again.

As soon as lunch was over the two of them set off for Casa Rossa. It was not difficult to find; the street was narrow, with tall buildings on either side seeming to press down on them, so that, at street level, it was cool and dark, as everything was in shade. A short flight of three stone steps led up to the doorway, above which a sign that would be illuminated at night was fixed above the door. They climbed the steps and pushed open the unlocked door, which led into a small reception area. There was a tiny table, with a hand bell on it, next to a guest book and beside that a sign in Italian, which Edward assumed would read 'ring for service.' He picked up the bell and rang it. After a short pause a rather stout but friendly-looking middle-aged woman emerged from the end of the passage. Smiling pleasantly she spoke rapidly in Italian, throwing her arms wide and shrugging her shoulders, to indicate she had no vacancies.

"No, signora," Edward said. "We are not looking for rooms. Do you speak English?"

"Jus a leetle," she said, looking puzzled.

"Show her the sketch," Edward said.

Robert opened his sketchbook and showed her the picture.

"Ah, Signorina Cabrossi," she said instantly.

"Si," Edward said. His heart was pounding, but he was filled with joy at the mention of her surname. Surely there could be no mistake now. It had to be Edwina. "We must find her. Do you have her address?"

The woman looked bewildered, clearly not understanding what had been said, but probably thinking the worst; that they may not have the best intentions towards the girl.

Robert pointed to the register on the table. "Her address?" he asked.

Instantly she snatched the book up and secured it beneath her left armpit. "Not poseeble," she said, shaking her head, clearly nervous at the turn of events. Edward could understand her anxiety. Two foreigners were trying to obtain information about a young girl, who had been a guest in her house until that morning. Who knows what their intentions might be. Perhaps that was why the girl and her friend had left so hastily.

Edward decided to take a chance. "Did she come from Castelfranco?" he asked.

At mention of the name the landlady looked at him with less suspicion, seemed to hesitate for a second and then decided. Taking a firmer grip on the register beneath her left arm, she waved her right arm in the direction of the door to indicate that the interview was terminated.

Edward did not argue. He thanked her and before Robert could protest he took him by the arm and led him outside.

"You seem to know this girl," Robert said, when they stood together on the pavement outside the Casa Rossa.

"I have never met her, but if she is who I think she is, then I am as keen to find her as you are. So we will join forces my young friend in the hunt for her. If I am right I will tell you all about it on our journey, but until then, my lips must remain sealed. Be patient."

"I will," Robert said. His respect and admiration for Edward had always been high, but now they had soared to new heights. He had realised from the conversation with the landlady that Edward must know a great deal about Eddy. Clearly he had recognised her picture when Robert had shown it to him, and also recognised her surname, when the landlady mentioned it. That, at least, had been one piece of positive information they had gained from their visit.

They spent the rest of the afternoon visiting the Accademia Gallery. Robert had been anxious to leave Florence immediately in pursuit of Eddy, but Edward restrained him. "We can't achieve anything further just now," he said. "I would like to talk to the young lady who brought you the message this morning. She speaks perfect English, you said, and she may be able to tell us more about Eddy. We may be able to meet her tonight. Also we can't leave Florence without seeing Michelangelo's famous sculpture of David."

At first Robert was reluctant to turn his attention back to art, but his enthusiasm revived after he saw the magnificent sculpture of David. Suddenly he wanted to explore. There was so much to see; other sculptures by Michelangelo, Botticelli and Potormo's 'Venus and Cupid' amongst others. Edward found the sculptures to be more restful than viewing the paintings. One could not help stopping, studying and admiring. All the time though his brain was in a whirl. He had come to Italy with a hope, nothing more, but after seeing the sketch by Robert and hearing the landlady call her Miss Cabrossi, he felt sure that his dream was a reality, but he still had to find her. That could be very difficult, especially as neither he nor Robert spoke Italian.

By the time they had satisfied their curiosity and returned to the Borghese Palace Art Hotel Edward had formulated a plan of action. As they ate their dinner he asked Robert where he had met Eddy on the previous evening.

"It was in a bar in the square, near to the road we turned down to find the Casa Rossa. It was like the others, with tables spreading out over the pavement, but larger than most and more crowded. It was noisier than the bar we were in, as there were a lot more young people. And the drinks were cheaper," he added as an afterthought.

"It's possible the girls will go there again tonight," Edward said. "I want you to meet them, but I will stay in the background. The sight of someone older might intimidate them. See if you can find the girl who speaks such good English."

"Adriana?"

"Yes, Adriana. Talk to her; tell her that it is most important that I trace Eddy. I don't think that is her real name, but we do know she is Miss Cabrossi. See if you can persuade her to come over to my table and talk to me. We may not find out anything, but even a small amount of additional information could be priceless in tracking her down."

"You know who she is, don't you?" Robert said.

"I think I do," Edward conceded, "but I don't want to say anything at this stage, as it will be such a disappointment if I am wrong. One thing I will say is that if I am right, I will be the happiest man alive."

Robert was looking puzzled, but grinned happily. This holiday was turning out so unexpectedly and he was intrigued to find Eddy, for his own sake, but also for the sake of Edward now who, he surmised, had an even greater reason to find her."

"So, what are we going to do tomorrow?" Robert asked.

"We will check out, after hiring a car and travel east. Hopefully Adriana will have given us a clue, but if not, I have a clue of my own."

After dinner they met in the foyer of the hotel. Robert had brought his sketchbook at Edward's suggestion. He wanted him to catch the girls' attention, as he had on the previous night, with his skill at producing quick sketches. They arrived at the bar early enough to be able to select separate tables, Robert's as near to the pavement as possible, Edward's tucked away in a rather gloomy corner, but where he had a good view of what was happening in the rest of the establishment. Edward gave his waiter a hugely generous tip with his first order for a scotch and water, assuring himself of good service for the rest of the evening. He had advised Robert to do the same and had supplied him with sufficient Euros to treat the girls, if they appeared, so that they would be less inclined to move on.

The bar began to fill up and both Edward and Robert feared the girls had either left Florence or had decided on a different venue for the evening, but suddenly, with much excitement, the girls arrived. They were delighted to see Robert and enveloped him with their extravagant greetings, including much laughter, many screeches and kisses on the cheek. Robert could not understand a word that was said, but he didn't have to, because their friendliness spoke for itself. The girls were even more voluble and excited when he insisted on buying them all their first drink.

Edward watched, satisfied, as the scene settled. After dragging tables and chairs together they were all eventually seated in a group. Robert had told him that Adriana was a blonde girl; she could be any one of three seated towards the outer rim of the group.

After a while Robert opened his sketchbook and began to draw. They were all keen to be sketched and were flattered by the results, giggling and passing the sheets around to be admired by the others. It gave Robert the opportunity to move among them and Edward watched the skilful way he worked towards a pretty girl, with long blonde hair. When he reached her he had a long conversation with her while he sketched. Eventually he turned and pointed out Edward. She smiled towards him and nodded her head. When Robert had finished her sketch, he tore it carefully from the book and handed it to her. She was obviously delighted with it and after it had been passed all round the table she folded it carefully, put it in her handbag and came over to sit beside Edward. She walked slowly towards him, sidling past tables, chairs and outstretched legs. She attracted a good deal of comment from the men at the tables she passed, but stood no nonsense from them, slapping their hands quite hard if they tried to touch her.

Edward rose to greet her as she reached his table, took her hand and guided her into the seat beside him, which brought forth an ironic cheer from some of the men, who had totally misinterpreted what was happening. It was easy to understand why though. She was a very attractive girl and moved with the grace of a model on the catwalk.

"You must be Adriana," Edward said. "My name's Edward. I'm so glad you agreed to talk to me. I'm trying to trace the girl you know as 'Eddy'."

"I know. Robert told me." Her voice had a musical quality and she tossed back her blonde hair as she spoke and gazed at him quizzically, with startlingly blue eyes. She was so beautiful. Edward was amazed that an American movie producer or a model agency had not signed her up.

"Are you trying to find her for Robert?" she asked. "I know they liked each other very much. Is he your son?"

"No. Let me explain. Robert is the son of a friend and neighbour and I brought him to Italy because he is going to be a very great artist in my opinion and he wanted to see the art of Florence, and I want to help him in his career. Also, and I have not discussed this with Robert, and would prefer him not to know just for the moment, I came to see if I could find my daughter."

Adriana looked at Edward with increased interest. "I don't want Robert to know that I have a daughter, not yet anyway, in case I don't find her, so I must ask you not to mention to him that I think Eddy may be my daughter."

Adriana put her hand up to her mouth in surprise. "How can this be?" she asked.

"I know it may seem amazing, but when Robert failed to meet Eddy this morning he drew a picture of her and I knew it was her, but the landlady at the Casa Rossa refused to tell us anything about her. I need to know if she put her address in the register there, or any other clue to where she can be found."

"And how can I help?" Adriana asked.

"It seems to me that she usually keeps the register on that small table in the hall, just inside the front door. I want to know what Edwina wrote in that book."

"You called her Edwina."

"That's her real name. Eddy must be a family name, or nickname as we would say."

"I know you are speaking the truth," Adriana said. "When we were talking two days ago she told me her name was really Edwina."

Edward let out a great sigh, tears came into his eyes and he buried his head in his hands to hide his emotion. He knew how Sir Galahad must have felt when he finally found the Holy Grail. Adriana watched as Edward slowly composed himself.

"Thank you," he said to her at last, taking her hand gently in his. "Now, at least I know she is here, but it's cruel to have missed her by such a small margin."

"I may be able to help you. The landlady goes to bed quite early. She locks the front door, but we all have keys, so that we can get in without disturbing her. Every night the register has been left on the table. If Robert comes with me I will tell him what she wrote in the register."

"Bless you," Edward said. "That will be marvellous. Her surname is Cabrossi and she may have left a clue as to where her home is."

"I think she must work in a library somewhere," Adriana said. "I overheard her talking to her companion one day and she mentioned books that were overdue, but it may relate to something else."

"But it could also be a vital clue," Edward said. "You have been such a help, Adriana. Thank you so much."

"We will find out for sure," Adriana said, rising to return to her friends. "Come." She held her hand out towards Edward. "You don't want to sit here on your own. There's plenty of room at our tables. Robert will be glad to have some male company and I will get the girls to help me. It will be an adventure for them. I won't mention anything about Eddy being your daughter. I will be speaking to them in Italian, so Robert will not understand. I will tell them he is very much in love and must find her." She giggled mischievously. "Come," she said.

Edward followed her dutifully back to the cluster of tables on the pavement and spent the next few hours, sitting beside Robert, surrounded by a colourful crowd of excited beauties, all planning how they were going to smuggle away the register, if the landlady was still up when they returned to the Casa Rossa.

In the end it was all so simple. By the time they left the bar it was quite late. They returned fairly quietly along the darkened street and while the girls all went into the Casa Rossa together Robert and Edward waited patiently out on the pavement. The register had been restored to the table and while the other girls crowded round her, to shield her in case the landlady should appear, Adriana turned the pages to find the important entry. Unfortunately there was only one word she could write down, but she scribbled this hurriedly onto a scrap of paper from her handbag, returned to the street and handed it to Edward, kissed him on the cheek and wished him good luck.

He and Robert made their way back to the hotel, each full of hope and expectation, although their hopes were different. Edward had put the paper in his pocket as it was too dark to read it on the street and he kept it locked in his fingers all the way back to the hotel, afraid to take his hand from his pocket for fear of losing the precious scrap.

When they were eventually seated in the lounge Robert was bursting to know what was written on that small piece of paper. He knew it was his only hope of seeing Eddy again. Edward took his hand from his pocket and smoothed out the paper on the tabletop. At first he thought it was blank, but then he could see there was just one word written on it. The word was 'Treviso'.

From where he sat opposite Edward, Robert could not see the paper. "Well? What does it say?" he demanded impatiently.

Edward passed the piece of paper to him. "It doesn't give her address, but it narrows the search."

"Treviso!" Robert exclaimed. "Treviso! Is that all?"

"That must be the town she comes from," Edward said. "Lots of people do that if they don't want to state their full details, particularly their address, so they just mention the town."

"It could be like looking for a needle in a haystack, particularly if it's a large town."

"Wait a second," Edward said. "I have a map and guidebook in my bedroom. I will fetch them."

A few minutes later he returned and spread the map in front of the two of them. Firstly he looked up Treviso in the guidebook, and quickly found it.

"It says in this that it is a city of approximately eighty five thousand people, situated close to and north of Venice." Robert groaned at the thought of the size of the haystack.

"One thing I haven't told you is that Adriana thought that Eddy worked in a library. There can't be too many libraries in Treviso, can there?" Edward chuckled as the look on Robert's face reflected his change of expectations and Edward's hopes soared also, as he noticed from the map the town of Castelfranco, just further to the northeast.

"I think we are on the right track," Edward said, rubbing his hands together in satisfaction. "We will hire a car first thing in the morning and set off towards Venice. There's something I have to tell you first. My object in bringing you to Italy was not entirely altruistic. I did want to enable you to see the great art of the fabulous Italian painters and sculptors. Of course I did want you to see that, but I also wanted to see if I could find my daughter, Edwina. That was why I told you that I wanted to spend part of our time over here, after visiting Venice, looking at some of the towns north of Venice."

"I never knew you had a daughter," Robert said, stunned by the announcement and the implication that Eddy could be Edwina. Edward's recent behaviour and willingness to help him trace this girl began to make sense. He remembered how shaken he had been at the sight of his sketch, and again when he heard the landlady mention her surname.

"You think Eddy and Edwina are one and the same, don't you?"

"I'm hoping. Your sketch convinced me."

"Then you have seen her before."

"No. I haven't, but I can't tell you how I knew. One day perhaps, in the future, but not now. Let's be content for now that we have a shared objective."

Robert was intrigued by the mystery. It was clear that Edward knew a lot more about Eddy than he was prepared to say. "I can hardly wait until tomorrow," he said.

41

Tuesday 11th May

Edward and Robert rose early on the following morning and, immediately after breakfast, Edward paid the bill and ordered a taxi to take them to the largest car hire firm in Florence. He had already contacted them by telephone and arranged for a car to be ready for them. He had specifically requested that it should have automatic transmission, as he found the gear change on the right-hand side on manual transmission cars awkward. After completing the paperwork they were soon on their way, heading out of Florence. Robert felt a thrill of anticipation at the thought of meeting Eddy again. He could hardly wait to see the look of surprise on her face.

Edward had decided to drive for the first part of the journey, as he was experienced in driving abroad, but he intended to hand over to Robert as soon as the younger man had familiarised himself with the road conditions and road signs. As the morning wore on, the day became hot and the road dusty. Fortunately, the car was air conditioned and had temperature control, so they were comfortable in their steel cocoon. When they stopped for a coffee and to change drivers, it felt like stepping into a furnace and after only a few steps towards the café Edward could feel the sweat breaking out on his forehead. It was cooler inside the building though and they sat beneath a huge wooden fan, which was attached to the ceiling and whirled noiselessly above their heads. They both sipped their coffee in silence after it had been served, each engrossed in their own thoughts.

"The distance between Florence and Venice is two hundred and fifty five kilometres," Edward said, "which is one hundred and fifty nine miles. So far we have covered about half that distance. We should reach Venice by midday, but we can skirt round it and head north to Treviso. I'll act as navigator from here on."

Robert smiled, knowing that Edward preferred to relax and enjoy the scenery, which became hillier once they had bypassed Venice. The hills were green with rows of vines and became ever higher as they travelled north. In the distance they could see a barrier of mountains. When he saw an interesting turning off the main highway into a village Edward asked Robert to turn into it, so they could find somewhere to have lunch. They both felt inspired by the morning's drive and soon found a small bar/restaurant with a dusty square at the front, where they parked. They enjoyed a typical Italian pasta dish, served with a salad and a glass of Chianti. It was a simple meal of the type eaten by many Italians at lunchtime, but they were both surprised by the quality of the food.

Fully restored, Robert drove the remaining short distance to Treviso, where Edward had reserved rooms for them at the Hotel Carlton, chosen and booked with the aid of their manager at the hotel in Florence, who had once worked in Treviso and knew the area well. Their hotel was very close to the centre of the city, which was an ancient walled town. The central square, which was close to their hotel, was enclosed on all sides by four-story red-brick buildings, but at ground level nearly every building was fronted by a bar or restaurant, with its tables spilling across the pavement and onto the street, their canopies adding much-needed colour to the background of red brick.

They walked around the square, which eased the stiffness in Edward's legs and eventually they sat at one of the pavement tables and ordered two beers. Their waiter, a short dark-haired young man, could speak a little English and from him they learned the location of the public library. It was quite close and after they had finished their beers, they set off to find it.

Stone steps led up to an imposing doorway, in what had at some time in the past been a council chamber or temple to some Roman God. Now it had been converted to the public library and thankfully it was air-conditioned. Their steps echoed hollowly on the tiled floor as they walked across to the only sign of life, a large wooden counter, behind which a bespectacled middle-aged lady was busy indexing what appeared to be a shipment of new books.

As they approached the counter the librarian looked up and gave them an encouraging smile. Robert left Edward to do the talking.

"Does Miss Cabrossi work here?" Edward asked, hoping that he would be understood and that if he was, he would not be instantly ejected.

"Si," the librarian replied, "but she not here now." She shook her head. "On vacation."

"Oh. When will she return? How long?" Edward added, seeing she had not understood.

She turned to look at a calendar behind her. "Here." She indicated the date on the calendar. She was pointing to the twenty-fourth. Edward could sense Robert's disappointment. He thanked the lady and they retreated back onto the street, into the glaring sun.

"Well, she could be anywhere now," Robert said, disconsolately.

"Or she could be at Bassano del Marostica."

Robert looked at him in amazement. "Bassano where?"

"Bassano del Marostica," Edward repeated, with a broad smile. He had recalled that, in the last letter Patrick had sent to Edwina, the very last sentence had read, 'I am convinced your mother is living in the village of Bassano del Marostica.' Robert looked baffled. "I'm following my last clue now," Edward said. "If she doesn't live there we will have to kill the next two weeks until she returns to work."

"Would you be prepared to do that?" Robert asked.

"Of course. I'm as keen to find her as you are. My instinct tells me that Bassano del Marostica cannot be far away. Let's go back to the hotel and consult the map. If it isn't too far away we might even be able to go there today."

Back at the hotel Edward produced his map and guidebook, but could not find a mention of the village on either of them. Finally he consulted the young man on the reception desk, who instantly recognised the name and was able to give them a brief explanation of how to get there. As Robert drove out of Treviso Edward felt a growing sense of excitement, but he also felt anxious. For days he had speculated about the chances of meeting Anna and longed for it, but now that the possibility was close to becoming a reality, he began to wonder whether she would be equally pleased to see him. After twenty-one years they would be complete strangers and his reception could be and probably would be less than cordial. He was equally anxious to meet Edwina. He knew he would recognise her, but to her he would also be a complete stranger. He told himself to be prepared for complete rejection by both Anna and his daughter, but at the same time his heart was filled with joy and anticipation at the thought of seeing them both at last. And so his spirits rose and fell on the short journey.

Robert, on the other hand, dreamed only of being reunited with Edwina. He could see her as clearly as if she was standing before him, almost feel the softness of her cheek and smell the perfume of her hair. He felt confident of his reception even though they had known each other for just a few short hours.

They travelled north out of Treviso, the road climbing higher into vine-covered hills, with glimpses of higher snow-capped mountains in the far distance. The bright afternoon sun reflected with an orange glow from the sandstone rock faces of the Dolomite range. They passed through a few small villages where nothing stirred and then, from the top of a hill, looked down on a larger village. The houses, with their gleaming white walls, were strung out on either side along the road, a spire rising from the church near the centre. They descended rapidly from the high ridge they had just crossed and soon were driving past the sign announcing Bassano del Marostica. Half a kilometre beyond they came to the church and Edward told Robert to stop in front of it.

"This must be the centre of the village," he suggested. "Now our problem may be just beginning."

"Why do you say that?" Robert asked.

"From information I had from a friend it seems the locals are reluctant to give out information to strangers about neighbours. Here we are in the village, but we haven't a clue where they live."

"I'm prepared to knock on every door if I have to," Robert said. "I'm not going to give up when we are this close."

"We have to be careful how we go about it," Edward cautioned, remembering how Patrick Plockton had been given the cold shoulder in Castelfranco when he was asking questions about Anna. "We are strangers here and we don't even speak the language."

"Then perhaps we should start here," Robert suggested, pointing to the church. "The priest usually knows everybody in a community this size and will be less suspicious."

"That's an excellent idea," Edward said. "Let's take it as a good omen that we pulled up outside the church."

They climbed out and walked up the gravelled path to the solid oak door. To Edward's surprise he found the door was open and they entered the dark interior. At first they were both blinded, coming out of the bright sunshine into the gloom inside. As their eyes became accustomed to the darkness Edward could tell that it was an ancient building, with large beams, blackened by age, supporting the roof. A dish of holy water, standing on a white cloth, was placed just beyond the porch on a small table and beyond that rows of pews led down to the altar, which was enclosed by wrought iron altar rails, with double gates, open at the centre. Three steps led up from there to the altar, which was sumptuously decorated with flowers, candlesticks and a tabernacle covered with a gold cloth. To the right of the altar gates stood a metal stand with three rows of candles burning at different stages of consumption. All was silent, but their entrance had been far from silent, as the heavy door had crashed shut behind them and their footsteps had echoed hollowly and noisily as they walked down the aisle towards the altar, where they paused. At last footsteps could be heard coming from the direction of the sacristy on the right of the altar and a priest in a dark suit emerged from the shadows. He was quite young and moved athletically, genuflecting in front of the altar, before descending the steps towards them.

He spoke to them in Italian, but Edward shook his head.

"I'm afraid I don't speak Italian father. We are wondering if you can help us?"

"Ah," the priest sighed deeply. "I speak a little English."

"We are looking for Anna Cabrossi and her daughter, Edwina," Edward said. He hoped that his direct approach would be the best way to avoid alarming the priest.

"Ah, si," the priest said, without a moment's hesitation. "Come." He ushered them towards the church door and they followed him out into the sunshine. He smiled at them and pointed to a cottage with whitewashed walls on the opposite side of the street.

"Grati," Edward said, using one of the few Italian words he felt confident about.

As they set off towards the cottage Robert could not contain his curiosity. "Who is this Anna Cabrossi?" he asked. "You haven't mentioned her before. You referred to her as Edwina's mother."

"Because that's who I believe she is. I couldn't be sure before, but now I'm certain. Your Eddy is my Edwina and Anna is her mother. This is going to be a difficult meeting," he added.

They came to the door of the cottage and Edward knocked. There was silence at first and both Edward and Robert felt deflated, as they had built up their expectations to such a great height, but then there was a sound of movement on the inside and footsteps approaching the door. When it opened he found himself staring into the eyes of Anna. Neither of them spoke. Although she was twenty-one years older than when they had met and become lovers in Venice, her face had not altered; in his eyes she was as lovely as when they had first met, the same as he had dreamed about for all of those years. Her hair was still long and black, her dark eyes still full of wonder and innocence. She was wearing a white sleeveless summer dress, pulled tight around her waist, which enhanced the perfection of her figure. It was amazing how much Edwina resembled her. There was a look of curiosity on her face, but suddenly it was replaced by a look of recognition in her eyes.

"Can it be you?" she said, her voice sounding as low and seductive as when he had first heard it in the dark street in Venice.

"Anna," was all Edward could say. "Anna," he repeated. "At last I have found you."

She smiled then and he thought how beautiful she was. She extended both hands towards him, her arms wide and welcoming. He stepped forward into her embrace and took her in his arms. She was trembling with emotion and tears came into her eyes. He took her hands in his, raised them to his lips and kissed them, then kissed her eyes, feeling her tears wet upon his cheeks.

"I always believed you would come one day. Please come in, you are very welcome."

As Edward moved forward it was only then that Anna seemed to notice that he was not alone. Robert had been standing quietly in the background, hidden by Edward, a fascinated observer of his meeting with Anna, wondering how it might affect his friendship with Edwina.

"Is this your son?" Anna asked.

"No, I never married. This is Robert, the son of my neighbour."

They shook hands. "You are very welcome Robert," she said to him. "You are both very welcome. Please come in."

She led them through the house to the rear, where she had been sitting in the garden, enjoying the afternoon sun, when they had disturbed her. The garden was quite extensive and well maintained, with an assortment of colourful shrubs and flowers. There were also several citrus trees, oranges and lemons, which acted as a sun shade, beneath which there was a table surrounded by a selection of wooden chairs covered with cushions. They seated themselves, while Anna bustled away, to return a few minutes later with glasses, a jug of lemonade and a carafe of white wine.

After she had poured a glass of white wine for the two men and a glass of lemonade for herself, she settled back in her chair.

"How did you find me," she asked.

Edward explained how Robert had met Eddy in Florence and they had decided to find her after she had left so suddenly.

"Her friends insist on calling her Eddy, but her name is Edwina," Anna said.

"I think I know why you called her that," Edward said, with a smile.

"Because she is your daughter," Anna said.

"Of course. I came to Italy to find you both. It was an amazing coincidence that Robert and Edwina should meet in Florence, but I knew instantly who she was, after Robert drew her picture for me. Robert is a very fine artist."

"I know. Edwina has shown me the picture he did for her and it is already framed and on the wall of her bedroom. I think it is very good"

"Thank you," Robert said. "Where is Edwina?" he asked.

"She has gone to see her friend, Bianca, at the other end of the village. It was Bianca's mother who supposedly took ill," Anna said scornfully. "I don't think for one moment there was anything wrong with her. She is a very selfish woman and was jealous of the two girls going off without her. Now she has spoiled both their holidays."

"So I will be able to see her?" Robert asked.

"Of course. Edwina will be home for supper. I hope you will both stay."

"We would love to," Edward said. He could not take his eyes off her; he was recognising again the same mannerisms that he had found so attractive on his first acquaintance with her, the sudden smile that lit up her face and toss of her head when something amused her. She had the same magical quality as when they first met and he realised that he was undoubtedly still in love with her.

"Edwina will get such a surprise when she finds you here," Anna said. "I can't wait to see her face. She has talked about nothing else since she returned from Florence but the young Englishman who was sketching all the girls." She laughed and Robert could feel his cheeks burning. "She was furious when she got home and found that there was nothing wrong with the wretched woman."

Robert was pleased to hear that Edwina had told her mother about meeting him. It gave him hope that she might be missing him as much as he had missed her, since she had not turned up for their meeting on the steps of the Duomo in Florence.

At that moment the front door banged and Edwina bustled into the garden. She had been hurrying to get home, so her cheeks were flushed and her hair dishevelled, which gave her the look of a schoolgirl returning from a busy day in the classroom, unaware of how lovely she was. The sight of the visitors stopped her dead in her tracks, as she was about to make some comment to her mother about something, which had happened to her since she had left the house earlier that day. She appraised Edward briefly, but when her gaze fell on Robert she gave a little cry of joy.

"Oh, good heavens, is it really you?" she said to Robert. Her face said everything there was to say. She could not believe that he was there before her. "How did you find me? I didn't think I would ever see you again."

Robert stepped forward and held her hand. "Let me introduce you to my good friend, Edward Grangelove," Robert said formally. "It was due to some clever detective work by him that we were able to trace you. I still don't know how he did it, but here we are."

She came forward shyly and offered her hand to Edward. He had been staring at her in amazement since she arrived. He took her hand in his and held it, feeling the soft texture of her skin, that he was familiar with, as he was with every feature of her face, from the soft dark hair curling around her cheeks, the slightly upturned nose, the ever present half smile playing on her lips and the dark eyelashes shading those lovely brown eyes. He had looked at that face so often in the mirror that he was now overcome with emotion, unable to speak, unwilling to release her hand.

"Edwina, my dear," Anna said. "This is Edward, your father." Edwina gave a little cry and put her hand up to her mouth. "I have told you how I met your father and how I panicked and ran away." Anna began to cry as she put her arms around Edwina and held her close. "I'm so glad this moment has arrived. I have longed for you and your father to be reunited."

Edward could see that Edwina was on the point of tears too, so he stepped forward and took mother and daughter in his arms and kissed them both on the cheek.

"Wipe your tears away," he said, "this is a time for celebration. Is there a restaurant or hotel nearby where we can go for dinner?"

"I can prepare supper for all of us," Anna said.

"I know, but you must share in the celebration. I want you to be sitting next to me, not working away in the kitchen."

"There is a hotel, with a very good restaurant at the end of the village," Edwina said. "There is a beautiful lake there and the grounds run all the way down to the shore. The whole area is a tourist zone, with hotels, caravan parks and campsites around the shore. The views are spectacular."

"But that place is very expensive," Anna said.

"Good," Edward said, "nothing but the best for you all from this moment on."

Anna laughed. "You haven't changed, have you?"

"And neither have you," Edward said, with a twinkle in his eye.

So that was decided. Edwina disappeared, to emerge a little while later in an attractive blue and white dress, while Anna telephoned to reserve a table, overlooking the gardens and the lake.

Robert took Edwina's hand. He thought she looked even more beautiful than he had imagined.

"Does this mean you are my brother?" Edwina asked gazing into Robert's eyes.

"No, it doesn't," Robert said with a laugh. "My father is a farmer and we live next to Edward." He could detect the relief on her face. "I have a brother and a sister, Rupert and Margaret. You will get on very well with Margaret."

"That's if I ever meet her," Edwina added.

"I'm sure you will," Robert said, squeezing her hand.

"Come along you two," Anna said. "We are ready to go." She had noticed how much they were attracted to each other and smiled to herself. There was a warm glow inside her that she had not felt for many years. Although Edward was a good deal older than her, she thought he was still a very handsome man, and she felt completely at ease in his company, just as she had on the first occasion they had met.

Robert fetched the car from where they had parked it in front of the church and after a short drive they parked again beside the restaurant. On the way they had climbed a small hill and on reaching the top had a glorious view down over the lake, which was much larger than either Edward or Robert had expected. It was easy to see why it was a tourist attraction. They were shown to a table with a large window permitting open views down to the lake.

"This is beautiful," Anna said. "I always wanted to come here."

Edward ordered a bottle of champagne and told them to order whatever they wanted from the menu and not to be influenced by the price. After their waiter had brought the champagne and poured the four glasses, Edward looked around the table and raised his glass.

"This is the happiest moment of my life," he said. "I want to drink a toast to all of you and hope that we will never be parted again."

They all raised their glasses and drank. The meal that followed was memorable for the excellence of the food and wine, but particularly for the relaxed way in which the conversation flowed. It was as though they had really been united into one family after just a short separation. After they had retired to the lounge, Robert and Edwina went off, to walk down to the lake shore. The sun was setting, creating a silver and crimson glow on the water. As they stood together Robert put his arm around her waist; Edwina inclined towards him, and he took her in his arms and kissed her for the first time in this life.

"I'm so glad you aren't my brother," she said. They both laughed and he kissed her again.

Edward and Anna sat close together on a settee in the lounge. One of the waiters served coffee and a liqueur for Anna and a cognac for Edward. Inwardly he knew that he had been dreading the moment when they would meet again, not knowing how much life had changed her. She could have married and there could be a husband and other children, in which case his presence would not be welcomed. Their meeting had been such a relief. "I feel like a young man again," Edward said. "It's so wonderful to have found you."

"I know, Edward. I know exactly how you feel, because I feel that way too."

He took Anna's hand in his. "Why did you run away that morning in Venice?" he asked.

"I don't really know. I couldn't believe it had happened so suddenly, when I had hoped and been expecting something to happen for so long, and nothing had happened. I just couldn't believe it. I was confused and frightened, I suppose, especially as you were from another country. Whatever it was, I regretted it for the rest of my life. I went back to your hotel two days later, but of course you had left. I wept bitterly then, because I knew it was more than just a moment's infatuation between us. I tried to comfort myself with the thought that you didn't care, but I knew that wasn't really true."

"And then you found that you were pregnant," Edward said sympathetically. "That must have been a terrible shock."

"At first, yes, but then I found comfort in it. I felt the child was a precious gift to me, to keep you in my heart forever. Unfortunately, where I lived, in Castfranco, it was a terrible stigma to have a child out of wedlock. The whole family was ostracised, so to save my family's embarrassment I decided to leave home. Thanks to my knowledge of English I was able to obtain a job as a translator and interpreter in the American embassy in Venice. My job was well paid, so after Edwina was born, I was able to pay for a nanny to look after her, to enable me to go back to the embassy."

"I hope you will let me look after you now," Edward said.

Anna smiled wistfully. "Things must take their course," she said. "We shouldn't rush them. Our lives are probably very different now. Perhaps I am too old to change."

"Nonsense, you are still a young woman. At least, let me show you how it could have been and then you can decide whether it could still be."

Anna looked doubtful. It was all happening too fast again, she thought, just like that evening in Venice. Her brain seemed to be in a whirl. Edward appeared to have such a mesmerising influence over her that she found it difficult to resist his suggestions.

"I think Edwina and Robert are in love," Edward said. "They may not realise it yet themselves. Perhaps they are like us"

"Out of control, you mean," Anna said, a smile playing on her lips.

"Yes, in a way I do mean that, I suppose."

"Edwina will make her own decisions. She knows what happened to me and will be more careful."

"They may decide to make their relationship permanent," Edward said, "in which case she may decide to move to England."

"Why should she decide to move to England? Why couldn't Robert decide to live here? He's an artist. He can work anywhere. Edwina has a good job, with a good salary."

"I know. I'm just saying that if she did move to England, I can give her a good job, with twice or three times more salary than she is getting now."

"How can you manage to do that?" Anna asked incredulously.

"She can become my business manager. I know she is more than capable of taking over from me. It will give me the opportunity to retire," Edward said, laughing, "and hopefully spend more time with you."

"I don't know," Anna said. "This all seems to be happening too quickly again. I don't think we should start making decisions before we know…" She failed to finish the sentence.

"I have had over twenty years regretting losing you in Venice and in that time I have had a long time to plan how not to lose you again."

Anna took Edward's hand. "You won't lose me again," she reassured him, seeing how solemn he had become. "I think we should just let matters take their course, and thank God for bringing us together. I always knew in my heart that we were destined to be reunited again."

The daylight had been fading as the evening had drawn on, slowly obliterating their view of the lake. For a time they sat in silence, contented in each other's company. For both of them it was a new experience, a new satisfying companionship.

Edward suddenly had an inspiration. "Edwina has had her holiday ruined," he said, "but she has nearly two weeks left. Come back with us, just for the duration of her remaining holiday. I will book the tickets and pay for everything else."

"You can't do that," Anna protested.

"Yes I can," Edward insisted. "Have you both got passports?"

Anna nodded. "You are just as impulsive."

"I know. It feels good to be alive again. I will make the reservations in the morning."

"It's all very well talking like this, but Edwina may not agree to go."

"Well, we can find out," Edward said, as the young couple came into the lounge, holding hands, their happiness reflected radiantly in their smiling faces.

"How would you like to spend the rest of your holiday in England?" Anna asked, as Robert and Edwina settled themselves on the settee.

"Could we?" Edwina cried enthusiastically. "Oh," she said, turning towards Robert, "that would mean spoiling your holiday."

"Not at all," Robert said. "I'm sure I could come over again in the future. It would be wonderful to spend the time with you in England."

"Can we afford it though?" Edwina asked, with a frown. "I lost quite a lot of money having to cancel my holiday in Florence."

"You don't have to worry about that," Edward said. "I will take care of the travel arrangements and you will find your accommodation at 'Highfields' is more than adequate."

"Then let's do it," Edwina said, rubbing her hands in glee.

And so it was agreed that Anna and Edwina should go to 'Highfields'.

42

Wednesday 11th May

As the airliner landed at Heathrow Anna and Edwina were both filled with excitement at the prospect of visiting England for the first time. Alf Pearson, who had taken on the duties of chauffeur in addition to gardening in the last few months, was there to meet them. He considered it a real pleasure to drive the Rolls Royce and Edward had been completely impressed with his driving skills and quite prepared, for once in his life, to luxuriate in the comfort of being a passenger. He had been able for the first time to appreciate what he had missed as a driver; time to see the countryside and how lovely it was as the seasons changed.

Edward sat beside Alf, while Edwina sat between Robert and Anna in the back. They had never been driven in such luxury and it added to the excitement and expectation. Robert had tried to give Edwina a description of 'Highfields', but felt that his words were inadequate, so he had sketched the house and some of his favourite scenes from the grounds. Edwina had been thrilled by his drawings and longed to see it all for herself.

Then, suddenly, they were there. The car swept past Hollytree Cottage and up the drive to the house. As the wheels scrunched to a halt on the gravel, Mrs Pearson appeared to greet them. She had been busy preparing a special meal for them and was happy that Edward would have some company in the house, if only for a few days. She had set the table in the dining room, laying out the best china, cutlery and crystal glasses.

Alf and Robert carried the luggage into the hall, while Edward took Anna and Edwina on a tour of the house. He had planned for this moment since his return, but never thought that it could become a reality. He led Anna and Edwina into the suite of rooms prepared for Anna and she was delighted to find that she had, in addition to her own bedroom and bathroom, a sitting room with a glorious view over the lake and her own small kitchen, but Edward pointed out that she would only be expected to use it to prepare drinks for herself.

"Oh, Edward," Anna said. "This is beautiful. Everything is beautiful." She took Edward's hand and squeezed it to show her pleasure. Then, reaching up, she placed her arms around his neck and kissed him. In that moment they both knew that they had found each other and would not be parted again.

Laughing with happiness, Edward released his hands gently from around Anna's waist.

"And now we must see where we can put Edwina for her stay," Edward said.

Then he led them down the corridor to the end room and opened the door.

"I knew this would be my room," Edwina said, "from the moment we entered the house." Then she stood in amazement as she studied every detail of the furniture, the furnishings, the colour scheme and the wonderful view from the window.

"Is this really my room?" she asked in a quiet voice.

"Your very own," Edward replied.

"How did you know?" she asked.

Anna looked puzzled, but Edward knew what she meant.

"It's just like the room I always imagined for myself ever since I was a child. I used to dream that I was a princess and lived in a wonderful castle with my mother and the king who loved us both and this was my very special room in the castle, but in reality there was no king and no castle."

Feeling her sadness creeping into her joy, Edward put his arms around her.

"Now there is a king, who loves you and is sorry to have been absent from your childhood dreams. Perhaps we can make them come true now."

"Yes," she whispered, drawing comfort from the strength of his arms. Anna came over and threw her arms around them both. She knew that all their lives were going to be changed completely and she felt an overwhelming feeling of relief and happiness that her patient wait was about to be rewarded.

With a crashing and banging Robert and Alf arrived at the top of the stairs at that moment, panting with the exertion of hauling the luggage up to the bedrooms.

"What on earth do you ladies pack in these suitcases?" Robert asked.

"Just a few dresses and some shoes of course," Edwina said, laughing.

"More like tweeds and hiking boots," Robert said.

"You must go and see your parents," Edward said, with a smile. "They will be eager to see you and hear about your travels, as short as they were. They will be interested to know why you are back home so soon," he added with a wicked gleam in his eye. "Alf will drive you over and you must come back as soon as possible to have dinner with us."

"That will be great. I won't be long, Edwina," he called out, as he raced down the stairs after Alf.

They all laughed as they heard him leaping down the stairs.

"Now I will leave you to explore your rooms, unpack and get ready for dinner," Edward said. "I will see you in the sitting room when you are ready."

He went downstairs feeling almost sprightly. Surely, he thought, all his hopes and dreams, enkindled by his transformation by Michael, were about to be realised. Surely that was what it was all about. What other purpose could Michael have had? Edward had always wondered though, throughout his recent experiences, whether Michael was a good or bad spirit or whether he existed at all, except in Edward's imagination. And yet he knew Michael must be real, as there was no way he could have imagined the experience of being Edwina, living as her, in her body, knowing her thoughts and feelings, even falling in love. He had been so sure, that he had planned to find Anna and Edwina, had gone to Italy expressly to seek them out and he had found them. He was sure too that it had been Michael who had led him from the start, eventually turning up that evening in the square in Florence. It was as though Michael was urging him on, giving him hope. That was not a dream, for now they were here in 'Highfields', just as he had planned.

Edward sank into his favourite seat in the sitting room, and relaxed in the comfortable armchair. Almost immediately Mrs Pearson came in with a gin and tonic on a small silver tray.

"I'm sure you will be needing this," she said, "after such adventures. I'm so happy for you."

"Thank you, Mrs Pearson. Just pray, that they will stay."

"I'm sure they will," she said.

Edward sipped his drink with pleasure and contemplated his favourite view, across the terrace, the rose garden, the lawns and the lake to the distant woods.

Soon he was joined by Anna, looking beautiful in a blue taffeta dress that swept down from her shoulders, to reveal her graceful neck and a curve of naked cleavage. Her skin was as smooth as alabaster and its paleness and texture was emphasised by the blackness of her hair and her flashing dark eyes. At that moment he remembered her as she was that night in Florence, when he held her naked in his arms.

"What a wonderful house you have," she said, as she sat on the settee. "And the grounds look lovely too. I want you to show them to me tomorrow."

"That will be a great pleasure," Edward said, "one I have been looking forward to for a long time."

"So, you anticipated finding me when you came to Italy," she said, teasingly.

"I did, but Robert meeting Edwina in Florence on our second night there made the search easier. What a coincidence that was."

"Maybe so, maybe not. What will be, will be," Anna said.

Edwina came in at that moment, looking so young and fresh in a delicate cream dress, which emphasised the curves and litheness of her body. Almost immediately Robert returned and Mrs Pearson served them with drinks, before announcing that dinner was ready.

As it had been a hot day Mrs Pearson had prepared a light meal, the main course consisting of a poached salmon, served with new potatoes and salad. As they sat around the large dining table, with all the old familiar pictures in place, Edward could see, as he, when he was Edwina, had seen that Robert's paintings would change the room entirely, adding colour and light. Somehow he knew that Edwina would change the room again. He hoped so.

After the meal Edward and Anna returned to the sitting room for coffee, but Robert led Edwina into the garden.

"We can walk as far as the lake, if you like, Robert said. "Tomorrow I would like to show you my favourite spot in the woods." He put his arm around her waist, feeling the warmth of her through the thin material. She shivered.

"Are you cold?" he asked. "We don't have to go, or you could fetch a cardigan."

"No, it's nothing," she said, pressing his hand against her. "It's just that I felt I had lived this moment before."

"Déjà vu," Robert said.

They walked in silence to the edge of the lake, blissfully happy, and stood in awe as the setting sun cast its last rays across the darkening waters. She shivered again and he pulled her close to him. They kissed passionately, knowing their love, although no word had been said.

In the sitting room Edward and Anna, sitting together on the settee, watched the sun setting over the lawn. "This is a magical place," Anna said.

Edward put his arm around her and they kissed. They both felt a great release of tension and Anna leant her body into him. She had not felt so relaxed in the company of a man since that night in Venice. She smiled at the recollection and cuddled into Edward's arms.

When Edwina finally parted from Robert she came into the house, feeling cold for the first time, and was surprised to find the sitting room in darkness. Edward and Anna had gone to bed. She felt so alive and happy. She knew her life was changed forever. Robert had invited her to Greenblade Farm to meet his family and had promised to show her his pictures. Yes, she thought, as she mounted the stairs, life would be very different from now on.

EPILOGUE

Edward lay prone on a lounger, his head supported by a crimson pillow. Close beside him, Anna also relaxed on a lounger. Their hands trailed across the gap to each other, contacting gently. They were both completely at ease.

Edwina and Robert arrived out of breath and laughing, tennis rackets in hand. Robert was wearing a white shirt and shorts, while Edwina wore an attractive tennis dress. As they threw themselves down on the blankets and cushions, there was a childish cry and two small children ran up from the lake, one a little boy, the other a little girl.

"Granma, Grandad," they shouted in unison. "We seed it, we seed it. We seed the kingfisher."

A PARALLEL LIFE